HARD LINE

A. D. JUSTICE

A.D. Justice
USA Today Bestselling Author

HARD LINE.

A CROSSING LINES NOVEL.

Copyright © 2019 A.D. Justice.

Cover photo by Wander Aguiar.

Cover model is Forest H.

Cover design by Sommer Stein, Perfect Pear Creative Covers

SYNOPSIS

My rule: Never let an old flame burn you twice.

Other people gave second chances—I didn't. My modus operandi was to move on to the next girl in line and forget the previous one.

So when Tawnee Milano said she needed her space, I let her go. Then I left our mutual employer for a new job with the CIA and didn't look back.

But a coded distress message from her sends me right back to where I was when we first split up. The possibility of losing her forever forces me to relax my rigid stance. With her life in danger, I'm finally facing my true feelings for her.

Mottos are all fine and good in theory. Not so much in practice.

Now my hard line policy is to get her back—and keep her this time.

PROLOGUE

Roman—Three Years Ago

"**I** can't do this anymore." Tawnee places her hands on her hips and burns a hole through me with the anger in her eyes.

"You can't do what anymore?" I know she isn't saying what I think she's saying.

"Us, Roman. I can't do us anymore. This isn't working for me. I've put up with too much, and I can't do it one more day. I'm sorry, but this is over between us." She snatches her bag off the bed and starts toward the door.

"You're breaking up with me? Are you fucking kidding me right now?"

"No, I'm absolutely not kidding you at all. I'm done. I'm so done."

"What do you expect from me, Tawnee? I mean, I gave you a drawer and everything."

Ah, shit. That was the wrong thing to say apparently. She's seriously considering drawing her gun and shooting me right now. She's weighing the pros and cons at this very second. I can see it in her expression and the way her muscles are tensed. I don't know what I've done this time to piss her off so badly. All I know is whatever we fight about always ends up being my fucking fault.

"You gave me a drawer? Yeah, let's talk about that drawer, Roman. Let's examine that gesture for a minute. One, it's the smallest fucking drawer in the whole house. Two, why the hell would I put a few items of clothes in that drawer when I still have to go back home for all the rest of my shit anyway? And, most of all, three." She walks over to the drawer I gave her and yanks it open. "You haven't even noticed I've never used the fucking thing!"

She releases it with a jerk, and it crashes to the floor as she walks away, leaving it where it landed.

We'd been dating on and off for a while before that eventful fight. I don't even remember what started the fight now. It was probably something stupid, like I said green is a better color than blue. Who the fuck knows or cares? The point is, she left me and said she was never coming back. I gave her two days to change her mind and her attitude. When I didn't hear a single peep from her within that time, I decided it was time to move on.

And that's exactly what I did. I went out the next night, I met someone new, and I enjoyed the pleasure of her company. Repeatedly.

I haven't seen the same girl twice since the day Tawnee walked out, and I haven't regretted one minute of living my life to the fullest.

૭ஜ૭

Present Day

"ROMAN, I SWEAR TO GOD, IF YOU TELL ME THAT fucking story one more time…I'm going to take this plastic knife I just used to smear cream cheese on my bagel, and I'm going to slit my wrists with it." Blake holds the knife at his wrist and pretends to saw his skin.

"I've told you that story before?"

"Only once or twice…a week…for three fucking years, man. Listen, I'm going to tell you this one last time as your friend. If you're my friend, you need to listen to what I have to say because I'm as fucking tired of repeating myself as I am of hearing you repeat yourself.

"One. It's time for you to face the truth.

"Two. You are not over being dumped.

"Three. You're not over her moving halfway

around the world and never calling you to say goodbye when she left the country.

"Four. You are nowhere near being over Tawnee.

"Five. You're in love with the woman. Still. To this very day. If she walked into this bakery right now and said she wanted you back, you'd jump for fucking joy. And so would I, because at least you'd have a new fucking story to tell." Blake bites into his bagel, tearing it with excessive force, and glares at me over his coffee cup.

"That's ridiculous. How do you get that from what I just told you?"

"Because I'm not a fucking moron, Roman. Unlike you. That's how."

"You're so full of shit. I don't give second chances, Blake. One and done—that's how I manage my relationship issues. Plain and simple. No fuss, no muss. No complications. No baggage. No unresolved issues."

"Yeah, I got it, man. You're still full of shit, for the record. I stick by my original statement and assessment of you."

We walk out of the restaurant and stroll down the street, keeping our target in sight without giving away our position.

My phone vibrates with an incoming text, so I fish it out of my pocket and quickly glance at the screen. My attention is on my mark, but when I glance down at the screen, I forget all about my mission.

I forget about my job.

I forget about my mark.

I forget why I'm following him.

After three long years, Tawnee has sent me a message. But it's not just any message. To anyone else, it appears to be a string of letters and numbers with no discernible pattern. But I know better. I recognize the secret code on sight. With a quick copy and paste into our own software program and our specific key, I decode the message and nearly let my phone slip through my fingers when I read what it says.

Send help immediately. Assassination plot. Extraction needed.

Her life is in imminent danger, and she's reaching out to me for help...from Dubai.

How can I not answer this call?

"What's wrong? Did you just see a ghost or what?" Blake looks over his shoulder at where I've stopped walking in the middle of the sidewalk.

"Something like that. Tawnee just texted me using Brad's secret message system. I haven't heard from her in three years, Blake."

"Yeah. Funny how I got that from the conversation we just had not three seconds ago. What did her message say?"

I hand Blake my phone and take his out of his hand. In seconds, I have my CIA partners, Silas Steele and Nick Tucker, on the phone and I'm relaying the message from Tawnee.

"What do you want to do, Roman?" Silas asks.

He knows damn well what I want to do, but he's testing me in more ways than one. It's not just my commitment to carrying out my duties as a CIA officer he's questioning. It's my commitment to her—someone who once worked alongside me at Steele Security. Someone who slept beside me, almost lived with me, and loved me. And someone I should have treated better than I did.

"I want to drop everything and leave a blazing trail on our way out of Dubai with her safely in my arms." That's probably the most honest statement I've made regarding her in the last three years.

"Have you done any research into what's going on and why she's involved in an imminent assassination attempt?" Nick asks, ever the level-headed hero.

"No, Nick. I just got the text and immediately called you two." I grit my teeth to keep my impatience under wraps.

"So, we could be walking straight into an ambush. It could all be a ruse to get you there for some reason. Or Silas. Or me. Or all three of us, for that matter. You have nothing but a simple text that could be from anyone pretending to be Tawnee."

"It came through Brad's encrypted system. Only Tawnee would know what secret key to use so I could decode the message. She sent it to me—not you and not Silas. Me. She needs me, and I'm going with or without you two."

"That's what I wanted to hear. Get your shit together, Roman, and screw your head on straight. If she's in a volatile situation, what do you think is waiting for us? We have no intel on what we're walking into, so you need to check your emotions at the door and think logically. What is she working on? Who is she working with? Who are their friends and enemies?" Nick has been in so many dangerous situations in his career, this line of questioning has become second nature to him.

He's right, though. I saw her plea for help, and I was ready to run headlong into the fire, no questions asked.

Maybe Blake is right after all.

"Tell Blake to pack his gear. He's going along for the ride too. I'll contact Langley and get all the intel we have on the situation. There's a flight leaving Miami today at 5:35. Let's meet at the airport and prepare for the long-ass flight to Dubai. Leave your guns at home. You'll never make it through customs with a weapon." Silas is the most seasoned CIA officer of us all.

Even though we're assigned to a joint task force with the NSA and CIA, we mostly perform under CIA rules. Meaning, there are none. This should be an interesting trip.

Tawnee

"RAFAEL, IT'S TIME TO GO. WE'VE CLEARED THE hallway." I approach my handsome Latin employer and try to urge him out of the luxury hotel suite for the third time this morning.

"Tawnee, you have to relax. You're far too pretty to be so stressed all the time." He finally stands from the overstuffed sofa and slides his sunglasses over his eyes.

"Unfortunately, my looks have no bearing on my stress levels. Ensuring your security does. You not taking your own security seriously also does. Why hire me and make me travel around the world with you if you don't listen to me?" I turn and walk back to the entrance to check the hallway before letting him pass through the door.

"There's nothing I have to worry about. I know you've already worried about it a thousand times over before I've even considered it."

"I don't doubt that's true. Not even for a second. Which makes me even more stressed since, again, you don't take your own safety seriously. We're caught in a vicious cycle, you and I. So I need you to help me out here and don't make me old before my time. Stay close to your security team, be vigilant about watching your surroundings, and do exactly as you're told to do."

"I love it when you're bossy like that. It's so sexy."

"I'm serious, Raf."

"So am I. And your ass looks awesome in those pants. You should wear those every day."

I stop and turn to look him dead in the eyes. "Rafael, I do wear the same style of pants every single day that I'm with you. They're basically my work uniform. And you can't possibly watch your surroundings if you're watching my ass."

His dark chuckle makes me smile. He knows he drives me crazy—that's why he does it on purpose. He's a shameless flirt, but he's also harmless. If he thought for one second his comments offended me or made me uncomfortable, he'd apologize profusely and buy me a mega yacht to make up for it. But then, he can afford to be so lavish since he's one of the richest men in the world. As the owner of a very profitable holding company, he controls the majority of shares in a lot of very high-powered, high-profile companies. Those businesses have made him an extraordinary amount of money, but he's still the same down-to-earth man he was before the cash starting rolling in.

All the money he has made is why I have a job today, albeit one that makes me crazy more than anything else in my life at the moment. Buying the controlling shares in companies whose owners aren't ready to give up control hasn't made him the most popular man on the Forbes Top 100 list. Corporate enemies can be ruthless. Kidnapping is a real threat for someone who is worth so much. Then there's the matter of his life insurance policy—it requires him to have private security in most circumstances…like when he leaves his house for any length of time, goes out on dates with unvetted partners, or when he's traveling to Dubai for both business and pleasure.

We're in the UAE for both reasons on this trip.

He's taking a tour of a recently built high-rise condo building as he considers expanding his interests. Not that he needs more income, but he's bored with managing his life against where the stock market closes or how a company performs. Expanding into real estate in one of the most popular destinations in the world makes good business sense to him.

Buying the entire building in this destination mecca isn't something many people could afford.

But Rafael Cruz isn't just anyone.

We finally make it to the waiting car and get him inside without incident. On the way to tour the high-rise, Raf makes another business call while I watch our surroundings.

"Tony, change lanes abruptly." Our driver, Tony, is used to my obsessive behavior by now, so he does as I ask without question.

All the hairs on the back of my neck stand at attention. I speak into the comms, alerting the rest of the team in the other cars. "We have a possible tail.

White Nissan Altima. Two males. Two cars behind and speeding up fast to catch up with us. Tony, make an unexpected turn, but not down a dead-end street. Make sure there's an easy out."

Tony's more alert now. His eyes are glued to the rearview mirror when he identifies the turn he'll make. Rafael, on the other hand, continues his conversation for a few more seconds before disconnecting the call as if nothing out of the ordinary is happening around him. The other car is traveling too fast in an attempt to catch up with us, so they're unable to make the same turn. They slam on their brakes, and the tires screech against the asphalt. Then they turn, and the front wheel jumps the curb before they speed up again, racing toward us.

"Tony, get us out of here. Now."

We race through the crowded city, drawing way too much attention in a culture that doesn't appreciate such outrageous behavior. But these guys aren't stopping. If anything, they're becoming more aggressive.

"Raf, you need to get down out of sight."

"Don't you have your gun? Shoot their tires out." He slides down in the seat, snatches his shades off his face, and looks at me with fear in his eyes for the first time since this chase started.

"Do I have a gun in Dubai? No, Raf, we're not residents here. We can't carry firearms without a special invitation from the sheik himself. Even you don't have that kind of clout here."

"Then how exactly do you plan to protect me?"

"By losing them and getting you to a safe place until we can work with the police to identify the owner of the car and the men inside."

Suddenly, another car appears out of nowhere and rams us from a side street. While we were watching the car behind us for the last several miles, they coordinated a sneak attack. Our car spins around in the middle of the street and slams into the side of a building. The initial shock of the crash takes me a few precious seconds to clear my mind, then I check on Rafael to make sure he isn't hurt.

He assures me he's fine, so I immediately survey our surroundings to get my bearings. Tony and the second car of security guys surround our car, ready to fight off our attackers. Raf's door is pinned against the building, so I turn and shield him with my body since there's no way out and nowhere to run. The ruckus outside the car is fierce, with aggressive yelling in Arabic and English. The men start to scuffle, leaving me exposed inside the car. Arms reach in, grabbing at me, trying to pull me out. But I plant my feet against the side of the vehicle and push with all my might, staying between them and Rafael.

Tony dispatches the man who had distracted him then rushes back to help me. Two other members of our detail soon join him, effectively beating back the attack with fists and brawn. The entire scene lasts mere seconds, but it feels like it takes forever. The next thing I see, the attackers run back to their cars. One turns to look at me again before he slides into the passenger seat. He angrily yells something in Arabic...but I distinctly hear him say my name right in the middle of his rant.

Now I'm not so sure Rafael was the intended target after all.

CHAPTER 1

Roman

Blake and I rush into the Miami airport as if we'll miss our international flight that doesn't even leave for three more hours. I'm so keyed up, it's not even fucking funny. Three years of no word from Tawnee evaporated into the Miami heat when I opened her message. Anything could happen in the eighteen-plus hours it'll take to reach the Middle East, including the layover time in Paris. Then there's the issue of actually finding her once we land. But one way or another, that's precisely what I plan to do. Then I'll carry her home, kicking and screaming over my shoulder if needed.

Both Silas and Nick are already here, waiting with

the flight reservations for Blake and me in hand when we approach them.

"Courtesy of Uncle Sam," Silas says with a smile when he hands us our itineraries. "Seems there may a need for us to be there in an official capacity after all. We have established contacts in the area who can get us what we need once we land, but there's a catch. We're not allowed to carry firearms in the UAE because we're not Emirati citizens and the sheik won't give us permission. Our big brass has already tried to convince him. The details are sketchy because Rafael Cruz is a private citizen who travels to foreign countries more than he stays in his own, but word has it he's involved in a lot more than what we see in his public persona."

"Such as—what?" Silas is fucking crazy if he thinks he can leave me hanging with a statement like that and get away with it.

"Go check in, then we'll talk more in the private lounge inside the international terminal."

I know waiting until we're in more secure quarters makes sense, but the rational part of my brain has taken a back seat to the impetuous man inside me. The man who wants to rush in with guns blazing and no backup plan. Even though I don't have a gun on me at the moment and won't have one for the foreseeable future.

The check-in line is too fucking long.

The agent is too fucking slow.

The people surrounding me are too fucking annoying.

"Look, I know you're worried about her, but she said she needs evacuation from the country. Not that she's taking heavy fire and about to be bombarded by cruise missiles. If you don't chill the fuck out, Silas will leave your ass here, and you know it. If you can't take the heat of this mission, you need to bow out on your own. Don't put all our lives plus hers on the line because you can't control your emotions." Blake keeps his voice low and controlled, but his aggravation simmers just below the surface.

He's right, and I know he's only looking out for me. I never would've dared to approach another case with this train of thought. Rash decisions and tunnel vision put my team in even more risk of danger... or worse. They have enough at stake as it is. I take a deep breath and slowly release it, letting the stress leave my mind at the same time. With my thoughts clearer and my attention better focused on the tasks we have to accomplish, I turn to Blake, the man who's been my best friend for more years than I can remember.

"Thanks, man. I appreciate your kicking my ass and making me deal with the problem at hand."

"That's what friends are for, Roman. I know this is more personal than any other mission you've ever had, but that's exactly why you always have to keep a clear head. Regardless of how unnatural that is for you."

Spoken like a true smartass. But his infusion of humor works, making us both burst out in laughter.

We get through security and find the lounge without a hitch then settle into a private corner with drinks in hand.

"Rafael Cruz made his billions from buying stock in companies until he had enough shares to influence the overall direction. Sometimes, he springs hostile takeovers on companies. His portfolio is vast—the more he makes, the more he invests into both upcoming and existing companies. He's involved in such varied industries, it's hard to find a common theme." Silas stops to sip his vodka.

"But you found one, didn't you?" I know Silas well enough to know he wouldn't bring up a specific topic without a good reason.

"I think so. They built Dubai to be a tourist destination because the sheik who owns it realized oil production can last only for so long. It'll eventually run out, and he didn't want his country dependent on a single source of income to sustain them. Mr. Cruz has recently started investing in multiple oil conglomerates that all directly compete with that very sheik. In fact, some of his investments even compete with one another.

"The working theory is Cruz's company is trying to

gain the maximum number of shares for each company under the radar. If he succeeds, he'll ultimately combine them into one company that makes him the biggest oil tycoon in the world. Imagine if the majority of the world had to get their supply from either Cruz or Russia. The boys at Langley are working on pulling the documentation to put the puzzle pieces together."

"Russia because it's a state-owned oil company, right?"

"Exactly. And Saudi Arabia's main production company recently went public. They're the most profitable company in the world. A Westerner taking over that business would provoke a lot of people in that part of the world."

"It definitely would. If news of that reached the general public, there would be riots in the street and lynch mobs out for his head. I'll call my dad when we land and ask if he's heard anything about someone making a quiet takeover bid for the world's oil. The time difference between Dubai and South Africa is only two hours." All I can see is Tawnee in the middle of that chaos, with angry men not caring if she is to blame or not. She'll be guilty by association, and they'll kill her because of him.

"What does your dad do?" Nick asks.

"He's the head chemist for the largest oil production company in South Africa. He moved there a couple of years ago to take over as the leader of his division. Since he's in senior management, he may be privy to information about potential mergers or acquisitions, but I doubt it. That information is usually reserved for the CEO and the board of directors to avoid massive stock dumps and insider information violations.

"But what we do know is time is of the essence. Silas, did you find out anything about the assassination attempt she mentioned in her message?"

"The oil shares piece is a working assumption. We don't have concrete evidence of that yet. As far as the message, my sources on the ground relayed information about a car chase that ended in a wreck. By the time the authorities arrived on the scene, the other vehicles involved had fled. They originally listed it as a hit-and-run, but they noted suspicious events surrounding it. Since then, the traffic camera feeds have been scrubbed, and any evidence has disappeared." Silas raises one eyebrow, conveying his distrust without a word.

"Scrubbed from inside Dubai?" They're not known for their dishonesty in state affairs, so that information shocks me.

"No, they were hacked from outside their network. Their computer forensics department is working on tracing the hack, but the sophisticated method is taking time to sort out. They're willing to work with us—to an extent. Remember, we're foreigners, but we're still expected to abide by their rules and their laws. They're lenient with tourists, but only to a certain point. But we're not entering their country simply as tourists, so don't expect to be treated as well as their guests would be."

"So, they know we're coming in an official capacity and will watch us closer?" Nick asks.

"Exactly."

Once we've mulled over all the details we currently have until we can recite them in our sleep, I stroll over to the bar and have a seat alone. After I've been lost in my own thoughts for about an hour, Silas slides onto the bar stool next to me and orders a double shot of vodka. He doesn't say anything for a couple of minutes, which I appreciate, but I know it's coming. Words of wisdom from the great Silas Steele.

"How are you holding up, Roman?"

"On the one hand, I'm okay. On the other, waiting is killing me. I'm not a patient man. You know that."

"I do. And I know all too well how being impatient can get you hurt or killed. Or worse, get someone else hurt or killed. You don't want that on your conscience. Trust me."

All I can do is nod, showing I understand what he's telling me. He's worked countless missions, putting his spies in harm's way every day. I have no doubt Silas felt terrible when his previous asset's cover was blown, but Tawnee is more than a resource to me.

"Have you stopped to consider why she contacted you after all this time? Why not someone else in Cruz's organization? He has more than one team. Tawnee doesn't work nonstop around the clock. So why bring you into the equation, halfway around the world, when she knows you can't get there immediately?"

"No. I haven't stepped back and looked at the entire situation as an outsider, honestly. I saw the message, my world blew up, and I started picking up the pieces without asking all the right questions. Do you think they coerced her into it? Are we walking into a trap? And, if so, what could they possibly want from us?" The wheels in my mind are turning at breakneck speed now. I'm not asking all the right questions or considering the various possibilities.

"Stop beating yourself up. If I got the same message from Kira, I'd find a way to teleport across the galaxy to reach her. These are just some of the questions I'm asking after sitting back and examining the entire situation. Something isn't adding up for me, and I think that variable is one that's still unknown. I'm not blaming you for not seeing it because I don't think it's been revealed to any of us yet."

"What fun would it be to have all the answers upfront and know exactly what to do when we arrive?" I finish off my whiskey with one large gulp and stand.

"Our flight is about to board. I can't wait to spend eighteen hours in the air with you. We'll have some great bonding time."

"Don't sit close to me." He throws back his shot and walks over to the others to get his carry-on luggage.

I'm close on his heels, laughing at his dry sense of humor and his way with words. It's good to have friends to keep me grounded regardless of the chaos around me. I have a strong feeling I'll need exactly that kind of friend once the wheels touch down on the tarmac in Dubai. When the shit hits the fan and we're scorching up the roads to find Tawnee—wherever she is.

We board the flight and take our seats in the first-class section. The enclosed window suite gives me plenty of privacy to sleep on the long haul, but I also have way too much time to think. Too many images of what could possibly happen to Tawnee before I reach her. Too many visions of her caught in the crossfire between some underhanded, unscrupulous businessman and his enemies. She'll do her job and defend him with her life—and he'll, no doubt, allow it. I've never met the man, but I already don't like him.

My thoughts drift to the last time I saw Tawnee and what our fight was truly about. The topic that kicked off that exact conflict isn't significant, but the underlying resentment that kept our relationship on edge is all on me. That's one part of the story I've never admitted to Blake, though he knows the truth anyway. It's not hard to figure out, considering how well he knows me. My reluctance to commit fully to her—to be a couple—created a sore spot between us that never healed.

Her words during that confrontation have haunted me since the day she left.

"Roman, do you want to be with me or not?" She met my gaze without hesitation, but then, that was just Tawnee in a nutshell. She stood her ground and never backed down from a fight.

"If I didn't want to be with you, I wouldn't be."

"Do you really think that answer is sufficient?" She put her hands on her hips and glared at me, her eyes narrowed and her normally full lips pulled into a tight line.

"It's the truth. What more do you need? Our relationship is self-explanatory. We're together, so that means we each want to be with the other."

Her hands flew to her forehead then her fingers started kneading her temples. She worked to remain calm, but the anger and frustration were building inside her like a volcano about to explode. *"You have about thirty seconds to make this right, Roman. I'm not exaggerating, and I'm not being overly emotional."*

"I don't know how you expect me to make it right. I don't even know what's wrong. We have a great relationship, sweets. What more do you want from me?"

"Roman, we've been together long enough now that we either move forward together or we should go our separate ways. I'm not some young kid fresh out of college. I know what I want. If you're still on the fence after all this time, tell me now so I'll know what I should do next."

"You know, pushing me into marriage before I'm ready won't work out well for either of us."

"Marriage? You think I'm pushing you into marriage? Why the hell would I want to marry you when you won't even commit to an exclusive relationship with me?"

"What are you talking about? I'm not seeing anyone else."

"Well, isn't that a relief." Her words dripped with sarcasm. "You're still waiting to see if someone better comes along. You've never said you love me. You've never talked about our future—how you see it, what you want, nothing. Apart from when we're literally having sex, we live completely separate lives. Is that all you want from us?"

"Look, I'm sorry, but I don't know what to tell you other than I'm content with our current arrangement. I think it works out well for both of us. We both have independent personalities, and we like our separate space. Why ruin a good thing by changing it now? You know the old saying, 'Don't fix what's not broken.' Well, I'm not broken, so stop trying to fix me."

"I'm not trying to 'fix you' or change you or make you do anything you don't want to do. All I want is for you to man up and finally tell me what it is you want for us—as a couple. For our future. For our relationship. For you and me together. Do you think you can manage that?"

"I don't think of it in those terms, Tawnee. I don't say, 'Roman, in exactly sixteen-and-a-half months, you're going to ask Tawnee to move in with you. Then, exactly five-years-and-nine-months later, you'll ask her to marry you. Then ten-years-eleven-months-and-twenty-nine-days after that, you'll start thinking about getting married. Then double that time, and you'll start thinking about having kids.' I'm more of a take-it-day-by-day kind of man."

The change in her expression and demeanor was instantaneous. Her face fell and her shoulders drooped. I saw something on her face I'd never seen before—defeat. She'd accepted it and waved the white flag of surrender in that very moment. While I never meant to hurt her, I realized that's exactly what my snide remark did. I confirmed all her suspicions and concerns about me and killed her love for me in the span of a few seconds with careless words. I wanted to take it all back right then—I wanted to drop to my knees and beg her forgiveness.

But I didn't.

I stayed rooted to my spot, hanging on to my pride instead of showing my true feelings.

It's not that I didn't love her; I just assumed she knew.

"Tawnee, look, let's not do this right now. Let's both just calm down, and we can talk about this rationally later."

"There's nothing left to talk about, Roman. You've made your feelings and intentions crystal clear to me now. If nothing

else, I do appreciate that, but I can't stay here with you one minute longer. I am calm, and I am rational—so don't expect my decision to change anytime soon."

"What are you talking about—what decision? You're not acting like yourself. Are you on your period or something? Oh fuck. You're not pregnant, are you? I definitely can't handle that shit right now."

Famous last words of a fool.

CHAPTER 2

Tawnee

"Tony, it's been two days since the incident. The report from the local police should be available now. Call them to ask if we can get a copy and see what else you can find out about their investigation. I'm sure there's information they're withholding from the general public, but we need eyes on everything we can get.

"Tabitha, Mr. Cruz's meeting is scheduled for next week, but he can't be late again when it's time to go. You know how he is about punctuality, and it's considered incredibly rude in this culture. They were very gracious about our mishap this week. Map out a new route and note any possible deviations so we're not caught unaware when we're on the move again.

"Carter and Jason, you two comb through the local news, online forums, and the dark web. Investigate anyone who posts or comments about the details. No one has claimed credit for it yet, which leads me to believe there'll be a follow-up attempt.

"John, talk to the head of security about getting the hallway camera feed sent to our secure laptops for extra monitoring."

After giving out the team's marching orders, I walk back into Rafael's royal suite and climb the elegant staircase in the entryway to complete a thorough search of the expansive accommodation for the third time since we got up this morning. We changed hotels and opted for this ultra-lux and uber-secure resort after the failed attempt to grab us, erring on the side of caution, though the manager of the original hotel tried his best to dissuade us from leaving. Having someone of Rafael's stature at a hotel only increases their bragging rights along with the number of people— mostly women—who frequent the bars and restaurants, hoping to run into him accidentally and have him fall madly in love with them at first sight.

If they only knew how many other women have attempted those same tactics and failed miserably.

He may be the world's most eligible bachelor, but he's also extremely discerning in choosing his dates. If there's no chemistry after they serve the main course, he politely thanks her for a lovely evening, excuses himself, and arranges her transportation home. That very scenario has happened more times than I can count. Not that I blame them for trying. He is one fine specimen of a man. At six-foot-four, he's an intimidating figure both inside the boardroom and out. His jet-black hair and dark brown eyes perfectly match his bronzed Latin skin. He turns heads everywhere he goes.

"How do you feel, Raf?" His usually handsome face is scrunched, and he's carefully kneading the back of his neck. "You're still in pain, aren't you?"

His sheepish grin is the only answer I need.

"Some days, I feel more like your assistant than the head of your security. Tabitha already rescheduled your building tour for later next week. The hotel concierge can arrange for a private physician to visit your suite. It's technically been thirty-six hours since the collision. You can't put off an exam any longer. If the doctor thinks you need X-rays or scans, we're going to the hospital, even if I have to taser you to get you there."

"Whatever you say, boss lady." He winks at me, knowing that term riles me up but also knowing I can't stay mad at him for long. "We've been together so long now that I think you know me better than I know myself."

"That's because I do. After the last three years of working for and traveling the world with you, I don't see how you could possibly have any secrets left I don't already know."

"You're my personal stalker. I kind of like that, Tawnee. Makes you even more mysterious and sexy, if that were at all possible."

"Did you hit your head in the wreck? Maybe I should take you for that CT scan after all."

He playfully bats away my hand when I reach to check his forehead for a fever. "Don't act like you don't know. I tell you all the time—you could wear a burlap sack and still be the most beautiful woman I've ever seen."

"And just like every other time you've said that, I call bullshit. You've dated Victoria's Secret models. I'm nowhere near their league."

"You have that backward. They're nowhere near yours."

I shake my head at his antics. "You are a shameless flirt, Raf. Do you need a bag of ice for your neck until the doctor arrives?"

"No, I don't think so. I'll just kick back here and relax until then. Thank you, though. I appreciate how well you take care of me."

Though it takes several phone calls and a lot of waiting, the doctor shows up and conducts a thorough exam. With no pressing business meetings this week, Rafael has plenty of time to rest and recuperate. Tony talked to the local police department, but their report isn't available yet—at least, not for us anyway. Without the additional information it contains, there's not much we can do at this time of day, other than finally relax and have a team dinner on the expansive balcony of Raf's royal suite.

The worried expressions on everyone's faces match my somber mood. What happened this week was much too close for comfort, and we're in a part of the world where I have no contacts available to help me out of a jam. Whoever is behind this and whatever their plans are, this team will have to handle it on our own.

"Penny for your thoughts, Tawnee." Rafael catches me staring into my wineglass.

"My thoughts are worth much more than that." My smile is as normal as possible under the circumstances. I don't want to add to the apprehension I already feel from the group.

"You know I'm good for it—however much you charge." He's like a dog with a bone.

"I'm thinking we should have your suite's assigned butlers clear the table now so you can get some rest after a very long and trying day. We'll all feel more refreshed in the morning."

"If you say so. That's not what you were thinking, but you're not wrong."

The entire security team stays in his suite while the staff cleans off the table and resets everything to perfection, watching every movement like a hawk stalking some unsuspecting prey. I'm not willing to trust anyone outside our circle at this point in the game. There are way too many variables still unknown. When the last of the waitstaff leaves the room, the rest of us follow close behind.

"I'll see you in the morning, Raf. But if anything happens tonight, call me immediately, and I'll come right back up here." I'm the last one out the door, hesitant to leave him alone just yet.

"Plan on joining me in my suite for breakfast first thing in the morning. I'll put the order in tonight so it's here on time."

"Okay. Goodnight."

"Goodnight, Tawnee."

HIS REQUEST FOR ME TO HAVE BREAKFAST WITH HIM isn't anything unusual. He hates to eat alone, even when he's in his room away from all the prying eyes.

His request to me *after* breakfast throws me for a loop, though.

"Tawnee, let's go down to the beach and relax. Just you and me—we'll leave the rest of the team here. We both need a break and some time to destress. We have all day to ourselves."

I stop walking, making yet another round after breakfast, and stare at Raf in disbelief. My jaw is slack, and my eyes fly wide open. "You've got to be kidding me right now."

"Not at all. No one will recognize us in bathing suits and T-shirts. They'll expect me to be in an Armani suit, silk shirt, and leather Louboutin dress shoes. I'll wear flip-flops and an ugly Hawaiian shirt with cheap sunglasses."

"As much as I'd love to see you in that get-up—and take pictures of it to blackmail you with later—I wouldn't be very good at my job if I agreed to your crazy request so soon after there was an attempt made on your life." I move closer to where he's sitting on the sofa, staring out the floor-to-ceiling windows at the inviting waters of the Persian Gulf. The people on the beach and in the water below look like ants from this height. But one fact is clear—Rafael is jealous of those ants and their carefree lives. "Talk to me, Raf. What's really going on? You've never mentioned wanting to swim in the ocean or wear Hawaiian shirts and flip-flops before now."

"I've made a lot of mistakes in my life, Tawnee. Some I'd give up every dollar I've made to go back and change, but we both know that can't happen. I've worked more than I've played. I haven't spent enough time with the people who mean the most to me. I've been on plenty of dates, but I've never felt that instant spark or connection with anyone." He turns and looks at me with deep sadness and regret in his eyes. "Except you."

I've never had an occasion to use the word flabbergasted to describe my own feelings and reaction, but now is as good a time as any. I've also never had a problem with using my vocabulary or conveying my thoughts—until now. An invisible tether holds our gazes in place. I'm staring into his gorgeous dark brown eyes, waiting for the punch line to pull us out of this awkward staring contest.

"This must come as a surprise to you, judging by your reaction. Or lack of reaction, I should say. Our flirting started out innocent enough—I used it as an icebreaker to get to know you better as a person, not just as my security officer. But the more time I've spent with you, the more my feelings have changed. Since the day we first met, I've compared every woman I've dated to you. Not one of them measured up to the high standards you set, though, and that's why I haven't kept anyone around."

Nope, this awkward moment will not pass by unnoticed. At all.

"Rafael—"

"Don't say anything yet, Tawnee. I haven't reached this level of success without being able to read people. You've always been the consummate professional, keeping any personal feelings separate from the job I hired you to do. Our relationship has always been one of employer and employee, and you haven't allowed yourself to consider any deviation from that course even though I flirt with you relentlessly. I understand why, and I respect you for it.

"What I'm asking of you is this—search for your true feelings for me, and I think you'll realize they run as deep as my feelings do for you. We've spent a lot of time together and grown to know each other very well. I've fallen in love with you, Tawnee. I believe you secretly love me too. Don't look at me as your employer. Simply see me as a man."

With our eyes still locked, I sit down on the couch beside him. I'm glad I was standing so close because my knees were about to buckle at any moment. "To be completely honest, I'm not sure I know how to separate my professional and personal life anymore. That has nothing to do with you and all to do with me. I've poured every bit of myself into my business for so long. I don't know if there's anything left of me outside of work."

His eyes soften as he watches me, understanding immediately lighting in them. "He broke your heart, didn't he?"

"Who?" I draw my eyebrows down in confusion for a moment. I'm certain I didn't mention any names. Or, more precisely, a single name.

"The man you loved once. The guy who wasn't

man enough to love you in return, not the way you deserved to be loved, anyway."

I'd feel less exposed in a two-piece thong bikini while standing in the center of the Dubai mall than I do fully clothed right now. He wasn't exaggerating when he said he could read people. He sees right through me as if I'm a transparent pane of glass.

"You deserve so much better than that. This week's events opened my eyes to how blasé I've been toward my own safety, even though you've warned me a million times. You know as well as I do, I've always considered the security measures to be overkill. I thought it was more that the insurance company was trying to save the money on my life insurance policy. Now I understand there's much more than money at stake. You may think my change of heart is only because I saw my life flash before my eyes, but what's really happening is I refuse to waste one more minute of hiding what I genuinely feel for you.

"That said, I'm willing to take whatever risks come our way to spend the day with you on the private beach at this ultra-secure resort. Do you have an indemnity waiver I need to sign first?" A sexy smirk covers his face, and his handsomeness strikes me with full force for the first time in the last few years I've known him.

His skin is naturally tanned, blessing him with a natural sun-kissed complexion. Those dark brown eyes and full lips are accentuated by his perfect cheekbones and strong chin. But it's that one dimple on his left cheek that's the finishing touch.

"Sorry. I must have missed something. What indemnity waiver are you talking about?"

"The one that absolves you of any liability when we put on our bathing suits and join the party crowd on the beach. My swimming shorts are calling my name. Did you bring a bathing suit with you?"

"Yes, I always bring a couple since I swim laps at night to get in my exercise."

"It's too bad I never knew that before now." He waggles his eyebrows and smiles seductively at me.

"Even though I have bathing suits with me, we're not going to the beach. I'm sorry, Raf. I appreciate your epiphany about taking your security seriously, but you've got to realize you're not doing that *right now*. Putting yourself out in the open on a very crowded beach is the opposite of being aware of your safety."

"You're right—see, I don't even consider these things because I know you will. We'll take my entire protection detail with us. They can take turns standing guard and playing in the water, so they'll blend in without being miserable in the sun. Just to be clear, I'm going either way, so…"

"Fine, only because I know you will. Then I'd either be forced to drag your ass back inside and cause a huge scene, or I'd have to quit and fly back home."

"You can never leave me, Tawnee, though the whole concept of you dragging my ass back to my bedroom has merit. Now, about that dip in the ocean. I'm going to go change into my bathing suit now, so I suggest you do the same. You'll sweat your ass off in those clothes outside."

With that, he walks off to his bedroom and leaves me on the couch, still searching for the best witty reply —though I come up short even with the extra time to think. Apparently, my only recourse is to give in to his whim and join him since he'll go with or without me. After I inform the rest of the team to join us at Raf's last-minute beach party, I head to my room on the next floor down to put on my bikini and slide a cute cover-up over my head. Dubai is more liberal than the other Arab nations, especially for foreign visitors, but strolling through the hotel wearing a few shreds of fabric held together by dental floss is still frowned upon.

The beach, however, is fair game.

When I walk out of my suite, the others are waiting for me in the hallway near the elevators. I hear Raf talking to them as I approach.

"To be perfectly clear, I'm the one pursuing Tawnee, not the other way around. In fact, the only thing she has agreed to so far is going down to the beach, and that's because I twisted her arm. She would never let me go alone, regardless of the professional cost to her. So, I wanted to be upfront with everyone in the event she agrees to go out with me on a personal level. I wouldn't want anyone to think she behaves in any way other than professional. I'm the one who confessed I'm in love with her. She hasn't admitted to any feelings for me yet, but I hope to rectify that very soon." Rafael's words stop me in my tracks.

It's one thing to have a private discussion with me about this, but quite another to share everything with my team without clearing it with me first. As he said, I haven't agreed to anything, but now everyone who works for me knows much more about my personal life, or potential personal life, or lack of personal life, than I wanted to share.

Yes, technically, he pays them, but they report to me. I'm the one who picked all his detail teams.

"Well, boss, this may surprise you, but we actually have a pool going on when you'd finally break down and ask her out. It's been clear to us for quite a while you've had a thing for Tawnee."

Thanks, Tony. That's exactly what I wanted to hear.

"Is that right?" Raf sounds proud. "In this pool, did anyone have any thoughts on how long it would take Tawnee to agree?"

Now, this, I have to hear. Only, the hallway is now completely quiet except for the nervous shuffling of feet. Then Tony finally opens his big mouth again.

"We pretty much agreed that would happen when

hell froze over. Nothing against you, boss. But she's pretty hard-core when it comes to her job, and we didn't think she'd jeopardize it for a potential relationship. That's not really her style."

"Interesting. Well, maybe I should fire her first then ask her out."

The group breaks out in laughter until I turn the corner to join them, then everyone has a sudden coughing fit.

"Very convincing, guys. Not obvious at all." I make it a point to glare at every single one of my team before turning my attention to Raf. "And you. May I have a minute in private?"

I turn and walk back to my room, open the door, and hold it open until he walks inside first.

"How you're still single is such a mystery to me when you're so romantic. 'Fire her then ask her out'? Really?" I roll my eyes and shake my head.

Raf laughs, clearly amused at the circumstances. "Don't blame them, Tawnee. That was my impromptu meeting. Just in case you come to your senses and realize you're as madly in love with me as I am with you, I wanted to avoid the uncomfortable conversation we'd have to have at that time."

"Well, why didn't I think of that? Yes, that makes perfect sense. So, instead of giving me more than fifteen minutes to absorb everything you said, you thought it was a good idea to have an uncomfortable conversation with the entire team today. Because, why not? We were just in a high-speed car chase then a wreck less than forty-eight hours ago, and now we're all going to the beach together after you announce your feelings toward me to my entire team. Just your average, ordinary vacation troubles."

"Exactly." He has the audacity to be proud of himself.

"Rafael, I really don't appreciate the position you've put me in at all. My personal life is none of their business. Your personal life is their business—to a degree—but you and I are not there yet. I haven't committed to anything more than our current relationship, which is employer and employee, borderline friends. If we progress into anything else, I'll be the one to have the talk with my team. Are we clear?"

"Crystal. But you have to admit one thing."

"And what's that?"

"At least you'd know life with me would never be boring." Rafael's smile crawls across his face, and his eyes twinkle with laughter. He turned what I intended to be somewhat of an insult into a positive.

"Always looking for the silver lining, huh?" I can't help but smile back at him.

"Absolutely, and I usually find it too. Now, let's go —the team is waiting, and they may get the wrong impression of us being in your room alone for so long."

He extends his elbow toward me and nods his head toward it. "We have to look like normal tourists, remember?"

"I do remember. I also remember any public display of affection here, even simply holding hands, can result in the police being called on us. I think we've drawn enough attention to ourselves today, don't you?"

"You win this round, Miss Milano. But the next one will be mine. I guarantee it." His predatory gleam sends shivers down my spine, but I mask my reaction

"I can hardly wait. Can we go now? We're burning daylight in here." I take the designer beach bag Rafael is holding and stuff my towel and sunblock inside before hoisting it onto my shoulder. We rejoin the others in the hall, and I press the down button for the elevator, ready for a couple of hours of relaxing with the ocean waves as my white noise.

Now that the tension is dispelled after Rafael's announcement, we can enjoy the rest of the day in the sun, sand, and surf. Stepping out into the extreme heat takes my breath away at first, but the breeze from the ocean helps me acclimate quickly. Each suite has a private cabana reserved on the beach with a lounging platform that resembles a queen-size bed. The four corners of the frame have gathered curtains, and the top has an optional cover for a shield from the intense Middle Eastern sun.

I set the bag down on the lounger and begin

pulling out the contents, specifically the sunblock for my shoulders, when Raf tosses his shirt in my face. Playfully, of course. When I look up at him, I have every intention of hurling an insult his way, but my eyes drop to his perfectly chiseled torso, and whatever thought I had leaves me.

Speechless.

Breathless.

And busted. So very busted.

"You aren't the only one who exercises." I can't see his eyes behind the mirrored frames and the bright sun, but I can feel the blatant satisfaction in them.

My senses finally return, and I grasp the hem of my cover-up and pull it off, leaving it in a heap on the outdoor bed. Now it's my turn to gloat and leave him speechless while he watches me rub the lotion into my skin before heading to the water.

It's been a long time since I've enjoyed flirting with a handsome man.

CHAPTER 3

Roman

"If you come over here one more time, I'll throw you out of this plane, Roman."

"You're not very nice when you first wake up, Blake. Has anyone ever told you that?"

"No, because you're the only one who has ever been brave enough to wake me up several times in one night. We've been traveling for too many hours to count, and we have several more hours to go yet. When they tell us we're coming in for a landing, that's when we'll be there. Not a minute before. So go back to your own suite and leave me alone until we get there."

"Here's what's bothering me." I ignore his loud groan—and when he turns his back to me—and keep talking. "I only received the one message. Nothing from her since then. If she hasn't been captured or killed, why wouldn't she have sent a follow-up message?"

"I understand what you're asking, but we can speculate for the next six hours until we get there and still be wrong. Write down all your questions, see if you find any common threads in them, and we'll be sure to cover all the angles as soon as we can. You're worried about her, I get it, but we can't do anything from here."

"You're right. These questions are just nagging at me. If she was okay, she would have sent a follow-up message. But she hasn't, so that leads me to believe—"

"That she's in a position where she can't send another message. Not that she's dead. Don't even go there, man. But *do* go back to *your own suite* and get some rest so I can too. We'll both need it in a few hours when Silas has us running nonstop."

I move back to my seat and spend the rest of the flight trying to rest, but the questions swirling in my mind make it next to impossible. Now that we've finally landed in Dubai, I realize I'm more keyed up than I was before we took off in Miami. Needless to say, after all the traveling and time difference, it's too late in the evening to canvass the area for information. Just my luck.

We walk into the FIVE Palm Jumeirah hotel, and I'm instantly floored by the opulence and attention to every minute detail. I've heard of Dubai and its growing popularity as the place for tourists, but I never realized the full extent of exactly how much until now. Our rooms are in one of the upper floors with fantastic views of the Persian Gulf, and we're all practically speechless over the lavishness surrounding us when we start to make our way to our rooms.

"And I thought Noah had a nice place," I mumble while we walk down the corridor.

"He does. This place is a completely different world altogether, though. Maybe we should send for the gang so we can all live here instead of Miami." Silas chuckles. He's kidding, but he still appreciates the beauty surrounding us.

"Just wait until tomorrow morning when you're not dying of jet lag and too many hours of flying. You probably won't want to leave the hotel grounds after all. Call Tawnee and tell her to come to us—we'll protect her from here." Blake unlocks his door, steps into the doorway of his room, and drops his suitcase. "Holy hell. Yeah, she needs to come on over and stay here with us."

When I open my door, I understand exactly what he means. Low lighting along the walls creates a soothing atmosphere, instantly sweeping stress away. The sliding glass door beside the bed gives an unobstructed view of the water surrounding the hotel.

Silas stops me before I'm able to take in the entire room.

"Roman, I assume she still hasn't answered any of your texts or encrypted messages since we landed?"

"No, and I've been checking every thirty seconds or so. I've sent enough unanswered texts to be considered a stalker at this point."

"I get it, man. Order room service for tonight. Get some rest. We'll meet out here at seven in the morning, grab breakfast, then pay a visit to the local police and see what we can find out. Don't go out on your own and get arrested—the laws are much different here than they are at home."

"That's over the line, Silas. You know I can't promise that at home, much less here." I flash a smile and shrug one shoulder.

"Don't make me have to lock you in your room for the night."

After looking over every square inch of my new home for however long it takes to find Tawnee, I unpack my suitcase and crawl into bed after ordering room service for the evening. I leave the curtains open so the rising sun will wake me, giving me the perfect morning view to set my mood for the day. I can only hope these small, positive touches help settle the sinking feeling in my gut. Tawnee has never ignored texts—even if she only responds to tell me to fuck off. The only way she wouldn't answer me is if...

Like Blake said, I can't let my thoughts go there again. One step at a time.

After enjoying a full four-course meal from the room service menu, I lie back on the bed and start listing all the things we should be doing right now that don't include resting, eating, or sleeping.

The next thing I know, the room is filled with bright sunshine. When I open my eyes, I fling my arm over them as a shield until they adjust. Then I catch a glimpse of the shimmering water outside. The bright blue sky above. The breathtaking view is exactly what I need to encourage me to rush through my morning routine and get dressed to accomplish my goals. First, find Tawnee. Second, take her home with me and keep her there forever. Third, make her fall in love with me again.

When I step out of my room, I'm surprised to find I'm the first one. After I glance at my phone, I realize I'm way ahead of schedule. Sunrise comes much earlier here than at home, one more thing to get used to, but I feel more rested than when we walked off the plane last night. I take a calculated risk and guess Silas is already up and rummaging around in his room while he waits for the rendezvous time, so I knock on his door.

As I expected, he's fully dressed and ready to go when he opens the door.

"A little eager, are we?" He smirks at me but holds the door open wide so I can pass through.

Then I turn to him, ready to get down to business. "You know I am. I was ready to go out and conduct a grid search last night when we got here. I was just thinking, maybe you should try texting her. You know, in case she's ignoring me for some reason but will answer you."

"I've already thought of that and tried. Although I didn't reach the stalker level you did, I did send her a few messages. She hasn't replied to me either, so it's not that she's avoiding you. She's off the grid."

"Is it strange that makes me feel better and worse at the same time?"

"That's a normal reaction—not strange at all. I've been looking into the guy she works for more in-depth this morning. I've already started a file on Mr. Rafael Cruz with some interesting information."

"You didn't sleep at all last night, did you?"

"Not much. I slept too long on the plane to make the flight go by faster, so I couldn't sleep once we got here. Did you know he's one of the richest men on the planet?"

"No, I didn't. I mean, I knew he was some bigwig in the corporate world, but I had no clue he was that wealthy. No offense to her skills, but does it make sense that Tawnee is his head of security?"

"First of all, never say that around her if you want

to keep your balls attached to your body. She'll snatch them off and have them stuffed and mounted as fuzzy dice to hang from her rearview mirror. Yes, it makes sense. She's good at what she does, and she has the experience to back up her decisions. That black belt in Brazilian Jiu-Jitsu doesn't hurt either—she knows how to use it to subdue much larger opponents. Plus, she has an efficient and logical approach to coordinating coverage. You underestimate her way too much, and you always have."

I've never really considered it in that light before, so I don't have much of a comeback to deny his assessment of me. I suppose he's correct, though. She obviously impressed one of the richest men in the world enough to nab that high-level job right off the bat. Makes me wonder what Cruz sees in her I didn't. Maybe I've just been wearing blinders where she's concerned without even realizing it.

"You're right. When we worked together for Noah, she was nothing but competent and reliable in every situation. In all honesty, I don't know what's wrong with me, Silas."

"Really? You don't know?" He looks amused, but I'm very serious.

"No, I don't. You think you do?"

"Oh, I know I do. I don't even have to think about it."

"Let's hear it, then. This should be good." I fold

my arms over my chest and wait for some enormous revelation about myself.

"You're selfish, self-centered, and take others for granted."

"Selfish and self-centered are the same thing."

"No, they're not. At all. You're selfish because you have no consideration for others. You're self-centered because you only focus on what *you* want or what *you* need, never putting anyone else's needs before your own. On top of that, you expect everyone in your life to keep giving their all for you, while you keep taking but never giving in return. Then you're shocked when they throw up their hands and walk away from you. That combination takes a lot of nerve—or stupidity. Which one is it?"

Fucking hell. The reflection I see in the mirror Silas just thrust in front of my face is not attractive.

Is that really how everyone else sees me?

Is that an accurate description of me?

Deep down, I already know the answer to both of those rhetorical questions. I also know that's exactly what Tawnee thinks of me—because I haven't given her any reason to believe otherwise. Now that I can't hide from the defects in my character, I'm one hundred percent committed to changing them, especially where she's concerned.

"Has anyone ever told you you're a shitty profiler?"

I know he's not, but I have to throw some kind of barb back at him.

"Nope. Never. I'm an excellent profiler, and everyone at the agency knows it. In fact, you should ask around and find out for yourself. It'll do you good." He quirks one eyebrow and nods toward my tightly crossed arms. "Even your body language says you're closed off. I knew you wouldn't accept what I had to say before I even said it. You don't fool me for one second, Roman."

"For argument's sake, let's say you're right about me. How would I go about fixing those character flaws?"

"Well, you could always say, 'What would Roman normally do in this situation?', then do the exact opposite. Or you could just stop and consider Tawnee's feelings for once in your fucking life. You're a grown man—start acting like it, for fuck's sake. I shouldn't have to tell you how to keep your girlfriend happy."

"Ouch."

"Tough love. You need more of it, along with a good, swift kick in the ass. Let's get the others and go to eat breakfast. I've made reservations for a late lunch at the Burj Al Arab Jumeirah."

"What's that? I thought we were going to the police?"

"We were, until I found out that Rafael Cruz is

checked in at the only hotel in Dubai nicer than this one. He's staying in one of the royal suites at that exclusive resort. There are also a few regular rooms are reserved under his company name, so we'll go over there and see what we can find out first. Without reserving a room, we can't even get on the grounds. The only way around that is to have reservations at one of their restaurants."

Silas's evaluation of me sticks in my mind, clawing at my sanity and making me second-guess my every move. But I can't deny what he said is true. Several times over breakfast, I wanted to rush the other men through their meals so we could get on the road. But I refrained from saying anything and simply listened to them while I drank another cup of coffee.

"Silas, you've been married for a couple years now. Can we expect to hear the pitter-patter of little Silas or Kira feet anytime soon?" Nick asks. He's been on Silas for the last year to give Amber, Silas's adopted daughter, a little brother or sister.

"You know, you're the sole reason why Amber asks us about that every single day now. Kira and I talked before I left to come here, and we've decided it's time. When I get back, we'll start practicing more." We all laugh, knowing exactly what he means. "When are you going to settle down, Blake?"

"Never."

"You're not allowed to hang around with Roman anymore. He's a bad influence on you."

"I don't know, Silas. I've been seeing this girl, but I'm hesitant to make our relationship a big deal. We're still taking it slow right now, nothing exclusive." Blake suddenly finds his fork very interesting.

"Do you love her?"

"I'm not sure."

"If you found out she'd been seeing some other guy while you've been away, how would that make you feel?" Silas already knows the answer. I can see it in his eyes.

Blake shrugs but doesn't look up.

"What if she told you she was in love with him and didn't want to see you anymore? What if she was letting him do everything to her body that you do?" Silas keeps pressing those buttons.

"I'd hunt him down and kill him." Blake pins Silas with an intense, murderous gaze.

Silas laughs in his face. "That's what I thought. You need to reevaluate those feelings you claim not to have before it's too late, my friend."

Too bad Silas didn't give me that exact advice three years ago. But I'm not sure I would have listened to him anyway.

CHAPTER 4

Tawnee

"Tawnee, are you awake?" If the pounding on my door wasn't loud enough to wake me, the yelling of my name from the hallway would have been. Fortunately, I've been up for quite a while already, trying to recall every detail about the incident without the police report as a reference.

We didn't stay on the beach for very long earlier this morning because I couldn't shake the feeling of being watched. When we adjourned to our rooms, I took a few hours of much-needed time off—and had an extremely productive nap.

I jerk the door open and face Rafael. He's dressed in his casual yet expensive attire, but he's carrying the same designer bag we used at the beach earlier. "Why are you out of your room without an escort?" I cross my arms and tap my foot while waiting for what I already know is an unacceptable answer.

"We're in the most secure hotel in the entire Middle East. This place is sitting on its own private island with a closed bridge manned by private security guards. They have a fleet of Rolls-Royces that pick guests up at the gate and drop them off at the front door. Who do you think can get me in here?"

"Anyone with the means to hire hitmen, Raf. You're not the only man in the world with money and who stays in fancy hotels when he travels. Whoever was behind that chase could have reserved rooms here too. You're making my job impossible. I mean, how am I supposed to get another security job if you get killed in 'the world's only seven-star hotel' on my watch?"

"Fooled you. Tony escorted me down, checked out the hallway, found no assassins, so I sent him back upstairs. But I promise I'll call you from my room next time I decide to venture out of my room… into the hallway… only one floor down from my suite."

"Since you're already here, come on in." I open the door wider to let him pass through. "What's on your mind?"

"First, I actually did try to call your cell a couple of times, but you didn't answer. You always answer, so that alone concerned me enough to rush down the flight of stairs to check on you." He takes a seat on the couch, his eyes never straying from mine. "Were you avoiding me?"

"You know better than that. With all the excitement, I didn't realize it until last night, but my phone is missing. Then with the impromptu beach excursion, I forgot to tell you. It must be in the rental car—maybe it fell under the seat when we crashed. I've looked everywhere else for it, and I know for a fact that I didn't take it to the beach with me. I was just about to call the wrecker service and ask them to look inside the car."

"Let me talk to them. Even though this area is more tolerant of women than others in this region, there are still plenty of prejudices. I don't think a wrecker driver would appreciate you asking him to search the car for your lost cell phone. In fact, that may ensure you never get it back. We won't be here long enough to have another one shipped. I guess you'll just have to stay close to me at all times. You can even move to my suite—it has three bedrooms."

"Yes, I guess I could do that. Or, here's a novel idea, you could just use the phone in your room to call me when I'm in my room."

He smiles, his dark eyes sparkling with dangerous flirtation. Dangerous to me, that is. "I like my idea much better. You can protect my body with yours much easier if we're in the same suite."

"If you don't open your door to strangers or go

wandering around the hotel alone, we won't have to worry about that, will we?"

"You never know, Tawnee. Anything is possible. We certainly didn't think we'd be chased and nearly nabbed this week, did we?"

"Actually, I always consider that it is a very real possibility. That's exactly why I was watching our surroundings so closely. Now, did you come down here just to try to convince me to move into your suite with you?"

"No, that wasn't why I came down here at all. I just now had that brilliant idea. The reason I've been trying to call you is to take you to the restaurant in the lobby for a nice lunch, then we can spend the rest of the day on the beach together. This morning was perfect. I haven't felt that relaxed in a long time, even though you saw ghosts everywhere. Since Tabitha rescheduled my meeting for later next week, we're free to do whatever we want to until then. What do you say?"

"Well, you are my boss, Raf, and it's my responsibility to make sure you're protected at all times. If you're on the beach, I'll be on the beach with you, along with several members of the team to keep an eye on the perimeter. But grabbing lunch then spending the rest of the afternoon in and around that crisp blue water sounds like heaven on earth. Give me a minute to change clothes and alert the guys then we can head down to the restaurant."

"I'll call Tony so he can alert the rest of the team to meet us downstairs. You just put your bathing suit on under that dress so we can start doing as little as possible as soon as possible."

⚜

"I'm not eating again today. My God, I'm so stuffed now I can barely move. You are a terrible influence on me." I plop down on the lounger in our cabana, ready to take another nap after the feast we just enjoyed.

"Au contraire, my love. I'm not a bad enough influence on you—yet. I'm working on it, though."

"Just lie down in the hot Dubai sun and shrivel up like a prune in silence, please."

He chuckles beside me. "Are you going to relax this time so we can enjoy it?"

"Yes, if you'll behave and not try to swim up and down the coast alone."

"Done. I'm staying right here beside you. I'm not quite up for the Iron Man today."

"How does your neck feel now?" I glance over at Raf as he stretches out beside me in the beach cabana, his bronzed skin already darkening in the sun.

"A little sore. Maybe you should massage it for me

and make it feel better." A smile plays on his lips, though he tries to hide it.

"Or maybe I should make you an appointment with the spa and let the professionals handle that for you."

"I'm positive I would feel much better if you rubbed it instead of someone I don't know."

My thoughts immediately stray directly where they shouldn't—ever—especially not about my boss. Nevertheless, I don't believe for one second that we're still talking about rubbing his *neck* at the moment.

"I'll call the doctor again and have him give you a hand sooner than expected. If you're still in pain, he should make sure nothing else is going on—even if that means a trip to the hospital."

"Nothing else is going on, *that's* the whole problem." Now he does smile, and his white teeth glimmer against his tanned skin. "I'm trying to fix that little oversight, if you'd just let me."

"Excuse me, sir. I'm so sorry to disturb you." The hotel concierge appears next to the cabana, waiting for Rafael to acknowledge him before continuing.

Raf opens his eyes and sits up when he sees the man is wearing a hotel uniform and name tag. "No trouble at all, Ahmed. What can I do for you?"

"There are four gentlemen at the beach entry gate who claim they urgently need to speak with you. They claim to be acquaintances of Miss Milano." His eyes momentarily skim over to mine.

"What are their names, Ahmed? Do you know?" Four men are here to see me? That's not ominous at all.

"Yes, ma'am. Their names are Silas Steele, Nick Tucker, Blake Mills, and Roman Scott." Ahmed reads the list from a piece of paper in his hand, then waits for instructions from us.

Since they aren't guests of this hotel, they're not allowed on the grounds without specific reservations for the restaurants or spa. But, I'm beyond shocked and concerned. What the hell are those guys doing here?

"Rafael, I know them. I used to work with all of them in Miami. If you don't mind, I'd appreciate your giving permission for them to join us. Something must be terribly wrong for them to be here, asking to see you."

"By all means. As long as you know them, they are welcome to join us. Ahmed, please show them to our cabana when they arrive. Thank you." When Ahmed walks away, Raf turns his attention to me. "What do you think all this is about?"

"I have no idea why they would be here. Miami is a long way from here, and there's an eight-hour time difference on top of that. Combined with what happened a couple of days ago, their arrival in Dubai is more than a mere coincidence."

"How would they have found us? It's not as if this hotel would give out customer information."

"They have the skills and means to get that information without calling the hotel. How they found us doesn't concern me as much as why they want to find us. Something big must be happening. We may need to cut this trip short and get you out of here on zero notice."

"I'm sorry, love, but that's not happening. If I don't see this through now, it'll never happen. The sellers weren't offended with the first change of plans because they're well aware most of the people here drive like a bat out of hell. But if I bail on them and leave the country, they'll never speak to me again."

"It really isn't my place to say this, but because I genuinely care about your safety, I feel like I should. Raf, you have more than enough money. Is closing this real estate deal really worth risking your life over?"

He pulls my hand to his mouth and kisses the back of it. "Thank you for worrying about me. I know you take your work very seriously, but I also know I'm more than only a job to you. But there's something you should know by now, Tawnee. There's no such thing as having enough money. Besides, I also trust that you'll keep me safe."

"You are an impossible man."

"Impossible to resist? Impossible to forget? Impossible not to love? There are so many possibilities to finish that thought. Which did you mean?"

"Rafael, I've worked for you for nearly three years now. If there's one thing you know about me, it's that I say exactly what I mean."

He laughs and nods. "This, I do know. Absolutely." He pauses for a moment, looking at me with a thoughtful expression, and part of me wishes I could read his mind. Then he lifts his knuckles and skims them over my cheek. "You're so beautiful. Your black hair shimmers in the sun. Your deep hazel eyes both captivate me and see straight through me. For the longest time now, I've been dying to kiss your luscious lips just to know how you taste. And, for the record, the more you blush like that, the more I'll tell you exactly what I'm thinking. That fact that you have no idea how fucking sexy you are makes you even more special."

Ahmed clears his throat from behind us, saving me from trying to come up with a reply. Rafael casually turns to greet his guests while I slide off the end of the lounger to say hello to my friends. Then I stop dead in my tracks when I see Roman's face, even though I knew he was on his way in. The red creeping up his neck to his face isn't because of the sun. His hands are curled into tight fists at his sides. His eyes narrow, crinkling at the edges as they draw tighter and tighter.

His teeth are clenched so hard, I can see the muscles jumping in his jaw.

After three years apart—because of his bullshit—he has the nerve to show up here and glare at me like that?

I don't fucking think so.

When I see Silas, Nick, and Blake, I ignore Roman and rush to hug the other men. I haven't seen them in three long years either, and I'm genuinely happy they're here.

"Silas, what are you doing here? It's hardly a coincidence that we're in the Middle East at the exact same time."

"It's not a coincidence at all, Tawnee." Silas looks over at Roman, who still hasn't spoken to me, before cutting his eyes back to me. The other men exchange curious glances—confusion, shock, relief, lots of questions—but no one says anything. "Roman received a coded message from you on our secure system. It said you needed immediate extraction from the country because of an assassination attempt."

"What? Are you joking? I haven't used that system in three years. That message wasn't from me."

All eyes shift to Roman as we wait for him to further explain this mystery message.

"What? Why are you looking at me? I showed you the message—I sure as hell didn't send it to myself."

"Oh shit." I close my eyes and mentally berate

myself for my stupidity. "We had an incident a couple of days ago that resulted in a wreck. There was also an altercation and a lot of commotion. My phone has been missing since then, but I just assumed I dropped it in the car while I was fighting off those men. What if one of them took it and cracked the code?"

"Cracked Brad's code? Come on." Roman automatically dismisses my theory. Seems nothing has changed in the last three years.

"Roman, think it through. That's the simplest explanation, no matter how improbable you think it is. We already know someone hacked into Dubai's traffic cameras and deleted all the footage of the wreck. Why couldn't that same someone hack Brad's system?" Silas turns his attention back to me. "Can we finish this conversation somewhere a little more private and a little less exposed to potential sniper fire?"

"Thought you'd never ask."

CHAPTER 5

Roman

Tawnee pulls on a summer dress over her bathing suit then heaves a massive bag onto her shoulder. Not that she's incapable of handling it on her own, but my mom raised me better than to stand by and not offer my help. The rest of the team is busy gathering their personal items and making introductions, so I take the opportunity to get a few minutes alone with Tawnee. When she walks between Silas and me on the way toward the hotel entrance, I grab the straps and slide it off her arm.

"Why do you have such a huge purse, Tawnee?" I chuckle as I turn and walk beside her.

"That's not my purse, Roman. It's Rafael's very

expensive designer bag." She shakes her head at me, but I see how she looks down at the ground, trying to hide her smile.

"Rafael carries a purse?" I know exactly what she meant, but I couldn't miss the chance to get a little jab in.

Her laugh bursts free before she can stop it. She turns to look at me and pushes her sunglasses up on top of her head. Fuck, I've missed those dark hazel eyes—warm golden-brown mixed with olive-green that sparkle and shine with her personality. "No, he doesn't carry a purse. You know better than that. Don't play dumb with me. You forget that I know you too well for you to get away with it."

"No kidding. I can't get away with anything around you. You're worse than Silas." I glance over at her and smile, trying to keep our banter light. My first thought took me back to when she left me, and how stupid I was ever to let her go.

"I'm going to take that as a compliment."

"You should—that's exactly how I meant it. Seems your team falls in line with your lead, following your orders to a T."

She doesn't respond right away, which naturally catches my attention. After a loud sigh, she meets my questioning gaze with a shrug. "You know how some of these macho former commandos are. To them, taking orders from a woman is the equivalent of... carrying a purse."

"So, you've caught shit for having the elite skills and the intense grit needed to be the head of security for one of the wealthiest men in the world? Sounds like they're more threatened by you than anything else."

"It's not everyone—just one or two who have been more challenging than the others. Let's just say I've had to prove that I mean what I say more than once, but they always see it my way sooner or later."

My first instinct is to come to her rescue by taking names and kicking asses of anyone who has disrespected her. But I push those feelings aside because it won't help our situation, and it won't earn me any points with her. If anything, my outburst would make her lose the hard-won respect she's earned so far. However, I am absolutely willing to put those assholes under a microscope and find out every one of their deep, dark secrets.

Jealousy makes men do stupid things, but when their masculinity is threatened, they can be deadly. That may be just the catalyst one of these guys needs to stage an attempt on their employer, making it appear as if Tawnee was caught in between. Since Tawnee wasn't the one who called me to her rescue, this could be a case of premeditated friendly fire. Maybe we should use this time to kill two birds with one stone—flush out any potential traitors and cement her place of authority.

"Which ones have given you the most grief?" I keep my tone nonchalant and conversational to avoid spooking her.

"Until recently, Tony seemed to be the ringleader. He was Raf's driver long before I came along and thought he could spot a seasoned tail with one glance. We've had a couple of instances occur where that wasn't the case at all, and we narrowly escaped. He resented my input on more defensive driving maneuvers. The last time he disobeyed a direct order, he and I had a 'come to Jesus' meeting, and I ended up telling him it was my way or the highway. He's still with us, so he chose my way, and I haven't had to give him an order twice since then."

Note to self: *Kick Tony's ass*.

"And what about Raf?" I can't keep the sarcasm out of my voice when I say his name. *Raf.* He makes me want to ralph.

Her head jerks in my direction, and I know without a doubt she picked up on the subtle change in my voice. "What about him?"

"What does he say about his security team disobeying your orders?"

She narrows her eyes at me but ultimately decides to leave it alone. For now, anyway. "Rafael offered to fire Tony and let me choose a suitable driver as his replacement. He fully supports me and my abilities to handle his safety—no matter what it takes."

"That must've chapped Tony's ass to hear that."

"I think it made him realize how seriously Rafael took my role in his organization and made Tony appreciate my input more." The words are there, but her tone lacks conviction. She may have believed that at one time, but now she's not so sure. "Wait a minute, do you think one of my own staff is behind this? Like they're staging a coup against me or something?"

"I'm not prepared to accuse anyone on your team of attempted kidnapping, but I also can't vouch for them. Until I've vetted them, I have to view everyone as a suspect."

"And who asked you to vet anyone? You know I appreciate you how you dropped everything at a moment's notice and came running because you thought I was in trouble. But as you can see, I'm not in trouble. I'm fine, and I'm not asking for your help or your interference with my job." She stops walking and confronts me face-to-face.

I'd expect nothing less of her.

"I'm not trying to take over your job, Tawnee. I have a job. The four of us are here for *you*—no one and nothing else. We didn't just come running at a moment's notice. We hopped on the next flight out of

Miami and flew halfway around the world. For you. After someone has already chased you and erased the traffic camera footage, do you really think they'll just slink back into the shadows and disappear? Someone hacked into Brad's system and sent an encrypted message to me—and only me—and made it appear to come from you. Only someone who knows you would know to contact me through that app."

A shocked expression passes over her features for half a second before she hides behind her mask again. Her chest rises as she takes a deep breath then she puts her hands on her hips. "You're right. None of this is a coincidence, and I'm clearly not thinking straight. I'm sorry for overreacting—I know you're just trying to help. Thank you, Roman. Your showing up here means more to me than you know."

We begin walking again, though the rest of the clan has nearly caught up with us now. "How have you been? You know, before this week went to hell in a handbasket."

"Fine." She glances in my direction but doesn't make eye contact with me. "I've been very busy, obviously. Rafael travels constantly, and his security team is always with him. We rotate days off, but we're almost always in a different country. We're scheduled to be here for a month before we get to head home and stay there until the end of September. I can't tell you how much I'm looking forward to that long of a break in his schedule."

"You two seem close." Yeah, I had to go there. It's eating me alive. Since the moment I saw her lounging in the ocean-side cabana with him in her barely there bikini, oiled skin, and carefree smile. He doesn't deserve that smile from her.

"We are."

That's it? No elaboration? No explanation? Only a confirmation of what I've already witnessed for myself. They're close.

We reach the entrance to the hotel, and I open the door to let her go in first. "After you." Then I follow her inside the elegantly decorated space.

"Thank you. And I should have said this before— thanks for carrying the man-purse for me. It was a little heavy." She doesn't even try to hide the smug grin this time.

"I have no shame in carrying the man-purse for you. I'd even drive to the store and buy the biggest box of tampons they have if you asked me."

"As always, you're too kind." She pushes the button for the elevator then quickly turns to me. "Oh, I forgot I need the room keycard inside the elevator."

She unzips the bag and starts rifling through the interior pockets while it is still on my shoulder. She's so close to me—her face is so close to mine. All I want to do is press my lips against hers right now. To feel the softness. To taste her one more time. To take back every fucking thing I did and said that ever hurt her.

Instead, I only watch her, unable to tear my eyes away from her face.

Just like my assessment of Rafael being undeserving of her smile, I don't deserve her kiss.

I haven't earned her affection.

Yet.

The others surround us as we wait for the doors to open, carrying on their conversation as usual. Silas asks Rafael about any enemies who feel strongly enough to act on their anger, before urging him to return to the US—apparently not for the first time since Rafael's response is a little terse. "I can't do that, as I explained. My business comes first. That's why I have a security team in place."

Nick is chatting with someone about the details of the wreck and the altercation afterward, asking a million and one questions. Blake has yet another side conversation with the only other woman of the group. The additional security members chime in here and there, adding tidbits of information that may or may not come in useful later. But in the several seconds we all wait for the elevator car to arrive, I feel the unmistakable sensation of angry eyes burning a hole through me.

When I abruptly turn to confront the glare like a man, Tony quickly averts his gaze and suddenly finds the adjacent wall riveting. Undeterred, I continue to stare and wait for him to grow a pair. The elevator doors open, and even though he knows he's being watched, he refuses to make eye contact with me again. We move into the elevator, Tawnee uses her card to access the resident floors, and the doors slide closed.

The silence inside the confined area is conspicuous and uncomfortable—for some. But I use it to my advantage while observing the other members of the security team. Beads of sweat gather on one guy's forehead. Another man shifts awkwardly, unable to stand still from nervous energy. A single glance at Silas, Nick, and Blake confirms my assessment. Their postures are relaxed and calm, and they remain completely still. No fidgeting whatsoever.

When we reach his floor and file out into the hall, Rafael's security team jumps into high gear, sweeping his gigantic royal suite before allowing him to enter.

"Wow, this place has multiple levels. I've never been in a hotel room quite like this one before." I look around the entryway, astounded at the ornate marble stairway leading up to the next story.

"I need ample space to stretch out." Rafael doesn't bother with the common courtesy of looking at me when he speaks to me.

Personally, I think he's compensating for something with this oversized suite for only one man. He must have a micropenis the size of a Tic Tac.

"Rafael, do you have any business deals in the works with the potential of putting you in harm's way?" Nick asks, getting straight to business as usual.

"My business ventures don't exactly invite new best friends, but I can't think of anyone who would want to hurt me—especially someone with Arab connections. Tony and I have had long discussions about this over the last couple of nights, going through all my recent acquisitions. But nothing has stood out to either of us so far."

"We need to review that information as well. There may be names on that list of business associates we recognize." I appreciate how Nick doesn't really ask for what he wants. He just says how it'll be, and that's the end of the story.

"Absolutely, we can arrange that right away. Any help you can give is very much appreciated. Where are you staying?"

Nick gives the name of our hotel then goes into full agent mode, talking with Rafael about hotel security, his security team, and a barrage of other questions. Silas and Blake join in when the rest of the security team rejoins us, and we're finally able to enter the main sitting area. While they're busy talking, I take advantage of the opportunity to steal some time with Tawnee.

"Which way is your bedroom?" I pat the side of the beach bag I'm still carrying.

"My suite is on the next floor down. I'm not staying in the same room as Rafael."

"Do you want to head downstairs to your room and change? I'll escort you." I gesture toward the door with my head, hiding my satisfaction at knowing she has her own room.

"Why would you assume I need an escort to my room?" She pierces me with her angry eyes as they narrow at the corners.

I cock my head to the side and draw my eyebrows down, trying to find the words to answer her. "Tawnee, I didn't mean it like that. I saw your face when Nick started questioning Rafael, and I know there's something you haven't told anyone yet. I thought maybe you wanted to talk about it in private."

She folds her arms over her chest, shakes her head, and rolls her eyes at me. "You know me too damn well, Roman Scott."

"Apparently not well enough to know why you're withholding vital information when you know how dangerous that is."

"Lower your voice, Roman."

"You're right—you know how pissed Silas will be when he finds out you haven't said anything about it yet. But I'm the one he'll take it out on. I suggest you come clean to me first, so I can help mitigate the damage."

"Fine, but only because I want to get out of this

bathing suit and into real clothes. Come with me." She steps forward into the room and gets everyone's attention. "Roman and I will be back in a few minutes."

Rafael doesn't appear pleased at all with her announcement, but Tony looks downright pissed off.

CHAPTER 6

Tawnee

My thoughts and feelings are all over the place when Roman and I step outside of Rafael's suite. Seeing Roman again immediately erased the three years we've spent apart, and I feel as if I'm right back at the moment when we split up. I mentally force my thoughts back to the present several times, trying to leave old memories and unresolved feelings in the past where they belong. We're in the middle of the most dangerous situation of my entire life, not to mention my career, and I'm distracted by a former flame like a foolish schoolgirl.

If anyone on my team knew how their head of security reacted when faced with a hostile opponent from her past, they'd band together and have me committed for losing my mind.

I wouldn't be able to blame them either.

This behavior isn't like me at all.

"Man, this hotel is so far out of my league, I'm afraid to even ask how much they charge per night."

"Well, Rafael's room is obviously more upscale than the rest of ours. His is around twenty-grand per night. Mine is much more economical at almost ten thousand a night."

Roman stops walking and gawks at me for a few seconds. "You're shitting me."

"Not at all." I can't help but laugh at that typical Roman response.

"You're talking US dollars, right? Not pesos or some fucking obscure denomination that equates to a hundred dollars a night." Roman pushes the elevator button, and we wait for the car to arrive.

"US dollars, yes."

"And you're here for how long?"

"A month." We step inside the elevator and move to opposite sides.

"Fuck me. I've never known anyone that rich before. Seriously, how do you amass that much wealth without being involved in some seriously shady shit?" While I'm almost positive Roman didn't mean that as a direct insult to Raf, I still feel the need to defend my employer and friend.

"I'm sure that's true for a lot of people, but Rafael made his money by learning the stock market inside and out, watching the signs, and getting in on the ground floor of stocks that paid huge dividends when the company took off. The more he made, the more he invested in his vision. It took years of hard work, losing large sums of money, and facing almost certain bankruptcy before he turned it all around. But that wasn't by doing anything illegal. He took a long, hard look at himself and his missteps, then he never made those mistakes again."

Roman simply watches me, his blue-gray eyes assessing my body language while he processes all the information I just dumped in his lap. But it's the intimate sensation his eyes evoke that rattles me to the core. The doors slide open and I step out of the elevator first, but I can feel Roman hot on my heels. The arcs of electricity are still there when we're near each other—regardless of how inconvenient or unwanted they are. One thing our relationship never lacked was sexual chemistry. Even now, my senses have kicked into overdrive from his closeness, and all my nerve endings are firing relentlessly.

It's as if my body craves him on a purely carnal level, and there's not a damn thing I can do to stop it.

My hand shakes when I lift the room key to open the door. As I should have expected, it doesn't work when I first attempt to open the door. It also refuses on the second try. After the third time, now I'm pissed off at the door, at Roman, and at the world. All for no reason other than I've allowed this man to affect me to the point I can't even open a fucking door.

Roman's hand slowly moves toward mine. I feel his chest barely brush my back, but the contact is enough to send chills down my spine.

"Let me try. Probably just needs an easy touch."

His mouth is too close when he speaks. The deep timbre of his voice combined with the feel of his lips brushing against the shell of my ear nearly makes my knees buckle underneath me. His fingers slide across my hand until they reach the room key.

All while I remain as still as a statue because I can't fucking move. Not that I'd ever admit this to him, but I'm equally afraid of brushing against him more... and not being close enough to him. My entire body is on fire in the best way—and this is a sensation I haven't felt since I was last with him. It's been three years since I've felt this alive.

He takes the card from me and tries it.

Naturally, it opens the first time for him.

"Oh, look, it opened for you. I warmed it up for you." I've got to dispel the mounting tension inside me with a little humor before I whirl around and mount *him* right here in the hallway.

"You certainly did." His voice is too low... too close... too intimate. "From the first second I saw you in that itty-bitty hot black bikini on the beach." He steps around me and holds the door open. The desire I see in his eyes not only matches mine, but reaches out and grabs me by the throat, making it impossible for me to say anything witty in return.

When I finally step across the threshold, he closes the door behind me but motions for me to stay put. Much like the security team did for Raf's safety, Roman silently moves through my suite, checking every possible hiding place for potential intruders.

"All clear, sweets. I thought I'd read this hotel had complimentary butler service to cater to your every need—even unlocking your doors for you."

The half-second hesitation in answering is only because I haven't been called "sweets" in so long, it hit me like a blast from the past. That was always his pet name for me. "Yes, they normally do. But for obvious security reasons, we declined the service. We like to know exactly who has access to our rooms at all times."

"I concur—I'd like to know who has access to your room at all times too. Let's make a list right now." He smiles from ear to ear, so proud of his little funny.

"You know my rule on that, Roman. It doesn't matter which hotel we stay in; I only allow them to make one key for my room, and I know where it is at all times. That way, if it's ever missing, I know not to return to the room alone, and I'll change rooms for added measure."

"Yes, I do know you—better than anyone else does. Want to tell me what you're hiding now? I have a sinking feeling I'll beat Silas to the punch and go ballistic before he even has the chance."

"I'm going to shower and get dressed before we have this conversation. But I will say one thing about it and leave you to ruminate on it."

"What's that?"

"You have good intuition. You should go with it."

"Fuck, Tawnee. I fucking knew it." He drops his chin to his chest and stares at the floor, keeping his hotheaded temper under wraps. He's trying to, at least.

I've got to give him credit for that—the old Roman would fly off the handle and pop off with something smartass. Then we'd end up in a huge argument because I'm every bit as stubborn as he is.

"You have a few minutes to digest it and come to terms with the terrible unknown, then we can speak calmly about it."

He nods, not making eye contact, but also not destroying the room in a fit of rage.

Baby steps.

"Is there any beer in the fridge? I'll probably need twelve or thirteen to get through this."

That makes me smile. "Yes, as a matter of fact, there's a twelve-pack in there. Don't tell anyone, though—I don't normally share my beer."

He finally looks up at me again, and what I see in

his eyes makes my heart skip a beat. Here I thought it was anger simmering just below his skin, waiting for the right moment to unleash hell on earth, when it was essentially deep-rooted fear he was fighting to control. Fear for me.

"You'd better call down and have another twelve-pack delivered before you're finished with your shower if you plan to drink any." The slight upturn of his lips betrays his halfhearted sarcastic jab.

"I'm not worried about it. I mean, technically, it's almost considered contraband here. But I have my sources if we need more."

"It's the butler you dismissed, isn't it? He's your beer source."

"Damn, you really do know me too well." I point toward the kitchen area. "Help yourself. There are snacks in there too."

I leave him to rummage through the suite and find whatever he wants while I head toward the master bedroom. When I'm standing under the hot water in the massive shower, my thoughts once again return to the problems in our relationship instead of focusing on the more pressing issue at hand. Since those thoughts won't leave me, I let them run rampant to get it out of my system so I can do my job.

His last words to me the day we broke up were to ask if I was either on my period or pregnant since the only reason for my outburst must have been hormone-related. I've never wanted to shoot someone before or after that event—but the fleeting thought was there. In my military and security careers, I've been required to shoot, but those instances were all about self-preservation and nothing related to revenge. In the heat of the moment with Roman, I finally understood the meaning of "crime of passion." Questioning my sanity and what I was possibly capable of doing haunted me for months after that encounter.

But it forced me to do a lot of soul-searching and being entirely honest with myself. The reason I reacted so strongly—and borderline violently—was because his flippant response to my legitimate heartbreak confirmed the facts I'd chosen to ignore for far too long. I loved him much more than he loved me, and that made me feel much too vulnerable and nowhere near good enough for him. His player days weren't far enough in his past to satisfy me, and his commitment phobia only reinforced the thoughts that constantly plagued me in those days. I couldn't shake the notion he was always waiting for someone better to come along… that I was only his "Miss Right Now" instead of his "Miss Right Forever."

Over the last three years, I've tried persistently to avoid comparing Roman and Rafael in any way. But there's no way around it. The stark differences are there in my face every day. One of the reasons I've been so loyal to Raf, even when he makes outrageous demands—such as going to the beach so soon after a deadly threat—is because of how well he treats me. Before he shocked me by professing his feelings for me, I knew the deep-rooted respect between us was mutual. I felt it, saw it, and we both appreciated it, never taking it for granted.

I've never felt as if my heart were in danger of being shattered into a million pieces with Rafael. With Roman, I waited for the other shoe to drop every day. Every time Roman started a conversation with the dreaded phrase, "We need to talk," I just knew it was to tell me he'd fallen in love with someone else. When Rafael says we need to talk, I feel no qualms about the unknown topic. The understanding that whatever we're facing, we'll face it together, is simply ingrained in our working relationship.

Until today, our relationship has been strictly platonic with only harmless flirting and innocent teasing. The line we crossed today put us in an all-new territory, and I'm not sure how to handle it. Roman showing up right at that moment only complicates the situation further, though my rational mind knows that's silly. It has been three years, for crying out loud. He shouldn't still affect me like this.

With my eyes closed and my head leaned back, I drop my hands to my sides and let the pouring water from the rain-like shower head rinse the conditioner out of my hair. My heart is racing, and I can barely catch my breath. When I saw Roman on the beach, looking at me with his dangerous and feral expression, the flush I felt had nothing to do with the temperature outside and everything to do with the desire that immediately engulfed me. He looked delicious enough to eat in his dress slacks, button-down shirt, and blazer.

The man I used to know thought dressing up meant wearing jeans with no visible holes in them. Back then, if I'd asked him to wear what the rest of the world considered dress clothes on the beach, I'd be in a psychiatric facility on a seventy-two-hour hold for a full mental health evaluation. Clothes do not make the man; that idiom, I firmly believe. But can a change in the man's choice of clothing signal a difference in the man himself?

Or am I putting too much stock in subtle variations and setting myself up for disappointment yet again?

"Fucking stop obsessing over this already, Tawnee. You'll end up driving yourself to the psych ward if you don't get a grip, girl." Talking to myself with a firm tone and a no-nonsense, practical approach usually does the trick.

I've been around Roman all of thirty minutes—max—and my thoughts are already running away from me. My cart and my horse aren't even in the same time zone at this point. With a shake of my head, I attempt to clear the fog from between my ears. Then I pick up my razor to shave all my lady parts. I set one foot on the tiled seat in the corner of the shower and slide the blade across my skin.

"Don't take this the wrong way, okay, sweets? I couldn't help but notice when I first saw you down on the beach that you look like you've lost quite a bit of weight. Not that you don't look fucking hot as hell, but I never thought you had any extra weight you could lose in the first place. You were always muscular for a woman, and it looked damn good on you. I've searched your entire kitchen and what you call snacks is more like raw rabbit food. I'm worried you're not eating and maybe even starving yourself or something.

"Fuck, this is coming out all wrong. I'm sorry—I know I sound like a complete dick, but I don't mean it that way. What I really want to know is if you're okay. That's all that matters to me, Tawnee—if you're happy and healthy and taking good care of yourself."

At first, the deep timbre of his voice emanating from inside my bathroom makes me jump. The sudden jerk of the razor against my leg nicks my skin, causing a tiny rivulet of blood to form instantly. The sheer audacity of him just waltzing into my bathroom while I'm obviously still in the shower and very naked strikes a chord in me. He's crossed a hard line—one he will immediately regret when my scrawny, too-skinny ass kicks his arrogant, self-absorbed ass to kingdom come. While he's mid-sentence, I grab the handle and swing the glass door open, ready to crack his skull.

Then three things hit me, one after the other, and they knock the wind out of my sails.

First, I didn't close the bathroom door all the way.

Second, he's standing in the opening with his back to me and his eyes closed.

Third, his apology is sincere and heartfelt—and so is his concern for my well-being.

Before he realizes I'm standing behind him completely naked and dripping wet, I step back inside the shower and softly close the door.

"I'm not sure how to answer the part about the weight loss. I guess I've lost some since you last saw me. But, yes, I'm taking good care of myself. We travel a lot, and you know how hotel gyms are compared to real ones. Their weights aren't as helpful, so I've been swimming laps and building up my cardio lately. And clean, healthy eating is not rabbit food. It's good for you—you should try it."

"Sweets, I'm not eating a plain stalk of celery. That's not a snack. A party-size bag of Cool Ranch Doritos is a snack. A giant Halloween-size bag of frozen Reese's—the best snack of all. Carrots, celery, and broccoli are meant to be combined with other ingredients to make a full dish—not to graze on like rabbits eating grass."

I laugh out loud as I turn off the water and grab my oversized plush towel. After a few quick swipes to dry off, I wrap it around me and step out of the shower. "Must be nice to eat all that tasty-good junk food and not have it go straight to your hips and thighs. Not all of us are as fortunate as you are, Roman."

"Is it safe to open my eyes and turn around now?" I can't help but think how sweet it is of him to ask that. Not that I should expect less from any man, but being respectful of anyone's privacy has never been in his nature.

"Yes, it's safe now. Thank you for being considerate of my privacy."

"No thanks needed, sweets." He looks over his shoulder, and his steely gray eyes darken with desire. He moves to face me fully while leisurely perusing the length of my body from my towel down to my toes. On the way back up, he notices the blood on my shin. "Your leg is bleeding. I saw some bandages in the kitchen cabinet. Have a seat and I'll grab them."

"Don't bother. It's only a small nick from shaving." I follow him out of the shower room and into the outer sitting area, but my protests fall on deaf ears. Within seconds, he's back with the small first aid kit I always take on trips.

"Let's have a look." He motions toward the chair in front of the vanity mirror as he opens the container.

"Really, I'm okay—"

"Sit."

"Fine." I plop down on the seat and scowl at him.

Then he hits me with that sexy smirk of his, and I forget why I'm irritated with him.

He kneels in front of me and picks up my leg to examine the minuscule cut. The rush of electricity that zings through my body makes me grip the sides of the chair, my fingers curling into the wood and holding on for dear life. I'm intentionally holding my breath to avoid saying something I'll regret later and praying he doesn't say anything that requires an intelligent reply. He slides his hand up the back of my leg to the bend of my knee. A whimper nearly escapes my throat from the warmth of his hand and the memory of his touch.

With a cotton swab soaked with peroxide, he cleans the area then leans closer and lightly blows on it to dry it. He's solely focused on my nonexistent wound, not at all affected by what is essentially foreplay for me.

I think I may die now... It's been way too long since I've been with a man.

He removes the smallest bandage from the kit, covers the cut, and sets my foot on his thigh before looking up at me. He doesn't move from his position at my feet. His hand is still on my leg, and his thumb lightly brushes back and forth across my skin...lovingly, reverently, longingly.

A sea of emotions washes across his features while we remain locked in a silent battle of desire versus reality. Part of me wishes I could read his mind, but a greater part is afraid of what I'd find there. Despite the number of times I've denied the truth since we parted, I can't fool myself any longer.

I've never really moved on from Roman Scott.

But I won't allow this old flame to be rekindled.

He not only shattered my heart beyond repair—he crushed my spirit and my belief in an eternal love in one fatal move.

"All better now. Thank you for taking care of me. I'll join you back in the living room once I'm dressed, and we can have that talk you're so looking forward to." My friendly smile is securely in place on the outside, but inside, I'm mentally hardening my heart.

Disappointment flashes across his face before he masks his features and gains control of his emotions. There's no doubt in my mind that he understands my underlying message. "As I said, there's no need to thank me. Taking care of you is my pleasure. Take your time, Tawnee. I don't mind waiting for you, regardless of how long it takes."

His hidden message isn't quite as ambiguous as mine... I hear what he's trying to say loud and clear.

The problem is, I took a hard-line stance against too-little-too-late men three years ago.

CHAPTER 7

Roman

Walking out of that room when I was so close to reminding Tawnee of what we once had was sheer torture. I was one step closer to convincing her to give me another chance. Then she completely slammed on the brakes and stopped the forward momentum I'd gained. Not that I can blame her, but I admit I was hoping our first meeting would've gone better.

So, I'll back off for now and give her a little space to deal with the changes and shocking turn of events that have been thrown at her in the last few days. My surprise arrival must make her feel awkward, to say the very least, but I know it sure as hell can't be as hard as seeing her cozy with another man. When I walked up and saw her with Rafael, I wanted to tear him apart. Silas's questions to Blake about how he'd react to seeing his girlfriend with another man echoed loudly in my ears.

Now I know exactly what it feels like—it fucking sucks, that's what.

She walks into the living room wearing tight-fitting black pants, a champagne-colored shirt, and a short white dress jacket. The way her thick black hair falls over her shoulders only accentuates her sex appeal, making me salivate like one of Pavlov's dogs on sight. Before she even glances in my direction, she sets her bag down and continues straight to the kitchen. When she returns, she has a beer in each hand, offers one to me, then sits in the chair across from me instead of on the couch beside me.

Aha, so this is how we're playing it. All right. If this makes her feel safer to keep her distance from me, I'll just use methods other than innocent touches or rendering first aid to win her over. That includes anything and everything under the sun. When I raise the longneck bottle to my lips, I keep her in my sights as the nectar of the gods slides down my throat. She stares at the bottle in her hand before taking a swig, then she starts peeling the label.

That act alone gives me more satisfaction than it should. Since receiving that encoded message, verifying her safety is the only thing that has made me feel better than seeing her make that little sign. At least she isn't getting any satisfaction from Ralphy-boy.

"You've been keeping a secret long enough, sweets. What is it you're hiding from us?" I prop my ankle on my knee and lean back against the overly plush cushions.

"You're not allowed to yell."

"Oh fuck. That's never a good sign." My deadpan expression really says it all.

"Promise me, Roman."

"You have my word. I don't fly off the handle and yell at people like a lunatic anymore."

"Good to know. Hold on to that thought for the next few minutes." She tilts the bottle up, and I'm mesmerized by the way the muscles in her throat work when she swallows.

When she turns her attention back to me, I purposely keep my expression neutral and my body language open. The last thing I want is to seem closed off to her. "Talk to me, Tawnee. Let me help if I can."

"I'll probably regret leading with this, but I don't think you'll appreciate the suspenseful buildup to it if I start at the beginning." I simply nod in understanding to avoid interrupting her. "I'm not entirely convinced Rafael was the intended target. When the Arab men heard the sirens approaching, they ran back to their cars. One of them was still yelling in Arabic, but I distinctly heard him say my name.

"Before you get your panties in a wad over this, I've gone over the scene in my mind repeatedly, dissecting every moment. During the altercation, I used my body to shield Rafael. His side of the car was pinned against the building, so there was only one way in and out— straight through me. Since I don't speak Arabic, I can only guess what he was yelling about. But it makes sense that if they'd researched Rafael, they would know I'm the head of security. So, he could have been cursing me because he lost that fight to a woman. Maybe he was mad because I dared to fight him off instead of bowing to his wishes. Or maybe he was pissed because I kicked him in the head. There are so many possibilities, it didn't make sense only to focus on a single reason at the time."

"At the time? But now you've changed your mind about that?" I know where she's going with this, but I'm trying hard not to be the overbearing asshole I usually am and simply blurt it out. But it's fucking killing me inside. My every instinct screams at me to throw her over my shoulder, march her fine ass out of this hotel, and put her on the next flight home.

"Yes. I can't stick my head in the sand and pretend I don't see what's happening. The team takes risks to keep Rafael safe—but we do what needs to be done to mitigate those risks as much as possible. Circumstances are different now, though, with the scrubbed camera feed, the hack into Brad's system, and the encoded message sent directly to you. All signs point to one fact. Their mark wasn't Rafael—it was me. And my staying here creates more danger for both Rafael and the team. I can't expect anyone to work double security details to cover both of our asses."

"Now that I know the finer details of what happened, I have to say I agree with your assessment. I know coming to this conclusion was especially difficult for you. You'd never voluntarily give up your responsibilities unless there was no other way. Those guys absolutely wanted you—but that doesn't automatically mean they weren't trying to nab Rafael too. Sending me the distress signal was a brilliant move. They get extra-credit points for that one."

As soon as the words leave my mouth, my spy senses start tingling all over.

Fuck me.

"Wait a minute... Let's talk this through, because something is way off base here. Sending me that message wouldn't help them get to you—they knew that. The only purpose that message served was to get *me* to come here to find you. What could they possibly have to gain from that?" Her lips part in surprise as my words sink in. The wheels in both of our brains are spinning out of control now.

"Do you have any Arab enemies? Anyone in this part of the world who would have used me as leverage against you?"

"No, I've never worked in this region before now. I don't know what this could be about or how I got on their radar."

"Roman, I have to tell you I'm freaking out a little now—and you know I don't do that. Ever." She jumps to her feet and starts pacing back and forth in front of me, unable to contain the nervous energy coursing through her veins. "But none of the scenarios in my mind included you as a target. Now that you've pointed out that someone wants both of us here—in Dubai, at the same time—that's all I can focus on. We should leave. All of us. Right now. Let's go explain it to the others and leave before they finish what they've started."

On her next pass toward me, I stand and block her path. With my hands wrapped around her biceps, I bend my knees to put us eye to eye. "Tawnee, slow down, sweets. Take a deep breath. I agree we need to talk to the others about this—but not *all* the others just yet. I'd rather start with Silas, Nick, and Blake, then go from there. Okay?"

She nods. "Okay, you're right. That makes perfect sense. They have the most experience with life-and-death situations in hostile enemy territories. Surely the five of us can put our heads together and come up with something resembling a good plan."

"You bet your *sweet ass*, we can." I waggle my eyebrows at her.

"Roman." She's using her stern voice. That's a good sign that she's getting her anxiety under control. "Did you have to remind me of the real reason why you call me 'sweets' right at this moment?"

"Yep, I sure did. It worked, didn't it?"

She's fighting against the smile that's trying to break free.

"In case you were wondering, I still think you have the sweetest ass in the world. Now that I've flown halfway around the actual world and have seen a lot of asses on my way here, I'm confident in officially claiming my title as the *numero uno* ass-expert now."

The smile wins.

"Well, you've certainly had enough experience in being an ass to make you an expert on the subject."

"Ha-ha. You're still so funny. Do you want to call up to Rafael's room and have the guys come down here to talk so we'll have more privacy?"

"I think it's best that we head back up there. Raf's suite is enormous—we can use one of the spare rooms to strategize then share the plan with the others when we're ready. Plus, Raf would probably be very suspicious of our motives otherwise."

By all means, let's not make Raf suspicious.

She cuts her eyes over to me, and I immediately wonder if I said that out loud instead of just thinking it. "Wait a second. You don't still think one of my security team is in on this, do you?"

"At this point, I don't trust anyone except for you and my team. Like I said earlier, I don't know anything about your employees, sweets, so I can't vouch for them. But I sure as fuck don't like the thought of your life in their hands."

"Don't hold back, Roman. Tell me what you really think."

"All right, I will. I absolutely think someone on your team is behind this whole thing, or at least involved. What's worse is you think so too, but you won't admit it yet. You hold on to this notion that everyone you trust is implicitly good and has your best interests at heart. But they don't, sweets. Not everyone."

"When did you become so insightful about other people?"

"Ever since I started working with Silas a few years ago. It's the only way to survive around that man. He's worse than a lie detector—he can read your thoughts."

"Good to know. I'll watch out for his telepathic abilities. Maybe I'll wear an aluminum hat or something."

"It won't help. I've tried it."

She rolls her eyes and shakes her head at me. "Let's go. We have work to do."

When we rejoin the others in the expansive suite, the eye daggers being thrown at me from both Rafael and Tony nearly make me laugh. Instead, I make it a little more interesting by pouring gasoline on the fire.

"Sorry to keep everyone waiting. Tawnee and I needed a little longer than we first thought." Nothing like leaving my comments vague enough to at least conjure the very images they're trying to avoid thinking about. "Silas, Nick, and Blake—can we talk to you privately?"

"Sure. Please excuse us for a few minutes." Silas stands and walks out of the living room without waiting for a reply from anyone.

We adjourn in a spare bedroom, Silas ensures his signal jamming device is on, and Tawnee and I bring everyone up to speed on the details she shared with me. When all their questions have been answered, the heavy blanket of silence covers the room as they digest the information.

"What do you think, Silas? Do we stay or do we go?" He rubs his hand along his jawline, weighing our options against the risks we face. But I already know what he'll say—his hesitation gave it away.

"We're staying until this is done. She's one of us— she helped you protect my parents when that lunatic was running around unchecked several years ago. I won't leave her to face this alone. Rafael is adamant he won't leave until he completes his real estate deal. If that's what he wants to do, that's fine with me. But I've got to tell you, it thoroughly pisses me off that he's so indifferent to his team's safety. Tawnee could head home and let someone else take over running the detail, but she can't live her life looking over her shoulder, waiting for some random man to grab her."

"Your director told you to stay on the job, didn't he?" Tawnee tilts her head to the side and raises her eyebrows.

"He may have suggested we need to identify who's luring Roman to the Middle East and neutralize the threat while we're here."

"Ah, you're shitting me. He figured it out before I did?"

"That goes without saying, and it's why he's the director. He's been doing this a lot longer than you have, Roman."

"Yeah, you have a point there. So, Tawnee... do you want to hang out in Dubai, put your life on the line with a group of Arab men who want to kidnap you, and cheat death out of the pleasure of using his sickle on you?"

"Well, Roman, when you put it that way...how can I possibly resist?"

Before this is over, she'll be saying I'm the one she can't resist. That is now my personal mission. It just so happens she and I will have plenty of time together in the very near future. I glance over at Silas and notice he's doing his Jedi mind trick shit again, reading Tawnee like a book. I've also learned to interpret the subtleties in his expressions better, and it's clear he respects her even more now.

"Nick, tomorrow morning, take Blake and go talk to the police. See what information they'll release about the scene or any angle they're working. I'll have a closer look at the security team members. Roman, you're on bodyguard duty for the time being. Don't let Tawnee out of your sight."

Thank you, Silas. I'll even babysit your daughter when we get home in return for giving me this assignment.

I will guard Tawnee's body with mine any time of the day or night. Vigorously.

Tawnee folds her arms over her chest and pins me with her glare. Maybe Silas isn't the only mind reader of the group. "Wipe that grin off your face and get *that* thought out of your mind right now, Roman."

Her direct order only makes me smile more.

CHAPTER 8

Tawnee

When we emerge from the spare bedroom, Rafael and the rest of the team stop talking, and all heads turn to us. Raf is the type of man that enjoys being the one in charge of everything, regardless of the circumstances or who else is involved. In this case, he doesn't have the expertise to be the one who calls the shots. And that really bothers him.

"Did the five of you solve the problems of the world in your impromptu bedroom meeting?" Raf asks with only a hint of sarcasm bleeding through his typically controlled tone.

"As a matter of fact, we did. Did you expect any less of us?" Roman throws his own sarcastic jab back.

Maybe all of us staying in Dubai isn't the best course of action after all. I can already see the frustration building in Rafael, and Roman isn't likely to back down to any man.

I'll be caught in the middle of their virtual pissing contest. That's just fucking great.

"Tawnee alone has my confidence. I don't know the rest of you from Adam. You could be the most incompetent of all the agents for all I know."

"Officers."

"Pardon?"

"We're CIA officers, not agents."

"So?"

"So, your assumption is wrong right off the bat. We're not the most incompetent agents at all." Roman's goading is intentional. He remains completely calm while Rafael uncharacteristically shows signs of his increasing aggravation. "But we're damn good officers."

"Rafael, Roman, that's enough from both of you. This isn't helping our situation at all." I shoot dirty looks at both men for putting me in this predicament in the first place. "Rafael, I can personally vouch for these men. They are the best at what they do, and they've already identified key factors I completely missed in all the chaos. You need to give them a chance."

"For you, I will do my best." His attention remains on me, not bothering to give the men helping us even a fleeting glance. I know exactly what this means. Rafael won't take orders from them out of spite. Instead, he'll wait until the word comes directly from me.

"Everyone—take a seat so we can talk as a team. Silas, I'm passing the speaking baton to you since you're the senior officer here. We're working together, but he's in charge of the plan." I glance around the room at every member of my team, wordlessly driving home my point.

"To be blunt, there are too many variables in this equation for anyone to assume anything. That's why I've already given each person on my team very specific marching orders. The message Roman received wasn't a fluke—someone wants him here for a reason. They may have been trying to kidnap Tawnee as a means to draw him in. When that didn't work, they grabbed her phone and used a system our IT guy created from scratch. It's not available to the public, so they have their own tech guru working behind the scenes too. Until we know exactly what they want with Tawnee and Roman, I've instructed them to stay by the other's side.

"As I understand it, Mr. Cruz, they rescheduled your real estate meeting for next week and that's your only business here in the Middle East. Is that correct?"

"Yes, it is." The skeptical expression is still firmly intact.

"In that case, it's best that you stay on the hotel

grounds with your security team around you at all times. We don't have enough intel yet to confirm if you are a target or not. It's best not to roam around out in the open like a walking bull's-eye. To be clear, I'll help keep you safe as much as I can. But I've been given orders from my superiors, and they don't include being your bodyguard. So, if you decide to venture off the grounds, know that you're doing so at your own risk and without my team or Tawnee."

I understand Silas's directness. As an officer in perilous situations, he can't risk being misunderstood. His edicts must be followed to the letter—dotting all the I's and crossing all the T's. However, Rafael isn't quite as understanding as I am.

Rafael deserves plenty of credit, though. He commands the room when he walks into a meeting. There's an innate air of authority about him that makes people flock to him everywhere we go. The way he carries himself, the way he dresses, and the way he speaks show a refinement most people don't possess. His charisma draws others in, but his shrewd business side leaves no doubt in their mind that he can be ruthless when he must be.

But he has a definite problem with authority. I think that's the underlying reason he started buying the controlling shares in various companies several years ago. He felt limited by the decisions and practices of the nameless and faceless company insiders. Since he had no power or influence to change their rules, he worked until he took over the company itself and changed what best suited him.

"So, if they're after Roman and were planning to use Tawnee as leverage to get to him, why would you put the two of them together? Doesn't that just make it easier for the bad guys to nab them both at the same time?"

"I can understand why you would think that, since you're not an expert in security measures. But, no, it doesn't make it easier at all. Think about it. If Tawnee is overseeing your security team, it divides her attention. She's responsible for making sure you're safe, that her team is following orders, and adjusting coverage on the fly when you decide to change plans at the last minute. She doesn't have the luxury of focusing on her own protection in that scenario. Whereas, by putting two highly trained and skilled operatives together, they can focus on their own safety and help each other. They'll assess their surroundings through a different lens automatically because that's what they're trained to do."

"If you say so. Tawnee and Roman can stay here in my suite. I have two extra bedrooms they're welcome to use." Rafael is speaking to Silas while looking at me.

Maybe I should feel flattered Rafael doesn't want me to be alone with my ex-boyfriend because he recently confessed his feelings for me, but his response isn't exactly a compliment. In the years since I met Raf, he's always had a domineering demeanor, but this reaction is different. His demand is more like a manipulation and control tactic, and I don't appreciate it at all.

"Rafael, that's not necessary. I'm already settled into my room downstairs, and there's plenty of room in it for Roman too. We'll be fine—no need for you to worry about us."

"We've had a long day. Let's all go upstairs to the rooftop restaurant and have dinner together. The sunset views are stunning."

Avoiding the subject won't make it go away and won't change my mind, Raf. But then you already know that about me.

"Good idea. Full bellies and empty bottles of wine are exactly what we need right now."

"My thoughts exactly. I'm glad to see we're on the same page."

My witty sarcasm is wholly lost on Raf.

Inside the elegant French restaurant on the highest floor in the hotel, the pissing contest continues when we take our seats. Roman slides into the seat beside mine before Rafael can claim it. The two men act out their juvenile charades with glares, passive-aggressive verbal jabs, and accidental hits with elbows. I choose to ignore them both and stare out the floor-to-ceiling windows at the Persian Gulf in awe.

The setting sun shimmers on the water like a million brilliant diamonds in full display. The lights of the city begin to blink on in the dusk of the day. Brief moments like this make me wish for a less hectic life. One that would allow me the chance to slow down and enjoy these exotic locales instead of only having a passport stamp to prove I've visited. A few cheesy tourist photos would be terrific—when I'm feeling nostalgic or want to show my kids what an exciting life I've lived. One day. Hopefully.

While everyone else is engaged in lively conversations around the table and enjoying the exquisite meals, I use the time to observe each person silently. After Roman and I split, I quit working for Steele Security and moved away from Miami. Noah Steele, Silas's younger brother, freely gave me advice and recommendations, viewing me as an ally rather than competition. Tabitha was one of the first people I hired for Rafael's detail. She's been with us almost from day one of venturing out on my own. Seated next to her is Carter, another long-term employee. While I haven't confirmed anything, I have my suspicions those two are more than friends after work hours. But all I care about is that they've both had my back in every situation we've encountered.

Next to Carter is Tony, a longtime employee of Rafael's. When Raf hired me to oversee all his security details, vetting everyone who had direct access to him

—that included Tony. A few questionable charges came up on his background check that made me want to dig deeper, but Rafael explained them away as cases of either self-defense or defending his employer. He assured me Tony had earned his place in the ranks several times over. He wouldn't allow the acts of greedy people who only wanted Raf to pay them off to make the charges go away tarnish Tony's years of loyal service.

The stories seemed plausible at the time, and I was willing to give Tony the benefit of the doubt—until the first time he disobeyed my direct order. Then I called in a favor to a law enforcement friend who provided more detailed information about those charges. Raf's explanations were generous, but it seems Tony was defending Raf against someone in every instance. Whether Tony committed the crime in question, or he simply took the fall for something Raf had done, was never firmly established.

Either way, Tony had gone above and beyond to prove his loyalty to Rafael, so I dropped the crusade against his arrests. Even though he and I still butted heads repeatedly afterward because he resented taking orders from a woman. If I had to guess, I'd say it bruised his ego when Raf didn't choose him for my role, especially after taking hits to his credibility because he covered for Rafael. *Allegedly* covered, that is.

Jason and John both joined Raf's protection detail

after they completed their stints in the military. They haven't been with us for as long as Tabitha and Carter have, but they've both proven their mettle on multiple occasions. Anyone would be hard-pressed to walk away with the high commendations those two men have.

Roman suspects someone on my team is behind this attack, but there isn't one person I can point an accusing finger at and still sleep at night. The security breach isn't on my team—I would bet my life on it. That only leaves one person who has the access, motive, and means to take me out of the equation. Only one man who would benefit the most from my permanent absence.

But the puzzle piece that doesn't fit is probably the most important one of all.

Tony doesn't even know Roman, so why send the fake distress call to get him here?

In fact, Roman and his coworkers' presence only makes the situation more difficult for Tony. So, what's his angle?

"There are tricks to flushing out a double agent. They all trip up eventually. It gets harder to keep all the lies straight. The reasons why they're sticking their necks out don't make as much sense anymore." Silas is answering someone else's question, but he's looking at me. "The signs are usually there if you know what to look for."

"What signs are those?" Tony asks. His tone is

more of a challenge than curiosity... or maybe I'm biased against him.

"In my line of work, it's almost always a large windfall of money that arrives out of the blue. I'm always suspicious of anyone who says their rich uncle died and left them a hefty inheritance."

Silas is right... the signs will present if I just keep my eyes open and watch for them.

"Tawnee, do you think we could go down to the lounge on the ground floor? I've read the terrace is beautiful in the evening, and that bar is the best place for evening cocktails." Tabitha's hopeful expression makes it nearly impossible to tell her no. She only wants some free time with Carter that doesn't involve a locked hotel room. "There are a lot of outdoor tables with triangle-shaped lamps to light up the veranda."

Hopeless romantic to the end.

"What do you say, guys? Think we'll be safe around the pool, in the waning light of day, with all of us together?" I glance around the table, waiting for a rousing round of "no" from the alpha-male league.

"I think that's a great idea. Let's go. We'll have a few drinks, listen to some music, observe the male peacock in his natural habitat." Silas lifts his glass to his mouth to hide his smirk.

Funny, but I'm not sure which strutting peacock he's referring to at the moment—Rafael or Roman.

"If there's music, then there's dancing." Roman turns to me and waggles his eyebrows.

"Do you have no sense of culture or propriety at all?" Rafael's patience is hitting a breaking point. "You are in Dubai, Roman. You don't dance in public unless you want to be arrested for indecency. By all means, have at it. Dance until your heart is content—but do it alone so no one else has to pay for your stupidity."

Roman's face burns bright red—even his eyes have a fiery flare in them. He starts to rise out of his seat, his hands curled into tight fists, but I put my hand on his arm to distract him.

"Sit down. You are not fighting in here." Roman does as I say, so I turn my attention to my employer. "Rafael, that was uncalled-for and impolite. Roman isn't here on vacation. He rushed here to help me. You'll have to forgive him for not researching the rules and customs ahead of time and be a little more gracious for the additional help."

"You're absolutely right, Tawnee. I offer my apologies to you, Roman. That was rude and condescending—two traits I abhor in other people. And, as she pointed out, I'm in your debt for helping keep us safe. I think a little time out on the terrace in the warm ocean breeze would do us all some good."

Roman keeps his gaze locked on Rafael, but he finally nods, signaling his agreement. I suppose that's the best response I can hope for from him.

"Thank you, Rafael. I appreciate the effort you're showing. I'm ready for some fresh air myself."

We take the elevator down to the mezzanine level and then ride the two-story-high escalator down to the lower lobby level. Tabitha and I chat and laugh, finally letting go of the stress I've been carrying. Until something catches my attention in my peripheral vision. When my eyes lock on to the source, my lungs seize in my chest, and I reach for the nearest source of comfort I can find. My fingers dig into Roman's arm, squeezing and clawing out of equal terror and disbelief.

"What's wrong? What is it?" His hand covers mine as the urgency in his tone increases. "Tawnee, talk to me."

"That's him, Roman. The one who tried to grab me in the back of the car." I point to the man strolling across the lower lobby floor as if he owns the place. He's not in a hurry. He's not concerned with being seen. He's staying in the same hotel as us.

"Which one? The man in the white dress with the red-checkered do-rag on his head?"

"He's wearing a thobe, the traditional Arab garment. And that's not a do-rag, it's his headdress. But yes, that's the one." At least Rafael doesn't sound as patronizing while he explains customary Arab clothing.

"I don't care what he's wearing. His ass is mine."

Roman winds around the people in front of us before sprinting down the escalator and across the lobby. Blake and Nick are close on his heels, chasing the unknown assailant. All three men disappear through the automatic doors leading to the expansive gulf front terrace.

"I'm taking Tawnee back up to my suite right now." Rafael wraps his hand around my upper arm and starts to push me forward.

"No, wait a minute, Raf. I'm a security professional too—I'm *your* head of security. I should help Roman chase him down and make him tell me why he was after us. We need to know who's behind this and why."

"Tawnee, I agree with Rafael on this one. Let's all go back up to his suite. One of your guys can stay down here and bring my guys back upstairs—with or without an extra visitor." Silas is a little too calm, making me question if he knows something he isn't telling. I narrow my eyes at him, looking for any of those clues he promised would surface. "Trust me, Tawnee."

"All right. Jason, you wait down here for Roman, Nick, and Blake. They can't get back upstairs without scanning a guest keycard in the elevator."

"Yes, ma'am. I hope they catch the bastard. If they do, we'll make him talk. Don't worry."

Fucking right, we'll make him talk.

CHAPTER 9

Roman

"He got away?" Tawnee stares at me in disbelief when I show up back in Rafael's suite empty-handed. "How? They built this hotel on a man-made island."

"Yes, he did." I want to fucking punch a hole in something. I pace back and forth, more aggravation building inside me with my every step. "We almost had him outside, but he pulled a fast one on us. The fucker in the white dress jumped on a speedboat that was already waiting right there."

"Which way did he go?" Silas asks.

"Straight out to sea, man, until we couldn't see the boat anymore. If I didn't know better, I'd say the whole thing was very carefully staged." Nick scans the room with his accusing glare, never one to hold back what he's thinking.

"Staged how?" Rafael sets down his drink and stands to face Nick. I almost laugh—as if Rafael could ever intimidate a veteran DEA agent who spent two years undercover with one of the most notorious motorcycle gangs in the world.

"Staged so that Tawnee would see the very man who caused a wreck, forcibly tried to drag her out of the back of the car, and said her name as he climbed into his car. Turn around and look out of the window right behind you. Do you see a dock out there anywhere? That boat was in that exact spot for a reason. This hotel wouldn't have allowed that to happen for just anyone." Nick takes a step toward Rafael, daring the man to challenge him a second time. "I think someone expected Tawnee to go after him. If I were a betting man, I'd say we would've encountered a shitload of resistance outside had she taken the bait. They would've disappeared into the horizon with her in the boat, and we would've had no way to stop them."

"Are you implying someone in this room is responsible for this? That one of us is a traitor?" Tony steps up beside Rafael.

I stand shoulder to shoulder with Nick and face down both men. "If Nick isn't saying that, then I am. I don't believe in coincidences."

"Neither do I. You know, at first, your accusation really pissed me off. But now, I absolutely agree with you. Someone in this room is responsible for all the bullshit that's happened this week, and I know exactly who it is." Tony glares at me with murderous intent in his eyes.

Bring it on, fucker. I've faced much worse.

"What are you saying, Tony?" Rafael asks, his eyes wide and his jaw slack as he stares at his right-hand man. "Do you know something about the attack we don't?"

"I've been retracing our steps, trying to isolate the one thing that would've given us away. We never give out our itinerary with enough advance notice for anyone to plan a well-coordinated attack like this. There's only one possible solution I've come up with... Roman is behind all of it so he can rush in, save the day, and be Tawnee's hero again. He's the one who staged the kidnapping attempt."

"Have you lost your fucking mind?" I'm about to go nuclear on his stupid ass.

"You're the only one who received this mysterious message from her. On a private, secure app no one outside of a select few people that you know can access. In a country where we have no means to verify anything you say is true. That's exactly why you weren't in any danger when you took off after that man—because you know he's not really after you.

You look pretty damn guilty from where I'm standing."

"You son of a bitch!" I lunge at him and slam my fist into his face. When he goes to the floor, I pounce on top of him and keep pummeling until I shut his fucking mouth for good.

Strong arms wrap around my shoulders and drag me off Tony. Everyone in the room stands between us as we continue to hurl insults at one another. I fight against the stronghold my team has on me, wanting to tear Tony apart for even suggesting this is all on me. Tawnee's life is in real danger, yet his main concern is that I want to play a hero game. He's a fucking moron.

"Everyone, stop!" Tawnee moves to the center of the ruckus and yells at the top of her lungs.

I mean, it works. Everyone shuts up and waits for her to continue, including me.

"Tony, you're way off base with accusing Roman. He is not behind this. He had no way of knowing where we were either. He and I haven't spoken in three years until he showed up here *to help us.*" She runs her hands over her face out of utter annoyance. "And you, Roman, have no right to accuse my team of doing anything underhanded. You've known them all of a few hours now. You may not trust them, but that doesn't give you the right to doubt them.

"I consider everyone here as a friend. Roman, Silas, Nick, and Blake are not private security contractors. They work for the US government, and they're here on official business. My team is private security, but we're all damn good at what we do. We've wasted enough time being suspicious of one another. Get your shit together or get the fuck out—it's that simple."

She's so fucking sexy when she takes charge. I don't know why some men have a problem with a woman giving them orders. I personally find it's a massive boost to my libido. Maybe that's because I also picture her—Tawnee—wearing a skintight leather suit, spiky heels, and brandishing a whip she isn't afraid to use. Shit, I have to get that image out of my head before a tepee forms in my pants.

She walks across the room toward me, and I watch the men move out of her path. While she doesn't appear to be especially pleased with me, I don't see that look she gets in her eyes when she wants to hurt me either. That's undeniably a good sign. When she reaches me, she picks up my hands and inspects my knuckles.

"Are you okay?" Her voice is low, only loud enough for me to hear her now that the crowd has dispersed.

"I'm fine, sweets. His hide isn't as thick as he likes to pretend it is." I wink when she finally meets my gaze.

"Do you need to ice your hands?"

"Are you trying to get rid of me? We're stuck

together now, remember? Mano a woman-o." I waggle my eyebrows at her suggestively, and she finally rewards me with a smile. She can't resist my juvenile wit and charm.

"Mano does not mean man, so your little catchphrase doesn't even make sense. However, I remember you chasing that man and leaving me on the escalator when you're supposed to be my personal security officer."

"I never would have left you had Silas not been right there to protect you. When you grabbed my arm like that, I knew you needed me to be the strong one even before you said the first word. Then when you told me he was the man who'd tried to grab you, I saw red. If I'd gotten my hands on him, I would've killed him right there in front of everyone. You may get a call from the front desk any minute now, telling you to get me out of here because I scared the other guests. They were tripping over their feet to get out of my way."

"Why, Roman? Why after all this time do you care so much about what happens to me? We haven't been together for a long time now." She looks down, afraid to look directly into my eyes and find something she's not ready to face.

But she doesn't have to worry about that.

Tawnee, time and distance have no influence on my feelings for you. I've loved and missed you more every day we've been apart. I should have told you forever ago, but I let my stupidity and pride stand in the way.

But I don't say any of that, because they're only hollow words. My recent good deeds are nowhere near enough to make up for my prior cruel actions. And professing my undying love right now will only drive her further away. I didn't make sure she knew how much she meant to me when I had her. Why should she believe it now?

"Ah, sweets, if there's one thing you should know about me better than anyone, it's that I'll always come running when you need me."

She peers up at me through her lashes, and the spark of hope shining there is unmistakable.

"Roman—"

"Tawnee—"

Fucking *Ralph.*

The invisible fetter holding her to me is broken by the sound of his voice interrupting our very private conversation. The moment is gone, and I'll probably never know whatever she was about to say to me, thanks to him.

"Yes, Raf?" She turns her back to me and faces him, which I'm sure was his intention.

He strolls across the room to her, not speaking but keeping his eyes trained on her. Yeah, we get it, dude. You just used your strutting peacock swagger to hold her attention. Whoop-de-freaking-doo. We're all so fucking impressed. I don't even bother trying to hide my disgusted expression.

He wraps his arms around her shoulders and pulls her closer to him. "It's been such a long and trying day for you. Why don't you lie down in the spare bedroom and sleep here tonight? I'd feel so much better knowing you're close to me and safe tonight."

I really want to tear his arms off his body and shove them up his ass right now.

"It's probably best that Roman and I head down to my suite. Silas, Nick, and Blake can use your extra bedrooms for tonight. It doesn't really make sense for all of us to play musical chairs with our belongings, especially this late in the evening."

"That sounds like a perfect plan to me." I beam with pride at Raf.

Roman—one. Raf—zero.

"Don't you need to go back to your hotel and pick up a few of your things?" He's trying hard to get rid of me for some reason.

"Give me your room key, Roman. I'll grab what you'll need for tonight and tomorrow, then we can assess our next steps." Blake steps up beside me and extends his open palm.

Have I mentioned how great my best friend is?

"Perfect. Thank you, Blake." I retrieve the keycard from my wallet and hand it to him. "We'll be in

Tawnee's suite when you get back, so stop by her room on the way up."

"I'll go with you, Blake. I can grab Silas's and mine too." Nick takes Silas's room key from him.

"Raf, do you mind giving them your extra room key? They'll need it in the elevator to get back up here. I have a master key, but I'd rather hang onto it, if that's okay." I'm glad Tawnee remembers the minor but vitally important details. I'll be tucked away in her room and not even thinking about where my coworkers are in just a few minutes.

"I don't mind at all." He's lying—he minds a lot. When he fishes his wallet out of his pocket, he removes the cards and hands one to Blake before putting the other two back in their place.

"You keep multiple room keys on your person at all times?" My brows draw downward, and the corners of my eyes tighten. I know Tawnee would have strongly suggested otherwise.

"Why wouldn't I? I never know when I'll need to ask one of my staff to fetch something from my suite."

Fetch? Does he think they're his dogs now?

I may be overly biased against him. Or maybe he's just a douche.

"Nick and Blake—be sure to bring back one of our business suits. There's somewhere else we need to be tomorrow that calls for us to look nice." All heads turn to Silas, who has been unusually quiet during this entire exchange. "Tawnee, you'll need to join us too. I wouldn't ask if it weren't important."

"Sure thing, Silas. I trust your judgment."

"Let's meet in the lobby at nine in the morning and go from there. Rafael, you should be safe with the rest of your security team here. But I still wouldn't recommend leaving the hotel grounds just yet."

"Even though that's exactly what you're doing with Tawnee and Roman tomorrow?" Tony counters. "After you've said they're both in danger?"

"Yes." Silas backs Tony down with his don't-fuck-with-me expression.

Most people don't understand Silas when they first meet him. He has two modes: all-business and all-family. When he's in all-business mode, he gets shit done. He rarely smiles, he's lethal when needed, and every move he makes is thoroughly calculated. When others say, "it's just business," they're justifying a decision that hurt someone else, rationalizing to relieve their own guilt. But Silas doesn't feel guilt over anything business-related. That's why he's earned the right to command respect at the agency.

When he's in all-family mode, no one from Langley would even recognize him because of the differences in his personality. He laughs, he plays practical jokes on family and friends, and he lets his daughter put makeup on him for their afternoon tea parties—it's almost as if he's an entirely different person.

The hard line no one wants to cross with Silas is questioning his commitment to his job, his country, his decisions, and especially his family—friends included. That seems to be a family trait because his brother is the same. Both men are my unsung heroes. The people I secretly wish I could be more like. But with all my character flaws, I don't see that happening anytime soon.

"Well, now that that's settled, maybe we should say goodnight and let these fine people get some rest." I take Tawnee's hand in mine and pull her out of Raf's embrace. I've watched him paw at her long enough.

My actions are as transparent as glass, which is why I refuse to acknowledge the dumbfounded expression on her beautiful face. In my defense, I don't mean to be a self-absorbed asshole who wants what he wants and pursues it with a vengeance. But that's also who I am, so I'm going with it for the time being. If Tawnee were to tell me she needed me to be something more, that would be different. I'd do everything in my power to be what she wanted because losing her the first time made me face my faults. Not that I'd dare claim to be perfect... but we are matched perfectly.

Raf cuts his eyes to look directly at me for the first time since the moment we met, but there are no warm and fuzzy feelings in those cold, dark eyes. He's severely pissed off—probably because he's not getting his way, but mainly because he's not getting Tawnee.

He steps toward her, puts his hands on her face, and gently kisses her forehead.

Right fucking in front of me.

Blake grabs my arm, stopping me before I even realize my body is in motion. I guess one round of fisticuffs isn't enough for me tonight.

Shit. Now I'm thinking about fists and cuffs in an entirely different light.

"Sleep tight, beautiful. I'll dream of you tonight." Raf's intimate whisper to Tawnee makes me want to punch him even more.

"Goodnight, Raf." Tawnee tries to act casual, but I can detect the subtle changes in her tone. His display of affection is out of the ordinary.

So… his majesty is threatened by the old Ro-Man.

Good.

"Come on, Tawnee. I'll tuck you in and get you some warm milk to help you fall asleep."

Blake covers up his snicker with an unconvincing cough, and I'm especially surprised to see Silas fighting a smile while he stares at the floor, suddenly refusing to make eye contact with anyone. As for me, I'm all smiles while saying goodnight to everyone on the way out of the multilevel, royal suite.

Dude must have more dollars than sense to pay that much for a hotel room.

We reach the elevator bank, and I press the down button, whistling a happy tune while we wait. Tawnee pulls her hand loose from mine, folds her arms over her chest, and cocks one hip out to the side—then glares at me.

"What?" Innocent. Oblivious. Charming. All at once. That takes real talent.

"I feel like a fire hydrant."

"Okay, I'll play along. How does a fire hydrant feel? Hard as steel? Holding back a lot of pent-up energy? Ready to squirt and shower someone with all that wetness inside?"

"Like every damn alpha dog in the surrounding vicinity has hiked his leg, pissed on me, and marked his territory without even the common courtesy of first asking if I enjoy golden showers."

My eyes bug out of my head, and my jaw drops open. "Are you into them?"

"No!"

The elevator bell dings, the doors slide open, and she stomps inside with her arms tightly closed over her body. She moves to the far back corner on the opposite side from the buttons and glowers at me from under her heavy brows. I push the button for her floor and face her as the car begins to move.

"Tawnee, come on, sweets. I'm sorry—forgive me. I didn't mean any harm—just trying to make you laugh. I swear I was kidding about that. Couldn't you tell?"

She draws in a deep breath, blows it out on a long

sigh, and releases her arms to her sides. "Yes, Roman, I know you were only kidding. But sometimes I need you to be serious. When I say something bothers me, you should know that it *really* bothers me. I need to know that you hear and understand me."

"You're absolutely right. Again, I'm sorry. So, if I've interpreted this correctly, you're saying you don't want me to compete with Rafael for your attention or affection. Does that sum it up?"

"Yes. No. I don't know. What? You're competing for my affection?" She clamps her mouth shut and steels her spine. "I'm not a piece of property for anyone to fight over. I have my own mind, and I'm perfectly capable of deciding who 'wins' my affections without being put in the middle of some juvenile turf war."

That's not at all what I wanted to hear her say, but I'll respect her wishes.

"Point taken. I won't get in his way anymore."

When the elevator stops, I hold the doors open with one arm and motion for her to exit first with the other. She walks past me, hesitates for just a moment as if she wants to say something, then thinks better of it. Once we're inside her room, she tells me to help myself to her secret stash of beer while she goes through her nightly bedtime routine.

But I don't.

While Tawnee is in the master bath, Blake drops

off my clothes and toiletries, which I stow in the second bathroom and change into my lounging pants. After locking the door, checking all the windows, and adding additional security to the balcony's sliding door, I grab the extra blanket from the hall closet and settle on the overstuffed couch to get some sleep.

A few minutes later, she emerges from the bedroom and stops when she reaches the darkened living room. I'm sure she expected to find me wide awake, beer in hand, and waiting to throw sexual innuendos her way. Maybe about the way her nightgown barely covers her sweet ass. Or how her toned legs look ultra-sexy peeking out from under the thin, silky material. Or even how her nipples appear to prefer the cold, air-conditioned air in here since they're standing at attention in perfect form.

But I don't say any of those things out loud.

Her eyes haven't fully adjusted to the dark room yet, so she stands over me, trying to determine if my eyes are open or closed. She chews on her thumbnail, unsure if she should say anything and chance waking me. Then she tiptoes back to her room and climbs into the bed... but she leaves the door open.

I close my eyes and let sleep overtake me.

CHAPTER 10

Tawnee

After a night of tossing, turning, punching pillows, and sleeping in short stints, I finally decide it's time to face the day. The enticing aroma of fresh-brewed coffee is so strong, I can almost taste it. In the living room, I find Roman is not only already awake, but he's fully dressed in his suit and has had breakfast delivered to the room.

"Good morning. Sleep well?" He's a little too chipper first thing today.

"Fine. You?"

"Like a rock. That couch is surprisingly comfortable. I think I like it better than my bed at the other hotel." He hands me a cup of piping hot java.

"Still take yours the same as usual—a little bit of coffee with your sugar and vanilla flavoring?"

I take a sip, close my eyes, and smile. "It's perfect. Thank you." He remembers exactly how to mix all the ingredients to suit my taste. How can that be? And why?

"Have a seat. Breakfast is ready too." He lifts the silver dome off my plate, and I lick my lips in anticipation. "You ordered pancakes? I haven't had them in forever. They smell so good."

When I finally come up for air after a few minutes of gorging myself, the subtle shift in my reality instantly slaps me in the face. My throat clogs with emotion, making it hard to swallow my food. The scene right in front of me could have been my idyllic life. The dream feels so real and so close that I could simply reach out and grab it.

A handsome man sits across the table from me, enjoying the breakfast he so thoughtfully made for us. The comfortable silence we enjoy means we don't have to fill every moment with words for our time together to be meaningful. The butterflies fluttering in my chest when I look at him are evidence my love for him will only increase every day. Our individual strengths and weaknesses only make us stronger as a couple.

But that's only a pipe dream with Roman. The man who barely gave me a drawer to keep extra clothes in. The man with an aversion to commitment and a fear of missing a better opportunity waiting around the corner. The man who prefers to remain a lifelong bachelor, never opting for marriage or kids to fulfill him. Like a bad case of déjà vu, I've been in this exact scenario before, and I recall how badly it ended.

I won't put myself in that position again. I won't give my love to a man who can't return it.

"Is anything wrong with your food? Do you want something else?" He lowers his fork to his plate and moves toward the phone to order whatever I want. Too bad it's not on the menu.

"No, this meal is delicious. No need to change anything."

"All right. Want to tell me what's on your mind, then?" He retakes his seat and directs all his attention to me.

"No, I really don't. Let's just focus on getting through today and whatever it is Silas has planned for us."

"All right, sweets. If you change your mind, I'm ready when you are."

"Ready for what, Roman?"

"Anything you want, Tawnee."

He seems so sincere, making it far too easy for me to be pulled under his spell and get lost in his eyes. That tug on my heartstrings? That's the direct line this man still has attached to me to this day. It's also the warning signal confirming how badly I want to believe him. And emphasizing why I always need to stay on guard. I never thought I'd fall back into the same old routine so quickly and easily.

If I were forced to examine why I don't simply ask him what I want to know or tell him exactly what I'm feeling, the conclusion would be something along the lines of… ignorance is bliss. I can't handle his rejection a second time around, so it's better that I don't go there in the first place.

We resume breakfast with idle chitchat, avoiding any topic that remotely relates to the two of us. When I manage to stop just short of licking the last few crumbs off my plate, I thank him for his thoughtfulness and disappear into my bedroom. All I know about today is Silas has plans for us that require dress clothes and leaving the hotel grounds. Since he hasn't shared intel on what's waiting for us out there, that helps me decide what to wear—black dress pants, a flowing shirt, and flats.

Once I'm dressed and ready to go, Roman and I meet Silas in the lobby.

"Where are we going?" Not knowing what's on the agenda makes me a little nervous.

"There's a conference nearby at the Dubai World Trade Centre that we need to check out." The smile Silas tries to hide makes me nervous. He rarely smiles while he's working. We all know and love this about him. Usually.

"Oh, a conference? That sounds… fun." That's a lie. Complete and utter bullshit. Conferences bore me to tears. I've attended enough as Raf's security to know I'd never voluntarily sign up for one.

"Doesn't it? I thought so too." Silas strolls through the main entrance, and the attendant opens the back doors of the Rolls-Royce limousine.

The two rows of plush leather seats face each other, leaving plenty of space in between to stretch out with the electric footrests. "I think I could get used to living in the lap of luxury like this. Have you ever seen anything like this before?"

Roman turns and looks out the side window, but Silas grins and nods his head at me. "This is very nice. It's way out of my price range, but I'm not above letting someone else pamper me for a while."

"I'm surprised your boss doesn't cart you around in one of these every day." There's no malice in Roman's voice, but there's an unmistakable deeper meaning to his words.

"Rafael certainly has the money for it, but he's not pretentious like a lot of men in his position are. Yes, he has nice things and travels the world, but he doesn't call unnecessary attention to himself by announcing to everyone around how much money he has. He has a security team in place to *avoid* trouble, so he doesn't want to do anything that will encourage it."

"Smart man."

"He is a brilliant man. There's no denying that." I'm stating facts, not boasting about my employer. But when I catch a glimpse of Roman's reflection in the glass, my heart drops to my stomach. The faraway stare. His down turned features. The clipped replies.

He's giving me exactly what I asked for—what I said I wanted. He's not competing with Rafael anymore. He's not trying to win me over or convince me he's the better man. When I said I'll be the one to decide who I'm with, I wasn't implying I'd chosen Rafael. But then, I suppose I haven't *not* chosen Raf either.

This is what happens when I'm around Roman. He makes me feel like a crazy woman. I'm never indecisive. I can't be hesitant—other's lives are literally in my hands in my line of work. But give me twenty-four hours with this man, and I'm the most wishy-washy person I know. If any of my employees were in the same state of confusion, I'd sideline them until they got their shit together.

When I turn my attention toward Silas, his knowing smirk makes my face burn red hot. Without conscious effort, my eyes jerk to the empty seat beside him. His light chuckle at my discomfort only makes it worse. My skin is melting off my bones by now, I'm sure of it. I take a deep breath, trying to calm my racing heart and erratic pulse, but it does very little good.

The driver stops to let us out at the exhibition center, and Roman extends his hand to help me out of the car. We follow Silas through the main entry doors, and I stop in my tracks when I find hundreds of people milling around, looking at the exhibits, and asking questions of the oil and energy professionals on hand. Why did Silas bring us to an oil conference? I feel so lost and completely out of my element.

Silas pulls three badges out of his jacket pocket and hands one to each of us. With a quick glance at it before clipping it to my shirt, I realize Silas has been hard at work. The badge already has my name imprinted on it. He didn't make this in his hotel room last night. Before I pepper him with questions, I peek at Roman to gauge his reaction. The only response he gives is a slight nod of his head before donning his badge.

No questions. No hesitation. No doubts.

Roman begins walking again, checking out several booths and talking with the men and women staffing them as if he's an energy expert. Since our badges show we all work for the same company, I follow his lead and try to sound somewhat knowledgeable about the topics at hand. I mean, I'm not, but I'm doing my best to bluff my way through the crowd. Silas loosely follows behind us, stopping at opposite stands and waiting for us to move ahead first.

When we finish one long row that spans the entire

length of the center, we stop at the refreshment center to get a couple of drinks. I've talked more over the last couple of hours than I have the past year combined. After a long gulp of ice-cold water, I twist the cap back on and look up at Roman.

The intensity in his blue-gray eyes steals my breath. Every time I look directly into his eyes, I have a physical reaction to him. My heart beats faster. I have a hard time controlling my breathing. Butterflies take flight inside my chest, swirling like a miniature tornado inside me. The man is dangerous to my sanity in so many ways.

"What are we doing here, Roman? What are we looking for?"

"I'm not sure, but I have a strong feeling we'll know when we find it." He lifts his water bottle to his lips, and I'm instantly mesmerized by the simple act of swallowing. Is it the way his tongue darts out of his mouth, barely grazing the opening of the bottle? Is it the way his full lips purse, kissing the rim? Is it because I want to lick the droplet of water left on his mouth?

The answer is most likely yes, to all three questions. And to anything else he asks me right now because I'm clearly out of my mind.

He cocks his head to the side and arches one eyebrow. One cheek rises with the most seductive half-smile. "Are you thirsty, Tawnee?"

I know that look—I've seen it all too often. He sure

as hell isn't asking if I want more water. But I have no words to answer him. I stutter and stammer before I give up and nurse my water bottle instead of trying to speak until it's empty.

"Let's keep going. We're bound to find something interesting." Roman tosses his empty bottle into the recycling bin, and we start down the second aisle.

From my vantage point a couple of steps behind him, I have an excellent view. His broad shoulders taper down to his slim waist. Even when he's wearing a business suit, his muscular ass looks fantastic. Other women stop chattering and check him out when he passes by them. Not that I blame them, obviously, since I'm doing the same.

"Tawnee?" A familiar voice in the crowd pulls me out of my reverie over Roman's ass. "Oh my God. Is that really you?"

When I locate the face behind the voice, I know without a doubt we've found exactly what we're looking for… or, I should say, *who*. "Gerald?" He wraps his arms around me, pulling me into a full embrace.

It's funny… and sad… realizing how much I've missed him after seeing him again.

"Dad? What the hell?" At least Roman looks and sounds as bewildered as I feel. "I've tried to call you several times, but you haven't answered. What are you doing here?"

"I'm working—this is an oil conference. It's sort of

what I do for a living, son. It's so late every night when I get back to my room, I haven't had a chance to call you. The real question is, what are you two doing here? And at this oil conference, no less? Why didn't you leave a message and tell me you were in Dubai too?" Gerald grabs his son in the same kind of bear hug he gave me, not the least bit concerned with the odd looks others send our way.

"First of all, I had no way of knowing you were even here. Second, I didn't leave a message because it's a sensitive topic. I couldn't leave it on your voice mail and chance someone else hearing it first. And last, I'm here helping Tawnee out—not for an oil conference."

"All right. Well, I can't leave the booth for a while since it's my turn to stand here and look pretty. How about we meet around one for lunch? Most of the crowd will be in breakout sessions by then. The session with my big reveal doesn't start until three."

"Sounds good, Dad. You're giving one of the session speeches here?" Roman's spy senses are tingling.

He stands up straight, drawing up to his full height, and begins carefully scanning the room. He shifts his gaze slowly and methodically, assessing everyone in his field of vision. When his eyes linger on one spot for more than a second, I follow his lead and find Silas standing off to the side with a satisfied smirk on his face.

"Yes, I am, and my topic is one of the more controversial ones, too. I can't wait to share my work with all the bigwigs in this industry." Gerald looks so proud. He makes me want to stay and listen.

"Do you speak fluent Arabic?" I don't mean to sound as shocked as I do.

He laughs. "No, sweetheart, I wish I could. They graciously hold this conference in English since it draws oil executives from all over the world."

"Ah, I see. So, what's your session about, Gerald?" I know he's a chemist for a major oil company in South Africa, but that's the extent of how much I understand about his job.

"I've created a synthetic product that can replace crude oil—and it lasts a lot longer. It'll revolutionize the entire oil industry. Instead of drilling and fracking and wrecking the environment, we can redirect our resources to manufacturing this synthetic compound instead. I'm so excited about it. Our initial trials are extremely promising."

I'm happy for Gerald—honestly, I am. But even with my limited knowledge of the oil industry, I understand he just painted an enormous target on his back. Roman stares at Gerald, his eyes wide and bottom jaw slack, shaking his head from side to side. He doesn't want to believe it either.

"Ah, shit." Roman drops his chin to his chest and stares at his feet. He's visibly uneasy in a way I've never seen him before. "There's no way it's a coincidence we're all three here at the exact same time."

Panic rises in my chest and stops at the back of my throat, nearly choking me as I work hard to restrain the scream that desperately wants to break free. He's right. There's no fucking way. Statistically speaking, that can't ever happen.

Yet here we are.

An Arab man who knows my name and tried to kidnap me.

Someone sent Roman an SOS message from an encrypted app on my personal phone to get him here.

Soon Gerald will reveal a creation that will effectively stop the need for oil production around the world at an oil convention with worldwide business leaders.

Ah, shit is exactly right.

"We've been set up, haven't we, Roman? We're here as the bait, aren't we?"

CHAPTER 11

Roman

"Tawnee, I didn't expect to find you here." Rafael sidles up next to us, resting his hand on her lower back in a passive-aggressive intimate display.

Is this fucker serious?

I'm just about to rearrange his face when I remember my discussion with Tawnee yesterday. She doesn't appreciate my ogre ways, so I throttle down my reaction before she sees my face. She's too busy staring up at Raf's face, anyway.

"What are you doing here?" She keeps her voice low and her anger controlled, but there's no mistaking the way she enunciates each word with purpose. "You weren't supposed to leave the hotel grounds."

"Yes, I know that was the original plan. But while I was working from the hotel room, I received an email about the topics for today. It's rather fortuitous that we couldn't reschedule the property tour for this week. This conference is one of a kind, and now I'm available to attend all the discussions." His smile reminds me of a used car salesman I used to know... slimy and underhanded.

"Don't worry, Tawnee. We have him on a short leash." Tony pats her shoulder while smiling. He knows his boss is a douche. "We'd better go find the meeting room if you still want to catch the session on industry trends."

"You're right, Tony. I can't miss that one. Let's have dinner together tonight, Tawnee. We haven't finished the discussion we started on the beach. I'm deeply interested in hearing your thoughts on the matter."

"Sure. Call my room when you get back to the hotel, and we'll complete our plans." She doesn't smile like I expected her to do. She's probably still mad that he disobeyed orders.

Like clockwork, I scan the area again for any potential threats and my eyes land on Silas in his hiding place. When Rafael walks off, Silas makes a walking motion with his two fingers, signaling for us to follow. Now I know Silas expected Raf to make his appearance here, but I can't wait to hear his explanation for not clueing me in on my dad being here.

My cell pings with a text, so I fish it out of my pocket.

Silas: *Don't worry. I'm covering your dad.*

Me: *Would've been nice to know he was here...*

Silas: *I had to verify it in person. Stick with RC. He's here for a reason.*

Me: *Copy that.*

"What was that about?" Tawnee looks up at me, knowing I'm only on my cell phone while working if it's an emergency.

"Silas said we need to stick with Raf. Let's go listen in on the thrilling topic of what's new and exciting in the oil and energy industry." I didn't lie... I just didn't tell her the entire truth of why we're following Raf around.

"Does Silas know of a credible threat against Raf?" Naturally, she's more concerned about his safety than her own.

"No, that's not what he said at all. But if he says we need to go with Raf, then we go with Raf without arguing over it. So, let's go."

The only seats left in the entire room are in the very back. Funny, those are usually the seats I scrap over to get to first. This subject must be more exciting than I thought. If we'd waited much longer, we'd have to stand. The tables along the front of the stage where Rafael and Tony sit are packed. When they announce the speaker, I understand why everyone is crowding the platform.

This is a fucking terrible idea. My brain screams at me to yank Tawnee out of her chair and bolt from the room before it's too late. My gut says to stay for as long as it's safe, gather the intel, and be thankful our seats are beside the exit door. Aside from Raf and Tony, every other guest at the other end of the room is wearing a thobe and head covering…much like the man who attacked Tawnee.

Only, from the back, they all look alike. There's no way to tell if that specific man is in this crowd or not. But the hairs standing straight up on my arms assure me he's here.

"Please welcome Saudi Arabia's Minister of Energy, Industry, and Natural Resources, Nizar Al Aiban. In his previous role, he was the CEO of the world's largest oil and natural gas production company, SAOR, Inc." The announcer steps aside and shakes hands with a sleek businessman before exiting stage left.

Nizar steps up to the podium and shares his insights on where we are today, where we should be, and how we will get there. He discusses environmental protection policies, company projected earnings, and the sustainability odds of current oil production. Though I have no interest in these benign topics at all, I know the other shoe will drop at any moment. I split my focus between what the speaker says and how the crowd reacts.

An hour later, he finally reaches the end of his prepared comments and opens the floor microphones for questions from the attendees. Numerous men clamor to one of the four stands located around the room. The announcer steps back up to the podium to quiet the low roar of voices. Though I don't speak Arabic, they sound angry to me.

"As a reminder for our international guests, please phrase your question in English. If you need a translator to ask for you, we have many in the room who will gladly help." He takes his seat off to the side again, giving Nazir the floor once again.

Nazir motions toward the man waiting at the first stand. "Please go ahead with your question."

"Thank you, Minister Al Aiban. As I'm sure you've already expected, many of us have the same question about the recent unpleasant developments. More specifically, the rampant rumors that have surfaced since SAOR, Inc. became a publicly traded company last year rather than remaining state-owned. Men whom I respect said a *Jewish woman* from the United

States is behind the company that has overtaken SAOR. Is this sacrilege true?"

Before Nazir says one word in response, the room erupts in a cacophony of angry shouts, low growls, and chairs scraping against the floor as more people jump to their feet. Although I don't understand what they're saying, I can take a few calculated guesses and feel confident I'm dangerously close to the mark. From citizens of a country that reviles Jews, Christians, Israelis, Americans, and basically all women around the world, their reactions are not hard to deduce.

Death to the Jewish-American woman.

Kill the foreign woman—take our oil back.

Allah forbids this blasphemy.

Tawnee leans over to whisper in my ear. "Um, wow. So much hatred in this confined space is stifling, isn't it? I've never seen a group of men have so much animosity toward women despite having four wives each."

"Their wives know their places—and that place is never equal to or above their man. A woman taking over the world's largest oil company, which happened to be Saudi-owned for the last three decades, is a direct slap in their faces. The fact that she's Jewish on top of that makes it even worse. I hope they never find out who she is because they will drag her body through the streets behind their vehicles without a shred of regret."

"How would they know she's Jewish? It's not as if they stamp our religious beliefs on our passports."

"Maybe she has a traditionally Jewish last name."

"Maybe that's her married name. It's just odd."

"Could be. Women don't take their husband's last name in Saudi Arabia. They're required by their religion to keep their father's name, so it's entirely possible they haven't considered that angle. But I will not be the one to enlighten them today."

When the room settles down enough for Nazir to answer, I notice more than a few heated glares cast in our direction. Seems they're willing to throw their anger in the direction of any woman unfortunate enough to be in the room.

"I can assure you these are all lies, carried out with the greatest of intentions. But their sole purpose is to undermine our operations and discredit our great country. We are working tirelessly to identify where these rumors have originated and stop them at the source."

He's lying. All the signs are clearly visible on his face, in his body language, and in the pitch of his voice. He's hiding the truth to save his own ass but also to keep this information out of the news. If the affluent Saudi investors find out a woman is taking over at the helm, they'll dump their stock so fast, the company will fold next week.

But then, maybe that's the whole point.

If I wanted to take over the most profitable company in the world at an unheard-of low stock price, that would certainly do it.

Rafael and Tony stand, say their goodbyes to their tablemates, and turn to leave. Raf's eyes land directly on mine. A visible jolt runs through his body when he realizes I've been watching him this entire time, studying his every reaction. Though he's unsettled, he plasters that same pretentious smile on his face to remind me I'm still beneath him.

That's all right, buddy. I've got your number.

Tawnee and I stay put as Raf makes his way toward us on his way to the exit. He stops beside Tawnee, addressing her rather than facing me. "I see you couldn't help yourself. Here you are, watching my back when you should be taking care of yourself."

"Roman and I have each other's back just fine right here. Don't worry about us."

That shitty grin Raf gave me just a minute ago? Yeah, I'm giving it right back to him now in spades. He focused solely on her, and she responded for the two of us. I really like how that minor action feels.

"Why don't you join us for lunch? Tony and I are eating with a few businessmen we just met. You're welcome to eat with us." He takes her hand in his, preparing to help her stand. Presumptuous much?

Not that he included me, but I feel obligated to decline his invitation, nonetheless. "What a shame.

Tawnee and I already have plans for lunch. Maybe some other time, though."

"Some other time, then." He leans over and kisses her on the cheek. "I'll see you at dinner tonight."

When Raf and Tony are out of earshot, Tawnee turns to me. "All right, spill. Gerald, Raf, you, and I are all here. This is not a coincidence. What is going on?"

"You know as much as I do, sweets. I'm sure whatever is coming will make itself known very soon. What fun would it be if our luck changed now?"

"Only you could make me see this situation as a game." She shakes her head at me, but her smile is there just the same.

"Sometimes it's better to think of these situations as a game. That way, you don't freeze up with fear or indecision. Everything we do is about moves and countermoves… beating our opponent's next play before it's even made. That approach helps me anyway."

"You know, that actually makes sense. I'll try that."

"Looks like we can make our way out of here now. The crowd around the door is thinning out. Let's go see who Rafael and Tony are having lunch with before we check on Dad again. I'm a little curious."

"Curious? That's not the word I'd use. More like suspicious." We stand and make our way into the crowd and through the doors.

"That word fits too." With my hand on her lower

back, I steer her clear of the masses and start walking toward the exhibit booths.

"Roman, I've worked for him for three years. That's a long time to be that close to someone and not know them inside and out. Do you not trust my judgment?"

"You know I do. But people change, Tawnee. Sometimes when you're looking right at them. The people closest to you know how to hide their lies because they know what you'd notice. You wouldn't see the most subtle changes, though. Psychopaths have this shit down to an art."

"Are you saying Rafael is a psychopath?" She arches one eyebrow.

"No. But I'm not saying he's *not* one either."

"You're impossible."

"Impossible to stay away from? Impossible not to fall head over heels in love with? I know. It's both a blessing and a curse, but I'll take one for the team and bear this heavy burden, anyway." I expect an eye-roll, maybe even a sarcastic huff, but I'm more than a little pleased to see an amused smile instead.

We take the long route along the deserted hallway and swing by the rear doors of the ballroom where the expansive buffet is underway. This affair isn't quite up to par with Rafael's usual dining preference, but no one would know that from the huge smile on his face. Even Tony is laughing and joking with several of the

Arab men sitting around them. Then Tony sees us standing in the doorway and lifts his hand in a small wave. The man sitting on Tony's right looks to see who he's waving at, and his cheerful expression instantly changes.

He points toward us, his finger exaggeratedly jabbing at the air.

Then everything turns black.

Someone slips a hood over my head.

Muscular arms wrap around my neck from behind, pulling me backward at a fast pace.

Tawnee screams my name from beside me, her cries for me muffled. But my captor has me effectively incapacitated and unable to help her.

I hear the heavy metal door of the conference center open, then we're thrown inside a darkened space, with Tawnee landing on top of me. More arms grab us, holding us down to prevent us from putting up too much of a fight. But they obviously don't know who they're dealing with, because Tawnee and I both let our legs and arms fly, contacting whatever flesh we can find.

During the fight, I realize we're in the back of a panel van from the unmistakable sound of a door sliding shut—just as the engine whines and the tires squeal in the rapid getaway. We're jostled around on the floor when the van jumps the curb and swerves right into the already heavy traffic, and several heavy bodies pounce on top of us. Horns blow from all directions and angry shouts soon follow, but our getaway driver never misses a beat.

"Keep your heads down and stay quiet if you want to live," the angry, gravelly voice commands as someone else binds our hands and feet with zip ties.

CHAPTER 12

Tawnee

"I recognize your voice, even though you're trying to disguise it. Take these cheap-ass cuffs off me, or you'll get a thorough ass-kicking when I get free." Roman controls his tone, but I sense the hostility behind his words. I'm still pinned on top of him despite the terrible driver behind the wheel throwing us around the interior like rag dolls.

"Wait a minute—I know that voice too." At first, I was too freaked out to realize who grabbed us. Now I know exactly who it is. "Take this bag off my head and untie me right now. Or so help me God, I will taser you right on your balls, film it with my phone, and upload it to every social media site known to man."

Laughter fills the vehicle, then the man lying on my

back slides off. Fingers wrap around my shoulders and upper arms to help me up since my hands are bound behind my back, then someone removes the thick black bag covering my face.

"Hello, Tawnee. So good to see you again." He has the nerve to smile at me.

"Rebel. Take these ties off my hands and feet right now."

"Do you promise not to punch and kick me again? You have a mean swing. That last one nearly broke my jaw." He raises his eyebrows, waiting for me to assure him I'll play nice.

"I promise if you don't release me right now, the damage will be much worse than a broken jaw when I'm through with you."

"Can someone take this fucking bag off my head? Now!"

All our eyes drop to Roman, who's still lying on the floor of the van, as if we forgot he was there. When I look back up at Rebel, Bull, and Shadow, we all burst out laughing, immediately dispelling the tension from just a moment ago.

"Yes. This is all real fucking funny. Just so you know, I'm kicking everyone's ass when I get out of here. Everyone involved. I don't care who you are." Roman's hands also are bound behind him, so even though he manages to sit upright, he still can't remove the covering.

"Leave Roman's on. That's a much better look for him," Reaper calls from the front.

"I should have known you were driving, Steele. You never could drive for shit," the talking bag retorts. After Bull releases my hands and feet, I help him free Roman. He glares at each man individually for a minute, contemplating a brawl in the back of the van. I can see it in his eyes. "Was all that shit really necessary?"

"We had to make it look convincing." Shadow shrugs one shoulder, as if we already should have known that.

"I meant being hog-tied once we were already in the back of the vehicle." Roman's eyebrows draw downward.

"Oh, that. Well, we weren't going to originally, but we came prepared just in case it came to that. You both fought like two feral cats in a burlap sack. You two gave us no other choice, so that was really your fault." Bull leans back against the side of the van and grins.

"You boys are enjoying this a little too much. Let me guess. Silas called you the minute they landed, and you decided to get in on the action too." I fold my arms over my chest then watch as each man cuts his eyes to the next one.

"Close, but not quite, Tawnee. We were here before you arrived. Shadow is here on official assignment, and he asked us to join him as private contractors. Silas called me when he got to his hotel room, but he didn't know we were already here until then." Reaper pulls into a driveway in a residential area and jumps out of the driver's door.

He slides the side door open, and we all file out, following him into an elaborately beautiful Italian-themed beachfront home. Strike that—this is a mansion. Should have known these guys wouldn't have anything less.

"Here's your new home sweet home for the next few days. The kitchen is fully stocked, but let me know if there's anything else you want. This neighborhood is safe for you to move around in, but don't venture out into the tourist areas. We want everyone to think you're being held for ransom." Shadow takes us on a quick tour to show us the layout and where to find everything we'll need.

"I'm starting to think I don't charge anywhere near enough for my services." I stroll through the interior behind him, amazed at the expensive marble on the floor and the walls. Every room is professionally decorated and offers every amenity anyone could possibly want. "This place is way out of my price range."

When we reach the back of the house, I realize exactly what love at first sight means. The entire wall is floor-to-ceiling windows, overlooking a lush, green yard, an outdoor kitchen with spacious seating, a gorgeous pool, and a private beach on the turquoise water of the gulf. I'm claiming this area for myself.

"There are some perks that come with the job. When you conduct business in an area known to attract the world's wealthy, you can't stay in a run-down shack. This house leaves no doubt about my status in society." Shadow is enjoying this part of his job a little too much.

"Yes, your image as a wealthy kidnapper is critical. Got it."

"Well, yeah. Even us kidnappers have to look good while doing it. Where have you been, Tawnee?"

"With my head under a black burlap sack, evidently."

"Good one. I knew I liked you for some reason." He smiles and winks, then moves to the refrigerator to grab a few drinks. He passes around the cans of beer, and we all take a seat outside.

"We knew something was up when we saw Silas hiding in the shadows at the convention center, but we didn't know what. How did you know we'd be in that hallway?" Roman takes a sip and waits for someone to fill us in.

"Silas called and told us which route you'd taken. It was the perfect timing. There were enough people around to authenticate the story, but none close enough to interfere. And, Rafael was right there in our line of sight—so it was perfect." Shadow quickly lifts and lowers his eyebrows before his smile covers his face.

"I don't get it. What am I missing?" I search their faces, waiting for the punch line—something—to explain what they obviously already know.

"You know, Tawnee... we had to ask ourselves if you knew what was going on. Ultimately, we decided there was no way you knew. But I've got to tell you, the evidence against you looks very damning." Reaper moves to sit down across from me and levels his assessing gaze on me.

"Evidence against me? What the fuck are you talking about? And how could you ever suspect me, Reap? You're the one who hired me after a thorough background check." I'm still so lost. I've worked on dangerous cases with these men. I've trusted them with my life, and they've trusted me with theirs. Reaper trusted me to protect his parents. But now they are looking at me as if I'm the criminal under investigation. "Someone needs to explain right now."

"Wait here." Bull walks into the house and returns with a file in his hand. "You need to read this. Just don't kill the messenger."

With an unsteady hand, I take the folder from him and flip it open. The first page is mundane business information, but I take note of the key details and move on to page two. As the pieces of the scattered puzzle start to fall into place, I flip the pages faster and faster. When I reach the end of their research and have the full picture clear in my mind, I slam the file shut and stare at it for a long, heated minute.

"Now you see why we needed a moment to gather our wits?" Reaper asks.

The sympathetic tone of his voice nearly shatters my outward façade. I need to hold on to this anger... this hatred... because the last thing I want to do is cry in front of these men. I haven't fought the stereotype of women in the security game all these years just to let it crumble in front of me now over this bullshit.

"Yeah, I see it all very clearly now... and I know what I have to do. I have a bullet with someone's name on it." My fingers curl around the manila folder, gripping until my knuckles are white. It strikes me as funny since I just watched my unconscious reaction happen right before my eyes.

But I'm not laughing right now.

The betrayal is far too fresh. The wound is way too deep. My revenge will be all too swift.

"You can't kill anyone, Tawnee. Not yet, anyway. You and I know who the villain is, but all of that is circumstantial. You'll take the blame for everything if we don't handle this exactly right. We're on your side, and you know we won't let you down." Shadow loosens my grip one finger at a time then takes the folder from me.

"Someone want to clue me in?" Roman stands and faces Shadow, waiting for his chance to read the file.

"No. We talked it over with Silas, and he wants you to remain in the dark about what's happening with this case. Tawnee needs to know what she's facing, but it's best that you don't know yet. Your reactions to everything that happens from this point forward must be genuine. No acting allowed on your part." Shadow walks back into the house, slides the folder into his laptop bag, and rejoins us on the lanai.

"You're fucking serious? I thought you were just pulling my leg with that whole keeping me in the dark fuckery. This isn't funny, man. What is Tawnee being blamed for? Who's setting her up? How am I supposed to have her back when I don't know what to watch for?"

"This is no different from any other job you've done before, Roman. It's no different from it was ten minutes ago when you knew even less. You'll never know all the variables, but you still have to find a way to account for every possible scenario. Stop putting your personal feelings in the mix and look at this from the same standpoint as you would for any other mission." Reaper stares Roman down until he submits.

"You're right, man. I know you are. Okay, if it's that important to Tawnee's safety, I'll be the odd man out and act all surprised over whatever's coming our way. Doesn't mean I have to like this shit, though." His sarcasm is spot-on. I only recognized it because I know him so well.

Plus, I know Roman better than to believe he'll just let this go with no further explanation. The first second he catches me alone, he'll grill me with every question under the sun. When I don't cave in, we'll end up in a huge fight and be right back where we started.

It's kind of our thing.

Or, it used to be our thing, anyway.

"Next steps are easy," Shadow continues, ignoring Roman's sarcastic digs if he even realized them. "Hang out here until we 'release' you. Try not to kill each other. If you do, hide the body so it doesn't smell. Don't do anything to get the police called on you."

"Where's the best place to hide a body around here?" I ask. Completely serious.

"Probably dump it in the gulf and let the sharks eat it. Tiger sharks are mean, you know." Shadow gets me.

"Are you guys not staying here in your posh kidnapper pad?" I ask when they all stand and walk toward the garage door.

"No, this place is way too shabby for us. We'll check back in on you soon, though." Shadow smiles and walks out first. They climb into a Range Rover parked in the second carport and wave goodbye.

Roman and I stand at the door to the garage and watch our captors leave. As soon as the garage door closes, Roman turns to me, folds his arms over his chest, and quirks one eyebrow.

"Let's have it, Milano. Don't leave out one single word of what you read in that file. I don't care what they say. I can't cover your ass as well if I don't know who and what we're up against."

"Sorry, Roman, no can do. I really do agree with the guys on this one. It's best that you don't know what was in there ahead of time."

"Fuck that, Tawnee. If I have to hold you down and torture you all night, you will give up the intel I need. One…" He takes a predatory move toward me with a sinister gleam in his eye.

I turn on my heel and dash through the house, trying not to scream and laugh too loud as I outrun him. When I reach the bedroom, I grab the lock on the doorknob, ready to turn it the second the door shuts, but a size thirteen shoe slips inside the opening at the last second. Then he squeezes his face between the door and the frame, his eyes wild and crazy, and a grin so big it shows all his teeth.

"Let me in, Tawnee. Open the door and let me in on your own. If I have to open it, you'll be very sorry."

I can't stop laughing. "No, Roman, I'm not letting you in here. You're not holding me down and torturing me. Now move your foot and your face before I cut them off with the door."

"Nuh-uh, sweets. My fingers are itching to get to

you. Every second that passes only makes it worse…for you. When I get ahold of you…"

"Roman, no. I mean it. No, no, no, no, no!"

When another fit of laughter hits me from the crazy expression on his face, he pushes the door open and rushes toward me. I stumble backward, trying to stay out of his reach, but the back of my legs hit the edge of the bed. It's too late to get away. He pushes me down on my back and pounces on top of me, placing his knees at my sides to cage me in. He holds my hands above my head with one hand and wiggles his fingers on the other while hovering over my ribs.

"Tell me… or the torture session commences."

"I can't tell you anything."

His fingers move closer, and I squirm involuntarily at the mere thought.

"Tawnee. You know I won't stop."

"Roman, this is not very nice of you at all."

"It's not nice to keep secrets from me. Last chance, Milano. Tell me what was in that file."

I shake my head. "You know I can't. This is Shadow's job. What he showed me in that file is classified."

"I don't care. I'm a CIA officer, too. I have top-secret clearance the same as he does. Two…"

"Don't do it, Roman!"

"Three!"

He is relentless. His brand of torture is to tickle the

information out of me. The bad thing is, it usually works because I can't stand it for long. He uses my weakness against me, and he enjoys it immensely. He releases my hands so he can use both of his to torment me more. I try to push his hands away, but he's much stronger than I am, so it does little good.

"Ready to talk yet?"

"Yes! Now let me up. I need something to drink after all that screaming."

His face is barely an inch above mine. His lips hover just over my mouth—so close, but so far away. The heady scent of his cologne envelops me, lingering in the air until all I want is to breathe him into me. "Hmm. I think you're trying to trick me. You know what'll happen if that's what you're up to, Tawnee."

Busted. I planned to run into the other bedroom and lock the door. To save myself from doing something even stupider than telling him what I read in that file. "Fine. You win. Just stop tickling me now."

"Good. Let's go raid the fridge and talk over a nice, long meal. I'll even cook for you. All you have to do is whisper in my ear and tell me all your secrets, sweets."

It's times like this that make me miss Roman more than usual. But that's one secret I won't spill tonight.

CHAPTER 13

Roman

Shadow wasn't kidding when he said they stocked the kitchen with everything we could possibly want to eat or drink. I'm keeping my promise to Tawnee and cooking a meal to make up for the lunch we missed earlier.

"You know, I wish they had let us stay long enough to hear Dad's speech. I'm not worried about him because I know Silas is watching him, but I would have liked to hear about his work." I start taking out all the ingredients I need to make our date night meal. Or, afternoon date. Whatever.

"I would have enjoyed hearing him speak, too. It's been so long since the last time I saw him. Too long.

I've always loved your dad. Don't suppose he got remarried in the last three years, did he?"

"No, there's no way he'll ever do that. Losing my mom so suddenly and at such a young age scarred him for life. He won't put his heart out there and risk having it sliced into a million pieces again." I drop the ground beef into the frying pan and chop it until all the small pieces crumble.

"Guess you still don't get to see him very often, huh?" Tawnee moves to the refrigerator to retrieve a bottle of wine.

"Can you hand me the lettuce, tomatoes, cheese, and sour cream while you're in there, sweets?" She pulls one ingredient out at a time and passes it to me. "No, I don't get to see him in person nearly enough. We video chat at least once a week, but it's always so bittersweet. I know his work is important to him, but I wish he'd move back to the States. He could have retired years ago and spent his remaining time with me."

"He loves you more than anything in the world, Roman. But he obviously never healed from his broken heart. Everything back home reminds him of your mom." The memory of the phone call telling us Mom had died of a sudden heart attack grips me, stealing my breath all over again. Tawnee continues speaking, thankfully pulling me back into this moment. "I'll never forget what he said to me one day. It struck a chord so deep inside me, I haven't been able to shake it to this day. He said, 'Tawnee, you only get one love of a lifetime. When you lose that, you lose the will to love again.' What scares me the most is thinking he's right."

I force air into my lungs again and quickly turn toward her. "I never knew—" Not realizing she was standing so close since I was in my own little world, I crash into her outstretched hand holding my glass of wine. The cold liquid splashes all over my shirt, soaking me until the fabric sticks to my chest. "Shit, that's cold!"

"Oh no—I'm sorry, Roman. I hope I didn't just ruin your shirt."

I chuckle to myself as she rushes to the sink to wet a dish towel. "Don't worry about it, Tawnee." Reaching behind me, I grab the back and snatch it over my head. "I'll throw it in the washer, and it'll be as good as new. No big deal. It's not like it's one of those thousand-dollar silk shirts your boss wears."

"Still, I feel bad for pouring wine all over you. You'll be all sticky now."

"I've been worse than sticky before. I'll survive." I wink at her and toss the shirt in the general direction of the laundry room. "How about getting me a refill while I start on our side dishes?"

"Sure. I'll try not to give you a bath in it this time." She tops off my glass and hands it to me.

After a few sips in between removing the skins and

pits from the avocadoes, I kick off my shoes and make myself comfortable. I'm focused on making homemade guacamole, adding all the ingredients, and ensuring it tastes perfect, when I remember what we were talking about.

"Hang on. You said you were afraid my dad was right about only having one love of a lifetime. I never knew he told you about his 'love theory.' He started saying that shortly after Mom died."

"Yeah, we were talking one day when he came home to visit. I think you were working. He was struggling with all the memories of Barbara hitting him at once, and I tried to console him. The hollow expression in his eyes broke my heart. He truly believed what he was saying. He doesn't think he can ever love or be loved again. It's sad because he can still have a full life, with love and laughter and family. From what you've both told me about your mom, I don't think she'd want him to be unhappy for one second. She certainly wouldn't want to be the cause of him not finding love again."

Tawnee's insight hits me like a bolt of lightning—all one billion volts strike me square in the chest. I have trouble catching my breath again while small black dots dance in the air in front of my face. My grip around the handle of the frying pan tightens, but I can't move the rest of my body.

"Here, let me help you with that. You're about to

burn our dinner. It takes a special talent to ruin tacos."
Under normal circumstances, I'd have a quick retort to
her joke about my culinary skills.

But I can't think of a single comeback now.

When I realize I'm no longer holding the pan or
the spatula, I take a step back from the stove and lean
against the island before I fall to the floor from the
smallest puff of air. She adds the finishing touches to
our meal and turns to me with her beautiful smile in
place.

Then it instantly fades.

"Roman, are you okay? What's wrong? Should I
call an ambulance?" The sheer panic in her voice
clears the fog from between my ears.

"What? No. Why would you think I need an
ambulance?"

"Because you're gripping your chest. Your face is
all contorted as if you're in pain, and you're suddenly
as white as a ghost."

"Oh." I look down and realize my fingers are
curled into my skin, over my heart.

"I thought you were having a heart attack or
something. You scared me. What's going on, Roman?
And don't tell me it's nothing because it's clearly
something."

"All right. Let me finish making the guacamole and
salsa for the chips, then I'll tell you. I promised you a
full meal after all."

The skeptical look she shoots me isn't exactly subtle, but she arranges the fixings for the tacos along the bar while I finish the sides. When we sit down together, she watches me expectantly, and I know without a doubt she won't let me off the hook with this one. Not that she should... I deserved that slap in the face of perspective and self-awareness.

"Tawnee, first I want to apologize for how we split up. You were right about a lot of my deficits, but I never corrected you about one assumption you made. I was selfish, immature, stupid, bullheaded, and all the other idiotic things. But I never—*never*—thought there was someone better waiting around the corner. I've always known there's no one better than you. There's no one I'd ever want more than I want you. There's no one who would ever compare to you."

Her throat muscles work to swallow the emotion bubbling up. Unshed tears glisten in her eyes. Her chest heaves, rising and falling rapidly with her ragged breaths. She gently shakes her head from side to side as if she doubts her own ears. This confession has been a long time coming, and there's a very real probability I'm too late.

But it's now or never, and I can't let this moment pass without trying.

"Mom and Dad's love was like a fire that could never be extinguished. It kept them warm, protected... alive. One thrived off the other, and everyone around them could feel how pure their love was. Even when they fought, it was always with the understanding that nothing could take their love away.

"But then she died. Without warning. Without a chance to say goodbye. There was no way to prepare for the devastation she left behind. My father's very essence withered up and died without my mother there to give him a reason to go on. Obviously, he loved me and provided for me. He was a great father. But he couldn't teach me the right way to love a woman, because he simply didn't have it in him anymore."

We both need a second to digest all that I'm throwing at her, so I empty my wineglass. She's still fighting the emotions raging inside, unable to verbalize what's she's thinking or feeling. So, I continue.

"It was devastating, losing someone I loved with all my heart. Somehow, I forgot how good it felt to love. My father's vow never to allow anyone into his heart became mine, although not intentionally. What you said to me just now nearly drove me to my knees, Tawnee. Mom would be furious with Dad and me if she knew how we'd shut ourselves off from sharing our love with someone special. She'd say we were cowards for being afraid of getting hurt again. She'd also blame herself for causing us so much unnecessary pain. She'd be so disappointed in us—in me. She'd be disappointed in *me*... for not making a life with the woman I still want more than anything.

All this time, I never realized the truth until you said it."

Tawnee stares at me, the silence stretching between us. She searches my eyes, part of her wanting to believe me, wanting to accept this is real. But then her shields fly back up. Her expression hardens when her self-preservation kicks in. She shakes her head harder this time, and her lips form a thin line.

"Nope. No way. I'm not falling into this trap again, Roman Scott. Do you have any idea how many times I gave you 'one more chance' over the years we were together? Too many, that's how many. I wasted so much time trying to give you love that you never wanted, and you made that painfully clear to me—repeatedly. Your little speech just now was very convincing, I'll give you that. For a few seconds there, I *actually* considered giving this dog and pony show of ours one more try. How stupid am I?

"You have this wonderful moment of clarity about how shitty you treated me and how disappointed your mommy would be in you, so you want to make it up to her. I mean, what the fuck, Roman? You're a grown man. Whether she's here, you know what love is… and you know what it isn't. You're trying to make amends to someone who isn't here anymore, not to me. I promise you this—I won't put my heart out there for you to trample all over it again. Any chance you had of reconciling with me has long passed."

She pushes back from the table, takes the wine bottle and her glass, and walks toward the back door.

"Tawnee, put all the other bullshit aside and answer one question for me with the full, unadulterated truth."

She stops in her tracks, only turning her head to look at me over her shoulder. "What do you want to know?"

"Do you love me?" I hold my breath and wait for her honest answer.

"Roman, if I thought any good would come out of it, I'd answer that question. But since I don't see anything changing between us, we should leave this subject alone."

"I deserve that after driving you away like I did. I've wanted to tell you how sorry I am every day since then. But I was too proud... too stupid... too scared to do anything about it. That coded message kicked my ass into gear—because I realized I didn't want to live anymore if I'd lost you for good.

"Then seeing you again nearly made me lose my mind. I've almost bitten my tongue off a million times since that moment to keep from shouting out how much you mean to me. But I knew if I just threw my feelings at you all at once, you'd run away again because you wouldn't believe me. I'm telling you now because it's the truth. If I die tomorrow, I want you to know no other woman has ever held my heart. Telling you has nothing to do with seeking my mom's forgiveness. I only want yours."

She lowers her face, staring down at the floor. I watch helplessly as big fat tears fall straight down from her eyes. I slip out of my chair and take a couple of steps in her direction. I don't want to crowd her, but I don't want to give her an easy out to turn away from me either.

"I'm right here, sweets, waiting for you with my heart wide open. All you have to do is step into my arms, and I'll shower you with all the love you can stand. For the rest of your life. For the rest of *our* lives together, Tawnee."

"I can't." Her whisper is so full of both pain and longing. She wants to, but she won't allow herself to chance playing the fool again.

My next play is a gamble... and I'm betting the house on it. I'm sending up silent prayers it works.

"Bullshit. You can, and you know it. You're just scared. You think you need this brick wall up all the time. Never let anyone see your weaknesses. Never admit to having any. Keep your emotions out of everything—including relationships—so you'll be taken seriously.

"You should know better than anyone that's not how any of this works. Teams are built based on the strengths and weaknesses of the individuals in them so there's a balance. Emotion plays its part the same as logic does. Brute strength is just as important as intellectual power. Persuasion can be more effective than force.

"Do you know what's both your weakness and your strength?"

"What?"

"Love, sweets. Love is. You are my weakness, Tawnee. I'd lay down my life for you this very second. But you're also my strength. There's nothing I wouldn't do for you. If you can honestly tell me you don't love me, I'll let you go right now, even though I know I'll never be happy again. But if it means you will be, that's all that matters to me."

Actions speak louder than words.

Sometimes the words need to be said, though.

Now that I've completely opened my heart and mind to her, the decision is all up to her. What will she choose?

Walk into my arms—or walk out the door?

CHAPTER 14

Tawnee

Roman takes another step closer to me. I want to believe him, and that's why I'm hesitant. Am I considering giving in and walking straight into his outstretched arms because I think he has changed? Or is being with him what I've wanted for so long, I can't see myself with anyone else now?

With my eyes closed, I drop my head back, inhale a deep breath, and slowly release it and try to blow the stress out on my exhale. When I envision my future, who do I see at my side? Who's there to comfort me, love me, and share even the most mundane details of my day with? I relax the tight control I've kept on my feelings and let the scene flow freely in my mind. I can see every detail as clearly as if I'm watching a movie on the silver screen.

When I open my eyes, I turn to face Roman. Those hypnotic blue-gray eyes are laser-focused on my every move. His inner turmoil swirls in them—fear, unease, and love. Now I know I'm not wishing it into existence. He's showing me in the only ways he knows how.

Hot tears spill over onto my cheeks, but I don't bother to wipe them away. They'll only be replaced by more waiting for their turn. My heart knows exactly what it wants, regardless of whether my brain agrees. My feet move of their own accord, rushing toward his waiting embrace. Somehow, in the few feet that separated us, I manage to put the wine bottle on the counter just before launching myself at him.

He catches me in midair, and his strong arms engulf me. I wrap my legs around his waist as I encircle his neck with my arms. He crushes his mouth to mine, and everything around us disappears. Our lips and tongues explore urgently, needing more and more, until we're consumed with unfulfilled need. The inherent electricity between us arcs, igniting our bodies with so much heat, our shirts seemingly melt off us and fall into a puddle on the floor.

My back hits the wall, jarring me out of a Roman-induced haze, and I break our locked lips for one more confirmation that I'm not in this alone. His arm, leg, and the wall hold me up while he searches my face, his love for me still shining brightly in his eyes. His gaze lingers on the wetness still on my cheeks. He wipes away the remnants of my tears with the pad of his thumb then leaves soft kisses in their place.

"I've missed you so fucking much, sweets." He leans his forehead against mine and closes his eyes. "Now that I have you back in my arms, don't expect me to let you go ever again."

There's so much regret in his voice and so much tenderness in his touch. Is it too much to hope the childish man I knew before has matured since we've been apart? Honestly, I don't want him to change everything about himself. He's still the man I fell in love with long ago. Our problems weren't all his fault. Now that he owned up to his shortcomings, I owe it to him to do the same.

"Roman, I…" His lips are back on mine before I can say another word.

"Unless you're about to talk dirty to me, and I mean *filthy, nasty*, dirty talk, whatever else you want to tell me can wait. But my balls are bluer than the water out there in the gulf. They can't wait one minute longer."

Leave it to Roman to make me laugh and put our current situation into perspective with only a few well-chosen words. "Yep, it can wait. Absolutely."

"Can't tell you how glad I am to hear you say that. I was about to strip those pants off you, bend you backward over the couch, and feast on you instead of the tacos still on the table."

"Oh, okay. Put me down, and I'll be glad to help you out with that."

His sexy smirk of reply is enough to dissolve my panties right off my body. He lowers my feet to the floor, skims his fingers down my chest, and relieves me of the rest of my clothes. With his arms wrapped around my waist and his hands resting on my ass, he walks me backward until we find the couch.

"Lie back, sweets. A growing boy needs to be fed. And I'm fucking starving."

Before I can respond, his mouth is on me. His tongue licks, flicks, and teases. Stars burst behind my eyelids when he sucks my clit into his mouth. His teeth barely graze over the sensitive bud, and my hands automatically fly to his head. I curl my fingers into his hair, gripping it tighter as each wave of pleasure crashes through me.

This man makes me crazy in so many ways. Every touch reminds me of when we were a couple years before. The memories of our good times have gotten me through so many dark patches when we were apart. The way he makes love to my body always left me more than satisfied and thoroughly spent. He takes his time, finding the exact spots that drive me wild, and uses it to our mutual advantage. Every touch, every kiss, and every bite only make me crave him more.

His hands slide under my ass, lifting me off the couch to give him better access. Then he begins his thorough feast yet again, until my screams fill the room and my body quivers from the overstimulation. He sheds the rest of his clothes and helps me upright again. The tender kisses he gives convey his feelings without words. The way his hands cover my cheeks, reverently holding me while our tongues perform their own mating ritual.

"I'm the luckiest fucking man in the world," he whispers in my ear, then leaves a trail of kisses and nips down the sensitive cord in my neck. "It's been too fucking long, Tawnee. Too long since I've tasted you, since I've felt you wrapped around me, since I've heard you scream my name loud enough for the neighbors to complain. I will rectify all of that several times tonight."

"They warned us not to have the police called on us." My breathy reply is hardly an objection. Merely an observation.

"I never agreed to that stipulation." He pulls my hair to one side and follows it around the back of my neck. "Now, be a good girl and bend over for me."

Goosebumps spread out across my skin, and a shiver runs down my spine when I do as he commands. I know what's coming next, so I grab the edge of the couch in a death grip. I feel him behind me, skimming the head of his impressive cock along my slit. Teasing.

Tempting. Torturing. The anticipation builds inside me, making all my muscles tense into tight coils while I wait for his next move. Every second that passes only adds to the thrill.

Then all of a sudden, he ends my anguish when he thrusts inside me. He fills and stretches me to accommodate him, and my body loves every second of it. The soreness I'll feel later is more than worth the intense pleasure he's giving me right now. His fingers dig into my hips as he holds tightly. His hips thrust harder and harder, punishing me mercilessly while stopping just short of inflicting pain. He is the only man who has ever had the power to make my body obey his every command.

After we christen every surface in the room and my body has been bent in more ways than a contortionist could manage, he finds his release. At last. My legs are about as useful as overcooked spaghetti noodles. My arms shake from overuse. Every inch of my body is covered in sweat—his and mine combined. I'm basically a pathetic bag of skin and bones lying in a heap on the floor, unable to move, barely able to speak, and incapable of removing the permanent smile that's now etched on my face.

"That was an incredible first round. Let's eat the tacos, chips, and dip then I'll be ready for round two." He springs up from lying on the floor to standing straight up as if he's an acrobat. Not a single sign of fatigue or lethargy in his demeanor.

"Make my plate and bring it over here. I'll eat mine from right here on the floor," I mumble into the throw rug. The one that gave me carpet burns in places no one should ever have carpet burns.

He chuckles from above me. "No can do, sweets. As much as I love looking at your sweet ass up in the air like it is...and all the ideas your current position gives me... we're still having dinner together. Come on."

His strong arms wrap around my waist, and he hoists me up to stand with no effort at all. With his hands on my cheeks again, he places sweet kisses on my lips.

"Thank you for getting me up off the floor." My weak smile is only because I obviously don't have his stamina. But he knows, so there's no explanation needed.

"My pleasure. Let me grab you a shirt to wear, and we'll finish the gourmet taco meal I cooked." He winks and jogs—*jogs*—to the bedroom to find whatever clothes the guys left here for us.

While he's rustling through the closet and drawers, I reheat the taco meat and shells. Taking a moment to examine the spread he made for us, I realize how much work went into it. He made the dips from scratch with all fresh ingredients. The toppings for our tacos are all neatly cut up in small bowls. The entire presentation was important to him… and it was all for me.

Tacos and guacamole shouldn't make me feel all emotional. This isn't the reaction of a normal, sane person.

The small gestures do matter the most. His attention to the details that others overlook shows how much he cares. The dedication to making every facet as perfect as possible confirms he values my opinion. Was his impromptu speech truly spontaneous and unrehearsed, or has he been holding in all those thoughts and feelings much longer than I realize?

"I found a T-shirt you can lounge around in."

When I turn from the stove to take the shirt, I realize he's been watching me, assessing my reactions while I didn't know I was being observed. "Thank you." I pull the shirt over my head and turn back to finish reheating our food.

"Want to share what you were just thinking about with me? You were latched on to something intense." He takes the reheated food from me and moves back to the table.

"I've been angry with you for a long time, and I just realized how I never gave you the credit you deserved. There were so many little things you did for me every day that I never even acknowledged. You took care of a lot of things without my asking you to or even knowing you did. If I hadn't reacted the way I did at the end, I wonder where we'd be today."

"You're not the one to blame for our problems, Tawnee. The little things I did never made up for everything you did for me. Not that I've changed *that* much, but I was immature and unappreciative. Your leaving me was the slap in the face I needed to wake the fuck up. At first, I thought you'd be back in a day or two. But then you struck out on your own, got this sweet gig with one of the world's wealthiest men, and you were gone.

"That made me grow the fuck up. I couldn't depend on you to take care of all my bullshit anymore. When I had to take responsibility for all the little things I'd counted on you to handle for me, I couldn't deny how shitty I'd treated you. As far as commitment goes, you had every right to expect that and more from me. For the record, I was always committed to you. I never even looked at another woman, much less thought about holding out for someone better.

"Where would we be if you hadn't left me? We'll never know. As much as I hate to admit this, I don't think we'd be right here, right now, in this new relationship we've found. For that, I can't regret losing you three years ago, because now I can promise I'll never do anything to make you want to leave me in the future."

His words still echo in my mind long after he spoke

them. He urged me to fix my plate before the hot food got cold again and the cold food got warmer. Every bite was better than the last, because I knew it was made by his hands with love—for me. He hasn't said those three little words yet, but his deeds have proven it to me time and again.

Over dinner, we talk nonstop, catching up on every insignificant detail of the last three years we can possibly think of. We intentionally avoid discussing any kind of romantic relationships that may have occurred while we were split up. As Ross so eloquently said, "We were on a break!" The truth is, it doesn't matter if either of us sought comfort from someone else—we're human, we're alive, and we both had to keep moving forward. Our love and our relationship are just that—ours. If we focus our attention on anything else, we'll be no better off than we were before.

Neither of us wants that.

For the first time, Roman and I are on the same page, and it feels better than I ever imagined it could.

"You know, I saw some bathing suits in there while I was rummaging through the clothes to find that shirt. What do you say to a long, leisurely dip in the ocean from our private beach? I think we've earned that perk after the day we've had. I mean, we were kidnapped today. That's very traumatic."

"I agree. We deserve a little fun in the surf. I'm sure

I've read somewhere that it helps prevent PTSD after a traumatic event."

"You read that in one of those tabloid newspapers you love so much, didn't you?"

"Let it go, Roman. I told you they have the best crossword puzzles."

This feels so right—the joking, the sarcasm only he and I seem to get, the way we know each other inside and out.

"Let's go change into our suits. I would love to skinny-dip, but I'm positive that would end in our arrest."

"You're absolutely correct. So will any public displays of affection out there, so don't even think about ocean sex. They barely tolerate it when tourists hold hands in public, so we're not testing them on anything else."

He huffs loudly, disgusted by my ocean sex refusal. I knew that was what he had planned. "Fine. But only because I know you'd be in a lot more trouble than I would."

"Whoever said chivalry is dead? We have living proof of it right here, ladies and gents."

"Tawnee?"

"Yeah?"

"You should be running right now."

I squeal and take off toward the bedroom. It's only when I cross the threshold that I realize this is exactly where he wanted me to go. Too late—he's already right on my heels and blocking the exit.

"I suppose I'll just have to settle for pre-ocean sex to hold me over." He waggles his eyebrows at me before stalking toward me with that damn sexy swagger and irresistible smirk.

Putty. I'm putty in the man's hands.

CHAPTER 15

Roman

"What types of sharks are in the Persian Gulf again?"

"The only shark you have to worry about is me, Tawnee. Now get your ass in this water with me right now."

She wades in, coming toward me with a sly smile on her face. "The water feels good."

"Yes, it does. I know how to make it feel better."

"No, Roman. I mean it. The answer is no, no, no."

"Spoilsport. Taking away all my fun." She rolls her eyes at me, but the smile on her face is genuine. I've missed seeing it and missed being the reason behind it even more. "Let's grab the masks and fins so we can snorkel over by the rocks."

After we put on our gear, we swim the short distance to a retaining wall that has large rocks piled against it, creating a man-made reef. We spend hours swimming back and forth, watching the small, colorful fish dart in and out of the rocks. When she reaches for my hand to get my attention, I don't let go. We move in tandem with our fingers laced together. I couldn't care less what anyone thinks about it—I'll hold my girl's hand whenever I want.

"I think we've worked off all the food we ate earlier. I'm starving." Tawnee looks up at me from her seat in the sand. She's removing her fins, beads of water drip down her face, and her smile is brighter than the desert's setting sun. "It's time to go inside, finish off the leftovers, and make something sweet for dessert."

"Yes, ma'am. Your wish is my command. Thrice-heated tacos and one homemade buttermilk pie coming up. Though I suppose it would be called laban pie here. Doesn't have quite the same ring to it, does it?"

"Those don't really sound like they go together." She scrunches up her nose and grimaces at the same time.

"Trust me. You'll change your mind after your first bite of pie." I extend my arm and offer her my hand to help her up.

"If you say so. I guess I should trust you—

everything else you made was delicious." She cups my cheek with her soft hand. "Thank you for doing that."

"My pleasure, sweets. Now it's time for you to eat and build up your energy again."

Her jaw drops open, and my only response is to wink at her. The nervous expression on her face is adorable. She turns to walk in front of me, but I hear her mumble under her breath, "I'm going to buy a chastity belt and hide the key for at least a week."

"That's fine by me, sweets. I know how to pick locks."

The house phone rings when we enter through the back door. I hesitate for a moment then decide to answer just in case.

"Roman, it's Shadow. We won't be back by the house for two or three more days. We can't leave our posts for the time being. Do either of you need anything urgently before then?"

"No, man, we're good. Thanks for checking, though. We'll be here when you're ready. Don't hurry on our account." Literally—I don't want them to hurry at all. We're good. We're so good here.

We disconnect, and I relay the message to Tawnee. "Looks like you're all mine for at least two more days. There's no way for you to escape from me. Isn't that great news?"

"On the one hand, yes. On the other, it makes me wonder what they're up to and what's coming next.

Did he tell you and you're just withholding information from me?"

"Nope. I wouldn't do that, sweets. You know as much as I know."

"Then I suppose we'll just have to find ways to entertain ourselves while we're held hostage in this house." She shrugs her shoulders and lifts her hands with her palms up. But I do love that grin on her face. "I'm going to shower and wash all the salt and sand out of my hair. I'll help you make that pie when I get out if you want an extra pair of hands."

"Don't worry about it. I've got it. Enjoy your hot shower in that enormous master bathroom. I'll take my shower while it's baking, then we can relax for the rest of the night."

She walks over to me, raises up onto her toes, and softly kisses my lips. "Thank you. You're spoiling me, and I'm loving every minute of it."

"It's about time I returned the favor. You spoiled me for a long time, only I was too thickheaded to realize what I had until you were gone. I don't want to lose you again, Tawnee. I've been miserable without you—just ask Blake. He caught the brunt of it."

She giggles, picturing the two of us going at it like brothers. "Remind me to send him a gift basket as a thank you for putting up with you in my absence. You know, after we're rescued."

"Hell, he'll be so happy to get rid of me, he'll send you a gift basket for taking me off his hands."

After we finish dinner and scarf down half the dessert, we settle on the spacious couch with a fresh bottle of wine. I sit at the end with my legs stretched out on the ottoman, and she snuggles against me in the crook of my shoulder. The familiar scent of her shampoo lingers in the air around me, and I inhale a deep breath, trying to remember the last time we took a moment just to chill and enjoy each other.

Not a single time comes to mind.

Did we never do this as a couple?

What the fuck was wrong with me?

We find an English-speaking channel and let the movie playing transport us to other worlds. We chat about the plot and laugh off the inconsistencies, unconcerned with reality versus fantasy in our choice of entertainment. We have so much in common in some ways, but we're polar opposites in others. But we can use all of that to our advantage if we simply focus on what's most important this time around.

Before long, I know she's fallen asleep by her rhythmic breathing and lax limbs. Watching her rest comfortably in my arms makes me feel ten feet tall. She feels safe and protected with me. She knows she can trust me and that I'm a man of my word. I'd die before I'd hurt her again… and anyone else who hurts her will be the proud owner of a shallow, unmarked grave in the middle of the desert.

The credits end on the movie we were watching, and another one begins, before Tawnee stirs. She lifts her head from my chest and glances around the room, momentarily confused, until her eyes land on mine.

"Hello, sleepyhead."

Cue the sheepish grin. "Hush. You're so warm and comfortable, I couldn't help but fall asleep. What time is it?"

"Not too late yet. We've just had a very long day. You can go back to sleep if you want, I don't mind. I'll stay right here and hold you."

"If we turn off all the lights in here, it's dark enough outside that no one could see us..." She lets her voice trail off, raises her eyebrows, and bites her bottom lip.

"No one could see us, huh? And what would we be doing that no one needs to see?" I like this adventurous side of her.

"Skinny-dipping in the pool."

Correction. I love this adventurous Tawnee.

"I will go turn off every light and night-light in the house right now. Are you wearing anything under that little silky robe?"

"Nope."

"Perfect. I'll grab a couple towels and meet you in the backyard in two seconds."

"Okay. Don't make any noise when you come out. I'll be the naked one in the pool waiting for you."

"You're killing me, sweets."

She slips out the door while I rush to grab the towels. If that thin, silky robe she's wearing gets wet, she may as well be completely naked. We're trying to avoid any jail time, if possible. I can't guarantee the neighbors won't hear her moans and cries after I catch a glimpse of the moonlight shimmering off her wet, naked body.

When I step outside, I drop the towels on the lounge chair beside the pool, kick off my shorts, and ease down the steps where Tawnee sits. I step in front of her, push her knees apart, and settle between her thighs. The warm water acts as a natural lubricant, and her body is a natural aphrodisiac.

She pulls my face toward hers and lightly brushes her tongue against the part of my lips before taking full control of our kiss.

Then she wraps her legs around my waist, pushing the warmth of her pussy against my cock, and all bets are off. With a slight adjustment, I'm poised and ready at her entrance. I drive inside her with full force, and her back curves from the intense pleasure. Her sexy moans only make me thrust harder. The water sloshes around us as her bare chest arches out of the water, and I slide my hand from her stomach to her throat.

"You feel so fucking good. I can't get enough of

you."

We twist and change places, with me sitting on the step and Tawnee straddling me. The grinding of her hips combined with her inner muscles tightly gripping me nearly pushes me over the edge first. With the first peep of her uncontrollable scream, I cover her mouth with mine and meet her stroke for stroke. In perfect sync, we reach the peak together and tumble over the other side in unison.

She collapses against me, and I lean back against the top step, holding her close with one hand and drawing lazy circles on her wet skin with the other.

"I didn't mean to attack you like that as soon as you got in the pool with me. I thought we'd have a few minutes to swim first." She giggles against my chest.

"You already know you can pounce on me anytime you want without permission or explanation. I truly do not mind one bit." I feel her smile against my skin. "We can swim now if you want. Wear you out a little more so you'll sleep like a rock tonight."

"I'm a little too comfortable lying on top of you to move just yet."

I pick her up and glide through the shallow end, semi-swimming but mostly letting the water flow over us. "How's this?"

"Perfect. Everything here is perfect. Feels like we're on an exotic vacation and makes me never want to go back to the real world."

A nagging doubt starts at the back of my mind. Like one tiny seed, just a fleeting thought, but it's taking root in my mind and growing faster than the speed of light. I've mentioned our future several times… over the last twenty-four hours… but she hasn't. Does she see this as a vacation fling? Having fun while we're here, but leaving it all behind when the fairy-tale escape ends?

But that's not Tawnee's nature. It never has been. She wouldn't use me like that. She wouldn't listen to my professions of love only to rip my heart out with pure spite. I push those thoughts out of my mind and refocus my energies on the beauty who's stuck on my body like a tattoo.

"Roman?"

"Yeah, sweets?"

"I think it's time to take me to bed, snuggle with me all night, and make sure I have sweet dreams."

"My pleasure." We exit the pool, and I wrap her towel around her. She peeks up at me from under her eyelashes, then places a soft kiss on my lips.

"If I'm already dreaming, don't wake me."

"You're not dreaming. This is all real, and it only gets better from here."

We head back inside and straight to the master bedroom. So much has happened over such a short time, all the other days start to blur into one. But not today. From now on, my hard-line stance is firmly in place—I'm not leaving here without her by my side. I won't lose her again.

We crawl into the middle of the king-size bed, our arms and legs wrapped around each other, and wait for sleep to overtake us. Tawnee is out like a light first, and I watch her sleeping soundly for a few minutes... captured by her beauty, captivated by her heart, and addicted to her love.

The next three days follow much of the same pattern as the first one. Shadow said they'd be back in a couple of days, but at this point, I don't care if he takes a couple of weeks. Or months. Years would be acceptable too. I've spent hours upon hours of making love to her, cooking meals together, swimming in the ocean and the pool, and enjoying a few days of having no responsibilities at all. We couldn't have planned a better vacation, or a more deserved break from reality.

Every day, I've considered pressuring her for information. What was in that file? Who was she threatening to kill? Why can't I know about it? But I haven't been able to bring myself to broach the subject. The mere mention of work or anything about our real lives may burst the bubble we're living in. Something tells me I'll need every possible minute to convince her we are real, what's happening between us is meant to be, and we can overcome anything together. I never gave her a reason to believe in me before, so I have to give her every reason to take a leap of faith now.

On the fourth morning of our captivity, Tawnee and I are at the table having breakfast together, joking about not knowing what we'll do today. Then we hear the garage door open, and a truck pulls into the empty space.

They turn the engine off, and we rest our forks on our plates.

Our eyes meet as the large door slides shut.

The knob jiggles just before the interior door swings open.

Shadow, Reaper, and Silas all file into the kitchen with their solemn, grim expressions in place.

Our small slice of heaven is about to turn into a pit of pure hell.

"Well, if it isn't the three horsemen of the apocalypse. To what do we owe the pleasure?" I lean back in my chair, preparing for the worst.

The three men glance at one another nervously, uncertain of who should be the one to share the bad news they're harboring. That truly makes me feel worse, because I've never seen any of these men hesitate to say what's on his mind. Silas steps forward, maintaining eye contact with me the entire time to keep my attention focused on him.

"Roman, there's something I need to tell you. It's about your dad."

CHAPTER 16

Tawnee

My hands fly to my face, covering my gaping mouth, and my heart drops to my feet. If someone killed Gerald because I didn't tell Roman what I know, I'll never forgive myself.

Neither will Roman.

Roman flies up from his seat, and Silas puts his hands up in front of him, signaling for Roman to sit back down.

"He's okay now. He—"

"Now? What do you mean *now*? So that means he wasn't okay at some point in the last few days?"

"Roman. This behavior is exactly why we've kept you out of the loop. You fly off the handle without having all the details. I know for a fact that you've been trained better than that." Silas straightens his spine, pulling up to his full height, and looks down at Roman with the stern expression of a displeased superior.

It works. Roman's demeanor changes immediately, and he nods in agreement. "You're right. When it comes to the people I love, my reactions may be a tad bit heated."

One side of Silas's mouth lifts briefly. It only lasts a split second, but it's enough to make me relieved to have seen it. "That's better. No more talking until I've finished briefing you. I promise to answer any remaining questions afterward. Deal?"

"Deal."

"As I said, he's okay *now*. He was attacked just after his speech at the oil and energy conference. There were quite a few people who didn't share his enthusiasm over his project. We were there, but a crowd surrounded him when he left the stage. Most of the people were peaceful and professional. They only wanted to ask more questions about his research after the panel said they had to move on to the next speaker.

"As the crowd dispersed, two men used that opening to move closer to him. One stabbed him and the other grabbed him, trying to drag him outside, very similar to the way we had you and Tawnee taken. Only they were stupid, because they didn't make sure he was alone before they made their move. Shadow and I immediately took him to the hospital, while Reaper and Bull cornered the two assailants. We have them in custody now and have been putting them through the wringer to squeeze every last bit of intel out of them.

"His injuries were not life threatening, but that doesn't mean he enjoyed it. They kept him overnight for IV antibiotics in case of infection. We arranged a privately chartered flight to get him out of the country and to Noah's house in Miami. Brianna is taking care of him now, and he's perfectly safe. She even took him in for a second opinion, against his will, but she managed it anyway. I received a message this morning from him. He sends his love to you both and said to tell you—and I quote—'Work your shit out so I can have grandkids before I die.' It seems he's fallen in love with all the kids coming and going at the house of Steele and wants his son to start contributing."

"Oh great, a new crusade for my dad to take an interest in. This one only involves my reproductive status. Do parents not realize they're encouraging their kids to have sex when they say shit like that? It just has the opposite effect. That's not uncomfortable at all." Roman's reaction makes me smile and stifle a laugh, but now that's exactly what I'll think about the next time I'm around Gerald.

"Our two idiot guests have confirmed our original suspicions that the three of you were not here by coincidence, but their boss only told them their part of the plan. We're confident they're not withholding information from us about that. The reason your dad was here is obvious. His name has been listed as a speaker on the agenda for months. But why the group behind this needed Tawnee and you here with him isn't clear to me yet.

"Now it's your turn to talk. What did I leave out?"

"Give me a second to process everything, man." Roman props his elbows on the table and rests his forehead on his hands.

Though I can't see his face, I can feel the full range of emotions flowing through him. I want to reach across the table and hold his hand, to show he has all my support, but I don't want to interrupt the moment he needs to collect his thoughts.

"Silas, I can't help but think this wouldn't have happened if we'd moved faster on investigating who was behind the documents you showed me. Is this my fault for not telling Roman about them before now?" I lean forward in my chair, my chest filling with dread at the mere thought.

Roman's head jerks up, and his eyes search mine. I know the underlying heartbreak he's dealing with right now—he's remembering when he lost his mother and thinking about how close he came to losing his dad too.

If I contributed to that by my inaction, by not telling him everything when I had a chance...

"You know, Tawnee, I've been over and over that in my mind. I've let the other guys go through every page and tell me if I missed the mark too. None of us has found anything that even remotely connects the information in that folder to what Gerald is working on. Not one single piece of it." Silas scrubs his hand over his face. I've never seen him look as weary as he does this morning. Makes me wonder if he personally escorted Gerald to Miami then flew straight back here.

"Here's a novel idea. Why don't we just tell Roman what's in the fucking folder so he can help decide if his dad is in any way connected to what everyone else fucking knows but Roman? Why don't we just do that?"

Shadow, Reaper, Silas, and I all stare wide-eyed and slack-jawed at Roman for several heartbeats. When he refers to himself in the third person like that, he's pretty much at the end of his rope. Then Silas folds his arms over his chest and levels Roman with his piercing gaze.

"You're doing it again, rookie. We didn't show you the file to begin with because you'll go ballistic when you read it. I know you all too well. There's still another part of this operation we'll execute next. You won't like it at all, but you'll suck it up and take it like a man, regardless. If you can't do your job, I'll get your walking papers drawn up right now, and we'll finish without you. You feeling me, Roman?"

"Yeah, man. I hear you. I refuse to say I'm feeling you."

I don't know why I bother trying to hide my outburst of laughter behind a cough. Shadow and Reaper respond with full belly laughs. Silas smiles—a genuine ear-to-ear smile—and nods.

"All right, then. Do whatever you have to do to find your Zen-zone. You will need it." He walks out to the garage and returns with his laptop case. When he hands the folder to Roman, I instinctively hold my breath.

Here we go.

He flips the front cover open and is mainly unimpressed with the list of Rafael's businesses. Then he turns the page and starts reading Exhibit B.

State of Florida.

Application to Marry.

Name of Spouse: Rafael Tomas Cruz

Name of Spouse: Tawnee Lia Milano

Both "spouse" signatures are in place, along with the first two state seal stamps to certify its authenticity. All that's needed now are the signatures and the seal under the "Certificate of Marriage" section that confirms the ceremony took place.

He holds that page in his hands a little longer than the average CIA officer would. His jaw muscles tick and flex with the gritting and grinding of his teeth. I remain silent because there are still several more documents to go through. He finally flips the page and begins reading the next one—the prenuptial agreement. After seeing Raf's and my names, he's not interested in the details, so he flips to the last page and sees the signature lines are complete, as is the witness' signature.

He blows out a hard breath, but the red creeping up his neck toward his jawline is a dead giveaway.

The next document is a copy of significant life insurance policies that were taken out on Rafael and me, listing each other as the beneficiary in the event of the other's death. Roman's empty hand curls into a tight fist, and his perfectly plump and kissable lips disappear into a hard line. Following the lump-sum payout are several property deeds showing my name has been recorded as the new owner recently. Though Roman didn't take the time to read it, the properties I now own are the ones that were negotiated in the prenuptial agreement, regardless if the marriage survives. The deeds to the homes, businesses, and land combined put my new tax bracket somewhere in the stratosphere.

He runs his fingers roughly through his hair in frustration, making his already tousled strands even sexier without trying, then he drags his hand along his short beard. He's working hard to keep from blowing up. The old Roman would have already smashed the glass table and stormed out of the room. The man sitting in front of me is earnestly trying to see past the betrayal he's feeling right now.

All eyes are on him, patiently—or impatiently, in my case—waiting for him to turn the page. I can't save him from self-destructing this time. His genuine reaction is important to me… and to us, but he doesn't realize that yet. He suddenly jumps to his feet, sending his chair flying backward from the force. But he doesn't leave. He plants his hand on the table beside the folder, takes a deep breath, and flips the document over at last.

Since I already know what he sees, my eyes are glued to his face. Just a second ago, his gorgeous features were distorted by rage and distress. Now they're slowly morphing into shock, then confusion, and ultimately understanding. He quickly goes through the remaining images, recognizing what he's seeing without realizing the significance yet.

"All right. I've memorized everything in this file. I can assure you that every single page is burned into my brain for all time now. Can someone explain to me why this is evidence against Tawnee? And why the fuck did I need to see this?" He's not looking at anyone when he speaks. In fact, he hasn't looked away from the last image at all.

"The answer to both of your questions is the same: because none of those documents are real, except the pictures of Tawnee and you at the very back. Those were printed from her phone… the same phone that was stolen after the car chase here in Dubai. And all of the documents are hidden in a single folder on Tony's laptop." Silas speaks slowly and calmly so Roman can follow the bread crumbs.

Roman looks up at Shadow. "So, when you said you had to make sure Tawnee wasn't involved, you meant in forging the documents so everything would go to her if Rafael meets an untimely death."

"Exactly. She'd be too smart to keep that kind of proof on her own laptop, especially if none of it appeared on Rafael's. But it would make sense if Tony was the keeper of one set of the documents. As Rafael's right-hand man, he'd be privy to their personal life together," Shadow explains.

"Wouldn't he need to update his will with all this for it to be binding?"

"Not in this case. The prenuptial agreement is evergreen, so there's no expiration date. It meets all the parameters of being fair and just to both parties—it even spells out the distribution of any properties, businesses, or financial gains after the agreement is signed. I'm waiting for a full copy of his will to verify who his beneficiary is, but prenups trump state property laws in most states, if they meet certain criteria. This one meets all the criteria."

"So how does a fake marriage and prenuptial agreement between Rafael and Tawnee connect to my dad and me?" Roman paces back and forth, the wheels in his mind spinning as he attempts to complete the puzzle. "Did the men who stabbed my father say anything when they got close to him? Anything at all?"

"Unfortunately, I wasn't close enough to understand their words. They just sounded like angry Arabs to me." Reaper shrugs his big shoulders, aggravated that he doesn't have more to go on. "I don't know what the fuck to think anymore. I've racked my brain trying to make a connection between all these bits and pieces."

Roman stops dead in his tracks, and he swivels his head toward Reaper. "Wait. What did you just say?"

"I can't make a connection." Reaper's eyebrows draw downward, and he cocks his head to the side in confusion.

"No. Before that. You said the men after my father were just angry Arabs."

"Yeah. So? Is that supposed to mean something?"

"Shadow, when you pulled this list of Rafael's companies, did you have the analyst look at Rafael's name only?"

"Yes. He's never been married. No kids. No family to speak of—not immediate anyway. What are you thinking, Roman?"

"I think you should have them run the trace again, but search under Tawnee's name this time."

"Let me help you out there," I interject. "The only business I have is my security business that you men have pulled me out of this week. Why would you think… *That motherfucker!*" I drop my head in my hands and bite back a scream. How could I be so stupid and blind?

"My sentiments exactly, sweets. *That motherfucker.* Now, can I kill him?"

"Only if you beat me to him, Roman."

Okay, now I get it, and I can't blame Roman for feeling this way ever again. The urge to throw shit, break glass, and pitch the biggest fit the world has ever seen almost overpowers me. I think I would feel much better if I could demolish everything in my path and get all this rage out of my system.

"Does someone want to include us in this big revelation? We may be able to offer some assistance if we know what's going on." Reaper waits for a reply from either Roman or me.

"Reap, if the information on the search comes back with what I think we'll find, I'll fill in all the holes. Since we can't dismiss the possibility that Tony's the beneficiary and the one behind all this, I don't want to get too ahead of myself. For once." Roman turns his attention to the other Steele in the room. "Silas, what's the next step in your plan? The one you said I wouldn't like. Might as well lay it all out on the table now."

Silas glances between Roman and me before a devilish smirk appears. "Rafael is paying the ransom for you two. The money drop is tonight. After we confirm the payment, we'll send him instructions on where he can find you. Once Tawnee is back on his team, her job will be to stay as close to him as possible, so he doesn't suspect we're investigating him. Our focus is still on both Raf and Tony, but one doesn't go anywhere without the other. Since Raf has professed his feelings for Tawnee, she'll confess she realized her mutual feelings for him after the harrowing ordeal with her kidnappers."

There's a pronounced moment of silence while the two men have a silent face-off in the breakfast nook. Not exactly an area conducive for the whole duel at twenty paces analogy, yet that's exactly where my thoughts go, anyway.

"Are you fucking insane, man?" Roman bellows and throws his arms up in the air, conceding to Silas. "You want to send her right back into the arms of the two men we suspect most of all?"

"Exactly. You can't say I didn't warn you first." Silas beams at Roman. He may enjoy this part of his plan a little too much.

CHAPTER 17

Roman

After that announcement, I need fresh air to clear my head and accept this ridiculous plan Silas is pitching. I turn and walk out the back door and straight into the ocean, where the waves lap at my bare feet and the soft breeze provides some respite from the scorching sun overhead. I close my eyes and drop my head back, soaking up the rays and using the salt and sand to calm this storm raging inside.

When I hear the door open behind me, I assume Tawnee is coming out to check on me. That was an intense few minutes in there, going through all the documents that suggested she was set to marry another man. My thoughts and emotions were all over the board as I moved from one piece of evidence to the next. What grounded me were the memories we'd made over the past few days. The woman they have held me captive with isn't someone who could spend several days in my arms then run off to marry someone else.

Keeping that in the forefront of my mind wasn't easy, though. Flashes of her lounging in the cabana with Rafael fought for their place in the equation too. I'd be stupid and careless and reckless if I didn't at least consider there was more than an employer-employee relationship between those two. I couldn't bring myself to look at her while looking through that folder—I had to work through my own issues with it first.

"How are you holding up, Roman?" Silas asks.

When I open my eyes, he's standing beside me, shoulder to shoulder. "Great. I'm about to send the love of my life right into the viper's nest. Other than that, really good."

"Unfortunately, I know exactly how you feel."

"I know you do, man. Would you do it again if you had to?"

"That's not a fair question, Roman. Kira's out of the game."

"Yeah, she is. But she'd jump right back in if she had no other choice. How would you deal with that?"

"You know what I'd do. I'd break shit, punch holes

in walls, and bite everyone's head off who dared to speak to me." His dark chuckle matches mine.

"That's what I thought. You couldn't patch into his comm lines and eavesdrop on his conversations since we've been abducted?"

"Do you honestly think I'd violate Rafael's civil rights like that? He's a private citizen, Roman. That hurts."

"Cut the bullshit, Silas. What'd you hear? And why are you keeping it from Tawnee?"

"My allegiance is to you, Roman. I'm trained to suspect everyone until they give me a reason not to— it's simply the way I'm wired now. Shadow and I talked about it beforehand. I allowed her to review that file, and I had him keep it from you for a reason, and it wasn't because of your temper. Though you do need to control yourself better.

"She's been with him for the last three years, practically around the clock. She excuses his behavior when she shouldn't. She gives him the benefit of the doubt when she should question his motives. That's all normal for someone who has an established relationship. We want to see the best in the people we're closest to, so it's not a big deal on its own. But I thought her reaction to the forged documents and life insurance policies would be stronger. And I thought she'd tell you everything over the past few days when you were alone. But your reaction to seeing the file for the first time was genuine. She didn't tell you about any of it—and what he did is just cause for a serious ass-kicking. Don't you find that odd?"

"Are you saying the documents are real and she planned to marry him? Or are you saying you think she's involved in something shady and trying to hide it from us?"

"After hearing Rafael's phone calls on what he thought was a secure phone, I don't believe she's involved in anything shady at all. But it's my job to question if the documents are forged or if they're legitimate. We need to know exactly where her allegiances lie, because when she goes back to him, she may realize how much she's missed him. That was a great call to search for companies in her name, by the way. Good catch."

"Silas, I don't know if anyone has ever told you this or not, but I think you need to hear it from someone who knows you very well."

"This should be good. Let's hear it."

"You should never, ever go undercover as a therapist. Especially not a relationship counselor. You can't say shit like that to people then follow up with an attaboy comment. That's not even in the same hemisphere of how that's supposed to be done."

"I felt it was important to end my little speech on a positive note. That didn't do it for you?" He has the nerve to look offended.

"No, it didn't work for me at all. Your people skills need a lot of work, man."

"I'll get right on that. I'll take sensitivity training or whatever bullshit it is all you pansies do." He gestures toward me when he refers to "pansies." Nice.

"That's Step One, right there, Silas. Self-awareness."

"Oh good, maybe I don't need that class after all."

"Just tell me what you heard on his secure phone calls."

"He called our Arab friends and very angrily demanded to know why they took the two of you early. Apparently, they were supposed to get all three of you at the same time. We caught wind of that plot a few days ago, which is why we took you and Tawnee when we did—because Rafael was watching it happen.

"He came to the conference to have plenty of alibi witnesses when you two were reported missing. But he was so focused on being innocent, he couldn't improvise and change his behavior when the deed went down. Even his table buddies were trying to alert you to the danger coming up behind you, but Raf didn't move a muscle. When he realized Gerald was still there, he lost his shit and called his buddies on their burner phones."

"What did they have to say about that?"

"They swore up and down they hadn't made a move yet and that they didn't know who had you.

When they finally convinced Raf they were telling the truth, that's when he really started panicking. He hung up and made another call to his lawyer, who advised him to get Tawnee back immediately because it takes seven years to have someone declared legally dead. Everything he has in her name would be in limbo without a body and confirmation. There was also a vague reference to multiple attempts in a short period of time being too suspicious and therefore not recommended.

"Just before we had our impromptu meeting in the spare bedroom of his suite, I slipped my own bug into the living room. It's a new design that's not detected by normal sweepers. He seems to spend more time in that room than any other. Perfect timing, too, since we wore out our welcome as soon as you two went missing. We've been listening to the others' conversations from our hotel room, too. So far, Tony is the only potential accomplice out of the people on his staff. He's overly stoic about her disappearance. Normal people would be more concerned than what he's displayed."

"Tony wants her job. Tawnee told me she's had trouble with Tony not following her orders and she's had to jump his shit more than once to get him in line."

"Makes sense. Maybe he thought he was about to be promoted from driver to head of security. But when Rafael agreed to pay the ransom for both of you, he squashed Tony's hopes. If that's the case, Tawnee may not be out of danger just yet."

"I don't think she's out of danger with Rafael either. It may not be smart to arrange another hit on her, but that won't stop him from doing it in this part of the world. Dubai may be relatively safe, but it borders Saudi Arabia, and we both know that country is not safe."

"Tell me why you wanted to check for companies in Tawnee's name. That wasn't just an off-the-wall idea you had. Something prompted it."

"Tawnee and I followed Raf and Tony into a breakout session at the conference. There were a lot of angry Arabs in there. They kept saying a Western Jewish woman was buying up the controlling shares of the primary Saudi oil producer. Think about it—they despise Westerners, they hate Jews, and they're widely known for their mistreatment of women in general. But this puts all three of those demographics together. Give a Western Jewish woman the controlling shares of their oil company, and you have an instant recipe for disaster.

"Rafael's business is buying the controlling shares of companies, right? So maybe he's staying under the radar on this one, using Tawnee's name to take the heat off him. His business model has never involved touring a real estate property before deciding to buy it. He's hanging around here for a reason. Now we have a bunch of marriage documents—fake or not—and he inherits everything when she dies. Milano is historically an Italian-Jewish name. Even though Tawnee's family isn't Jewish. They were raised as Christians. These men could easily find out she's from the US, though. Rafael may be the one who released the rumors to get the old-fashioned Arab men up in arms about it."

"That does up the ante. We need that report back immediately. If she's the shareholder they referred to, they won't believe her when she says she didn't know. They'll charge her with some other high crime and execute her after a one-day mock trial." He retrieves his phone from his pocket and sends an urgent email to his analyst at Langley.

"Are we still sending her back in there knowing all this?" I already know the answer, but I'll make him confirm it.

"We have to. We expect no less of our assets in hostile territories. We push them to get us the information we need to carry out our jobs. Tawnee has a business to run too, and her sole client is paying for her release. Just be glad he didn't negotiate for her release and not yours."

"That doesn't make me feel any better, Silas. Now I have to live with thinking he bought and paid for me… and know that he sees it exactly in that way." That pisses me off even more.

"We'll split the ransom money. That'll make you

feel better. You'll get his money for your abduction. Pretty sweet deal, huh?"

"Until he has the real kidnappers come back and finish their job. Did he ever say why Dad and I were part of his plan?"

"The working theory is your dad was a target because of his new compound. The oil investors aren't ready for it, especially not Rafael if he's trying to corner the market with the Saudi oil company. You were most likely on his radar because of the pictures still on Tawnee's phone. The coded message was probably a test to see if you'd answer her plea for help. When you came running, they confirmed you as a threat. If she disappeared, he knew you'd never stop looking for her.

"Taking all three of you out at the same time, in the same place, would have been easily explained. Your dad was here for a conference, you'd reconnected with an old girlfriend, the three of you went off together and got lost in a bad area. Accidents happen to tourists every day."

"We should take this back home to finish it. The odds of this playing out in our favor in this part of the world are slim to none. And who would believe Tawnee would want to stay here and stay on the job, after being kidnapped? No one."

"Roman, listen carefully, because you'll only hear me say this once. You're absolutely right." Silas smiles, and this time, it isn't his usual sarcastic grin. "But the bosses have declared your dad a higher priority for national security than Tawnee, so we don't have a choice. We finish it here, one way or another. Gerald is safe at Noah's, but if we bring two more targets back to Miami—or anywhere in the US—we put him in more danger. They'll revoke our passports to keep us out if we force their hand."

"We are surrounded by motherfuckers."

"Speaking of, we need to review our strategy for picking up the money and releasing the hostages tonight. Nick will be here any minute now. Blake, Bull, and Rebel escorted your father back to the States, and they're taking turns standing guard over him. You know they'll keep him safe."

"But can they protect Dad from Liz? That's the real test."

"No one is safe from Liz. There's a new national security threat level named after her. Maybe we should have brought her with us—she'd have them confessing to crimes they didn't even commit in no time."

We both crack up over that. Laughing again feels so good after such a stressful day.

"I know we have to consider anything is possible, but you should know I trust Tawnee with my life. Maybe she does want to see the best in everyone and gives too many chances, but I love that about her. She wouldn't have stayed with me for as long as she did if that weren't part of her personality. And she wouldn't be back with me right now if she weren't willing to see the best in me, because we both know I didn't deserve a second chance. If you don't think she's part of anything illegal, you should tell her what you know before she walks back in there. She deserves to know... She deserves that much from us."

"I'll think about it. We have a few hours before this goes down. We'll all be around the table while we build our strategy. I'll be able to get a better read on her before we release you tonight."

"You already know if you don't tell her, then I will. Don't you?"

"Do I look like I was born yesterday? I'm not stupid."

With my temper cooled off and my head screwed on straight, Silas and I head back inside with the others. Tawnee eyes both of us skeptically when we step through the door. She has her own sixth sense, and I know her Tawnee-senses are tingling all over right now. Silas and I had a long conversation, and that is out of the ordinary.

"Did you two finally decide to ask my opinion before running off to solve a problem that revolves around me?" She glares at both of us. Apparently, she thinks we were discussing her role in this plan without her. As if.

"That never crossed our minds, Tawnee." Silas

keeps a straight face for as long as he can then bursts out laughing. "Just kidding. I would love to hear your thoughts on sending you in to spy on your employer."

"I'm in. It's the only way we can get to the bottom of this anytime soon. You'll never get anything against Rafael out of Tony. I believe the rest of my team is loyal to me, but they're also not close enough to Raf to have anything useful or incriminating. It has to be me."

"You do realize what I'm asking you to do, right? You'll have to convince him you're interested in pursuing more than a friendship with him. Hopefully, he'll drop his guard easier that way."

Her eyes float up to mine. We don't have to speak the words to know what the other is thinking.

This will be the hardest fucking assignment I'll ever have.

I'm not exactly the sharing type.

CHAPTER 18

Tawnee

After hours of walking through the plan for the money drop, the hostage release, and what'll be expected of me as an undercover double agent, we take a much-needed break for food and adult libations. Lots of them. I load the machine with ice, alcohol, and drink mix for an extra-large pitcher of frozen margaritas. The guys work on grilling steaks and making baked potatoes and tossing a side salad.

We carry everything outside to the lanai to enjoy our last day in our private paradise. Roman has been exceptionally quiet and withdrawn most of the day. Not that I don't understand—I don't like this setup any more than he does, but I don't know of another way to find out what Rafael's endgame is. Though, to be honest with myself, it doesn't take a genius to figure out what he's doing after creating all those documents with my signature forged on them.

Being near him without stabbing him in the neck with my pen will be hard.

Not recoiling when he touches me will be very difficult.

Pretending to be romantically interested in him knowing everything I do, especially after reconnecting with Roman, will be nearly impossible.

We finish our meal, with Nick, Reaper, Silas, and Shadow carrying the conversation while Roman and I only occasionally engage. The margarita pitcher is empty, so I walk back inside to replenish our supply. One last drink as a team to toast our upcoming success —because failure isn't an option. While the machine shaves and crushes the ice, I'm lost in my own thoughts and memories. Rafael's betrayal stings worse than I've outwardly shown. Not because I'm in love with him or anything remotely like that, but I thought we were truly friends. I believed he'd have my back the same as I've had his all this time.

I've learned firsthand how much it hurts to care more for others than they do for me.

But there's no time to dwell on that when it's painfully obvious he has more nefarious plans for me than I ever believed him capable.

"Are you okay, sweets?"

Roman's voice in my ear makes me jump almost out of my skin. "Holy shit, Roman. I didn't even hear you come in with the ice grinder running. You scared me."

"You were deep in thought. Want to share what you're thinking?" He brushes his knuckles along my cheek, and I instantly melt into his touch.

"I'm dreading this assignment for so many reasons. You know I don't do well with hiding what I'm thinking—I don't have a poker face at all. I really don't want to be thrown into a Dubai prison for murder, but that could very well happen if they find my fork sticking out of Rafael's neck. And…"

"And?"

"I don't want to leave you. These few stolen days have been amazing. I'm afraid to leave and break the magic spell we've been living under."

He pulls me into his arms and holds me, reassuring me as only he can. "Our magic spell can't be broken, sweets. Nothing will come between us again. I've been waiting all day for Silas to tell you the other part of the story, but he hasn't. I'm not letting you walk into this trap without knowing all the facts. I'll pour us a couple of drinks, and we'll talk in here."

When he reaches for the margarita pitcher, I put my hand on his to stop him. "We'll keep the straight tequila. Give them the pitcher."

"Good idea." He presses his lips to mine then takes the pitcher outside.

When he comes back in, I have several shot glasses lined up on the bar, and I'm pouring the tequila in each one. "If Silas is keeping information from me, I have a feeling we'll need these. It'll be harder for me to inflict injury on him if I'm shit-faced."

Roman begins laying out the backstory Silas shared with him earlier. The plot to kidnap all three of us and leave our dead bodies somewhere to be found at a later date. Raf's calls to the Saudi men demanding an explanation for their fuckup. The call to his lawyer and the vague reference to not making another attempt so soon after the first. Raf's inaction when they grabbed us right in front of him.

Silas questioning where my loyalties lie—with Rafael or with Roman.

I've already downed several shots, but I have so much adrenaline and rage coursing through my veins, I don't even have a buzz yet. I'm still fully capable of causing massive damage. So many thoughts swirl through my mind as I pace back and forth along the length of the kitchen and dining area. The longer I walk, the madder I become.

"Tawnee? Did you hear anything I just said?"

With quick strides, I walk toward Roman until we're standing toe to toe. "Look me in the eye, Roman

Scott. Where did you say my loyalties lie—before you told me everything?"

"I told Silas I trust you with my life. My trust in you has never wavered."

He's telling me the truth. I can see it in his eyes. "As long as you believe in me, I don't care what Silas thinks. Now, what did you just say? I'm sorry, I didn't hear you."

"I asked if you're still sure you want to do this. Knowing Raf's behind everything and wants you dead, are you sure you want to go back in there with him?"

"More than ever."

He drops his head back and stares at the ceiling, clearly not pleased with my decision.

"Roman, is there something else you're not telling me?"

"Nothing concrete yet. Just the theory on the secret company in your name we're waiting to confirm. I know in my gut we've hit the nail on the head, and that makes this charade even more dangerous. That oil company was state-owned since it began decades ago. The government took a gamble by putting it on the stock market, but the more traditional nationals never approved of that move. So, if Tawnee Milano, an Italian-Jewish Western woman, dares to attempt a hostile takeover, a lot of angry men will be gunning for you."

"You know, when I first saw those documents with

my signature forged on them, I actually believed he was just so cocky, he assumed I'd accept his proposal on the spot. That he'd had them prepared ahead of time because he doesn't like to wait for anything. He'd just shared his feelings for me not long before you showed up at the cabana. He'd always been a flirt, but I never took him seriously. When he confessed that he was in love with me, I was too shocked to give an intelligent reply. Then he told my entire staff he was pursuing me and not the other way around, I believed he was legitimately trying to save my reputation. How stupid am I?"

"You're not stupid at all. He had a long time to plan and scheme to get to this point. You couldn't have known what he was up to or how far he'd go to pull it off. But you can't underestimate him now, sweets. He's dangerous, and we don't know how much Tony is involved in this. You've got to assume he's just as bad. Bury your feelings deep inside, knowing you can tell me all about them when it's over. But you can't give anything away until we get the notice to make our move on him."

"Am I trying to get him to admit to conspiring to kidnap and kill us? Or to forging my signature on documents? Or to working with Saudi nationals? Or to creating a fake company and buying shares in my name? What is our endgame, Roman?"

"We can't return home until we neutralize the

threat. Dad is a high priority for our national security, so we can't go back and put all three targets close together again. If we can get a line on who Raf is working with inside Saudi Arabia, maybe we can shut it all down at once. That's why Shadow was here first, and why he recruited the others to help him. This is bigger than just three Americans in trouble in the Middle East."

"Well, I have to tell you... none of that makes me feel any better. At all."

We both start laughing, knowing it's the truth but there's not a damn thing we can do about it except ride the wave wherever it takes us.

"We have several hours left before we put our dirty clothes back on and stage our release. Is there anything special you want to do until then?"

"Yes, there is. Tell the guys to leave and give us the rest of the time alone. Let's swim in the ocean, snorkel along the rocks, have more pool sex, eat junk food, finish off the margarita mix, and snuggle on the couch while we watch movies. One more day of our real world before we have to leave here and pretend to be someone we're not."

"Sounds perfect to me, sweets. I'll tell them to hit the road right now."

Roman walks outside, and I hear him ordering his friends to "get the fuck out of here right now." The guys walk through the house to the garage door, each with a knowing grin on his face. Not a single one even tries to pretend he doesn't understand why we're kicking them all out. But that's fine with me—I don't have to hide my feelings for Roman here. Silas stops at the bar on his way out, watching my reaction for a moment before he speaks.

"You two are good for each other. He loves you, Tawnee. He never stopped loving you. Hold on to that until this is over."

I simply nod, unable to speak, then Silas continues walking to the garage. When the large automatic door shuts, confirming we're alone again, we rush to change and grab our gear. We have a short time left to do all the things we enjoy together, so we'll make the most of it. All this will change as of eleven o'clock tonight.

I just hope and pray it's only a temporary inconvenience rather than a permanent situation.

"THE MONEY DROP HAPPENED WITHOUT A HITCH, JUST as we knew it would. He wants you back more than he wants the money he paid for your ransom. We've had the hostage exchange site under surveillance for the last several hours with no suspicious activity detected. We'll still cover you from all sides, though. We're not taking any chances. Are you two ready?"

"As ready as we'll ever be." Roman glances over at me. "You got this, sweets. You'll do great."

"Yeah, I got this." I'm not as convinced as I sound, but I can't go home until this is finished. And I'm more than ready to go back to the US now.

Shadow drops us off on the sixth floor of a deserted parking garage. He drives up to the top of the garage, ditches the van, and uses a keycard linked to someone else to enter the office building. Keeping his face covered and turned away from security cameras, he makes his way out the side door and into a waiting car. Though I can't see them, I know the other guys have eyes on us because I have the distinct feeling of being watched.

A few minutes later, the unmistakable squeal of tires and an engine revving echoes through the garage. Roman and I are tied together, back to back, with the thick black hoods covering our faces. Our clothes are dirty, our hair is matted and stuck to our heads, and we have splotches of dirt smeared all over us. I'm also missing a shoe, which I heavily protested because I really like these shoes. Silas promised I'd get it back when this is all said and done.

"Tawnee? Is that really you? Thank God you're safe! Did they hurt you?" Rafael is obviously a better actor than I gave him credit for. He's laying the brokenhearted hero bit on thick while untying our restraints and removing our hoods. He holds my face in his hands and kisses me squarely on the lips. I think I just threw up a little bit in my mouth. "I'm so happy to have you back, love. What did they say? What did they look like? Who are they? I'll pay someone double the ransom to hunt them down and bring them to justice."

"We're okay, Raf. It was terrifying, but they didn't harm us. I guess they wanted the ransom money more than anything. They spoke very little English, and even that was broken, but I didn't get a good look at any of them. Did you, Roman?"

"No, I didn't. But I'd recognize their voices if I heard them again. Thank you for paying the ransom. That couldn't have been easy for you to negotiate with terrorists like that." Roman extends his hand to shake Rafael's. There's a brief hesitation on Raf's part, but he does accept the olive branch.

"Don't mention it. I wouldn't have it any other way." Raf and Roman share an uncomfortable moment of simply looking at each other, so I clear my throat and force a fake cough to break the tension.

"Tawnee, it's so good to see you." Tony pulls me into a full embrace. "I'm so relieved you're okay. Let's get you out of here before they decide to come back."

On the ride back to the hotel, Raf turns to Roman. "Which hotel are you staying at, Roman? We can drop you off."

Subtle.

"I'm staying in the suite with Tawnee. I'm not convinced she's out of danger."

"No offense, but I think she'd be safer staying in my suite with me at this point. You both were taken from a very crowded conference. I will hire additional staff to stand guard outside my door around the clock to ensure no one gets to her again. After my business concludes next week, she'll be on a private jet headed back home."

"It's okay, Roman. I appreciate your offer, but maybe Raf has a point. I'll stay inside the resort and wait this out. We only have a few more days until we can make our trip home." Keeping my tone neutral is much harder than I thought it would be.

"If you say so. I'll be around for a few more days if you need me. What about the police, Rafael? Do we need to go give any statements or anything?"

"No, the kidnappers were very clear about that. If we contacted the police, they would kill you both. I wouldn't take the chance they weren't bluffing about that, so I didn't involve any of the authorities."

Isn't that convenient? The problem is, I remember Silas said he didn't give that stipulation, purely as a test.

You just failed that test, Raf.

CHAPTER 19

Roman

The smug bastard drops me off at my hotel and barely waits for me to get out of the car before telling Tony to drive away. Silas and Nick are already here, waiting for me to join them in Silas's room. I can't stop the sinking feeling in my gut as I watch Tawnee drive away with him. No matter how many bugs we have in his suite or how closely we watch him, we're not there if—*when*—something happens.

After a quick rap on the door, Nick opens it, and we walk straight back to the command console where Silas is. The bug in Rafael's living room is on speaker, so we have a front-row seat to hear all his conversations. I just wish we could listen to what was being said inside the car while they're on the way back to their hotel. We couldn't slip a phone on her since they stole hers in the wreck. Someone would be sure to check her for listening devices after being out of their clutches, so there was no use in even trying.

In her capacity, she wouldn't have allowed a device to stay on her person, anyway. If she'd walked in and gotten caught with one, Raf would know instantly, and she would be in danger just as fast. We have to trust her to get the information we need and get out of there as soon as she does.

"How'd they act in the car?" Silas asks.

"Rafael couldn't wait to get rid of me. I said I was staying in Tawnee's room with her, but he shut that down real fast. He wants her in his suite in no uncertain terms. He said they're leaving here after his meeting next week instead of staying for an entire month. That means whatever he has planned will go down soon. He said he'd hire additional security to stand guard around the clock. He could be lying, or that could be how he betrays her again."

Tawnee's voice comes across the speaker, and I can breathe easy again for now.

"I'm going to take a shower now, Raf. I can't wait to get out of these dirty clothes and into my pajamas."

"Are you hungry? I can order room service and have it here waiting for you when you get out."

"Can I pass on it for tonight? I'd love to have breakfast with you in the morning, though."

"Breakfast is our thing, isn't it? That's a great idea, love. I'll order it tonight, and it'll be delivered first thing in the morning."

"Thank you again for everything, Raf. I wouldn't be here now if it weren't for you."

"It's my pleasure. A feast fit for a queen will be waiting for you in the morning."

Silence on the speaker means Tawnee escaped to the shower. I don't know if I can listen to this guy much longer without stabbing my eardrums until I'm completely deaf. I don't know how she's endured it for the last three years.

"Silas, can I just go over there, strangle him to death, and close this case once and for all? The world would thank me if they could hear him."

"Yeah, Roman, for once, I think your anger is warranted. I'm very tempted to send you over there and put us all out of our misery."

The shrill sound of a cell phone ringing comes across the speaker, making both Silas and me perk up.

"Hello?"

"No, you listen to me. You will do exactly as I say, when I say to do it, and not one second before or after. This must be executed flawlessly. I understand you're not accustomed to perfection, but you will learn quickly."

There's silence, presumably while the other party

responds. What I'd give to have that comm line in my ear.

"Yes, Yousef, I'm back in my room now. She just went to bed. Bring Omar, Khalil, and Ahmad with you first thing in the morning. Don't be late."

"Don't be late for what? Do those names mean anything to you?" I turn to Silas and Nick, ready to bolt.

"Other than being four of the most common names in Saudi Arabia, no, they don't. Sit tight. We don't want to show our hand unnecessarily. That could be his additional security team coming on duty." Nick continues to concentrate on the speaker.

"Have you heard him order a team since we've been out of the picture?"

"No. I haven't. But that doesn't mean he didn't do while he was away from the bug where we couldn't hear him."

I know Nick's right, but that doesn't stop me from wanting to tear down the place to get her out of there. Now we wait and see what happens next. I know Tawnee is capable and a badass; that's part of what I love about her. It's because I love her that I don't want her to face this alone.

After Rafael hangs up with Yousef, he calls room service and orders one of everything on the breakfast menu to be delivered to his room by seven o'clock tomorrow morning. That may be a slight exaggeration because I can't stand the guy, but he's definitely overcompensating now. He's desperate to impress her and show her he can give her the world on a silver platter.

Or the illusion of it, anyway.

He doesn't want to stay with her any longer than it takes to pull off his scheme without being the target of a nation of angry men.

"That shower felt so good. These clean pajamas feel even better. Thank you for having my clothes brought up here ahead of time. That was so thoughtful of you. I just wanted to say goodnight."

"Goodnight, Tawnee."

Silas turns to me and shrugs. "I'll leave the speaker on and listen for anything out of the ordinary tonight. You two can go back to your rooms and get some sleep. We'll probably be very busy tomorrow."

"As much as I hate to leave her in there with him all night, I guess you're right."

"She may be in there with him for several nights before we get any real answers. Now it's a waiting game, and I know how impatient you are. If you stay in here and drive me crazy, I'll have to hide your body beside his." Silas cuts his eyes at me and lifts one brow.

"Fine, fine, fine. I can take a hint. I'll be back in the morning. Silas, wake me if anything happens."

"You got it."

❧

As promised, I'm back in Silas's room at first light, bearing gifts. When he opens the door, I offer coffee, donuts, and breakfast sandwiches. That seems to brighten his mood some.

"Nothing exciting happened last night?" I know he already would've told me if it had, but I can't resist asking.

"Not a peep all night."

"In a way, I hope today is more exciting because I'm ready to take this motherfucker out and go home."

"You and me both, man. You and me both."

When they finally stir, several voices carry through the speaker at once. I distinctly hear "good morning" and "sleep well," standard early morning greetings.

"You've been through quite an ordeal, and I'm sorry to put such an imposition on you by asking for a favor."

"Are you kidding? You saved my life, Raf. Any favor you need isn't an imposition. What's on your mind?" She's very convincing. I know she hates every second of being fake.

"I'd really appreciate if you could find the energy to finish the conversation that we started a few days ago but never had a chance to complete. I know my timing is terrible, but I almost lost you, and I don't want to let more time slip away."

"I understand what you mean. We can talk over breakfast.

Thank you again for ordering in—I'm not ready to face a restaurant full of people just yet."

"I actually prefer it this way because I get you all to myself. I hope you're hungry—I may have ordered an overabundance of food. It'll be here any min—" A chime rings throughout the spacious suite. *"Ah, that's probably the food now. Tony, can you get the door, please?"*

"Sure thing, boss."

"Raf, did you leave anything for the rest of the hotel to eat?" Tawnee laughs. To the untrained ear, it's a normal laugh. To my Tawnee-tuned ears, it's forced.

"Only the very best for you. Would you like to eat at the formal dining table?"

"Actually, no, I'd rather eat in here if that's okay with you. The couch is so comfortable, and I've had enough of hard chairs and floors this week."

Good excuse, sweets.

"That's perfect. I prefer the more intimate setting for our discussion, anyway. Shall I make your plate for you?"

"That's very kind of you to offer, but I think I can handle it."

When they settle down on the couch, their voices come in loud and clear.

"I realize this is very sudden and may seem completely out of the blue, but I assure you I've given the matter a great deal of thought. Even before this week and everything that's happened. This ordeal has only magnified the importance of not wasting

another moment. Tawnee, will you do me the honor of marrying me?"

Silas and I turn our heads to look at each other at the exact same time.

"No fucking way. He did not just ask her to marry him."

"He did. He's escalating his timeline." Silas picks up his phone and texts the rest of the team to give them a heads-up.

"Raf, I don't know what to say. This is very sudden." Tawnee doesn't hide the surprise in her voice, but she's careful to keep her tone from sounding harsh.

"We're in one of the most beautiful cities in the world. We can get married on the hotel grounds. The wedding coordinator can arrange for a local Christian minister to officiate the ceremony so the courts will recognize it. It'll be the perfect setting, and you won't have to lift a finger."

"They can't get married here. They're not residents —the UAE courts won't recognize it. Right?" I'm grasping at straws here.

"The Dubai courts will recognize it if a minister of their faith conducts the ceremony—especially since they're of the same faith. Dubai is much more accommodating to visitors than the other Emirates. They know this place is a wedding destination gold mine. Had Tawnee truly been Jewish, they obviously wouldn't allow it."

"I really don't know what to say, Raf."

"Say yes, and make me the luckiest man in the world."

"Say no, and make me the happiest man in the world, Tawnee," I yell at the speaker, willing her to hear me.

"I'm very flattered, Raf, but I have to say no. It's too fast for me. We've been friends and have gotten to know each other after all this time. But if I do get married, it'll be for the rest of my life. We need time to get to know each other as a couple before we even think about marriage."

"I completely agree that marriage should be until 'death do us part.' We are on the same page there. But I think you know if someone is your match or not. When someone is your soul mate, you can feel the connection regardless of the distance or time apart. And when you're close to that person, your very essence tells you. Electrified touches, knowing glances, finishing sentences for the other, and understanding deep feelings without the words to describe them—these are all signs that your soul has found its mate."

Not that I ever thought I'd agree with this tool, but he's one-thousand percent correct about soul mates. All of that is what I feel when Tawnee is near... what I've always felt around her, but I was too stupid to realize it. I used to think love made me weak. Now I recognize love makes me the strongest man alive. I'm nothing without her in my life and by my side. When I get her back—this time—I'll hold on to her for the rest of my life. Now that I know exactly what I've been living without, I see I haven't been living at all.

"That explains so much." I can tell by the inflection in her voice that she's lost in thought. She's thinking about what she feels for me.

"It certainly does."

"Be ready to move at a moment's notice, Roman. Nick is packing his stuff now. She just turned him down, and she just confirmed she's still in love with you. Even though she didn't say your name, he can tell she wasn't referring to him with that last comment. He won't wait much longer to get rid of her now. There's something else I need to check—your question about them getting married raised a red flag for me." Silas opens his secure CIA laptop and starts clicking away.

I try to watch what he's looking for and listen to the speaker for strange noises at the same time. If someone rushes in and nabs her, the only signal I get could be a muffled cry for help. Silas zips through the website, letting our special encryption translate each page while hiding his online presence.

"You're looking at the deeds for the property he's touring next week? Why?"

"I have a hunch from something you said before… Yep, there it is. He already owns that building. He's not here to consider buying it—he already owns it. That means he has an automatic resident visa. Now, let's go to one more site and check one more thing… Son of a bitch. They just processed Tawnee's resident visa as his employee. He must know it's approved for her to stay here long term as his employee. He's not planning to return to the US in a few days. He's staying in Dubai, gaining control of the most profitable oil company in the world, and setting up residence as an expat right here on the Saudi border."

"We know everything has been a setup from day one. The trip to Dubai, the wreck, the attack on my dad—let's just go in and take him out of play altogether. Don't give me the company line that the CIA doesn't assassinate people. I know better than that shit. We are the elite team that goes in when others can't or won't. Get her out of there, remove him from the picture, and let her dump all the shares. She'll make a ton of money, and they'll leave her alone since they'll have their company back."

"Not a bad idea. Maybe we can sell that to the State Department so that they'll let us back into the country—it's still iffy. We have direct orders to identify the conspirators because of the high probability of terrorism. We may have to stop over in another country first to give her time to close out the sales and get her name off all the dark web hit lists. She'll have to change her name for a while too." Silas is thinking out loud.

"She can change her name permanently—to mine. Let's just go over there and get her the fuck out of that place, man. Before it's too late." I'm already on my feet, moving toward the door.

"All right. Go pack your shit and take your suitcase with you. We'll have to gain entry by sea. The only way in or out of their hotel by land is blocked by guards. Rafael won't let us in again. As soon as we have her, we'll have to flee the country."

When I step out of his room, I hear him calling Shadow and Reaper to let them know we're making a move on Rafael today. I don't even feel the least bit guilty—he's plotting to kill my girl, but he's the one who will get a six-foot-deep surprise.

Before the door closes, I hear voices on the speaker again, so I stop and listen.

"Oh, yes, I almost forgot. I have a surprise for you. Stay right here, and I'll fetch it from the bedroom."

"Raf, you really didn't have to get me anything."

"Nonsense. I enjoy spoiling you. It's quite breathtaking. One moment."

"Okay, if you insist."

Silas's cell pings with a text then his laptop signals an incoming secure email. When he double-clicks on the attachment, he leans back in his chair with his bottom jaw hanging down to his lap.

"What? What the fuck is it, Silas?"

"Hey! What are you doing in here? Get out before I call security! Let go of me! Noooo…"

"Tawnee!" I scream at the speaker, as if she can hear me, as if it'll stop whoever is doing whatever to her. "Silas—fucking say something!"

"Rafael listed Tawnee as the beneficiary for his entire estate—everything he owns is automatically hers upon his death."

"Good. But his death isn't the one I'm concerned about right now. Move your ass—we have to go help her!"

"They have also recorded a will in Tawnee's name, leaving everything she owns to Rafael in the event of her death. It was dated six months ago." He jumps up as he speaks and opens a zippered compartment of his suitcase, retrieving a packet of guitar strings and two short metal poles. "Here. You'll need this."

When I realize he just handed me a garrote wire, I'm impressed with his knowledge and skills all over again. I was ready to go in with fists flying. This will be much more effective. Steal up behind Rafael, wrap the guitar string around his neck, and twist the poles until he's dead. It results in a silent kill, no need for a gun, and no ruckus to alert security.

"Perfect. I hope this cuts his fucking head off."

CHAPTER 20

Tawnee

Four large men in expensive Armani suits stormed into Rafael's room, dragged me off the couch, and down the steps to the first floor of the suite. Raf casually strolls down the stairs with a carefree grin on his face.

"Ah, I see you've met my associates. Good. Formal introductions aren't exactly necessary at this stage. You know, I wasn't sure about going through with this at first. After all this time you've been my head of security, I thought you were loyal to me. I was confident I could convince you to marry me by confessing my love for you.

"But all of a sudden, your entire personality changed. You didn't argue when I had your personal belongings moved from your room to mine. That's not the Tawnee I know. She would've raised hell with me over that. Then you kept favoring a certain seat on the couch, and you wanted to eat on the couch instead of at the table. Those signs were just a little too telling. We didn't find your bug, but I know it's somewhere in that room. Your friends have been listening to our conversations, checking up on me." He turns his attention to the brutes holding me. "Get her ready."

One wraps a roll of thick, black duct tape around my head, covering my mouth and underneath my chin several times. Another man binds my hands behind my back. The third man approaches with a boshiya, a thick black veil that completely covers my head and face. There isn't even a hole for my eyes. Then they cover me with an abaya, a traditional Muslim dress that hides my regular clothes underneath, all the way down to my shoes, and makes me feel as if I'm wearing a heavy tent.

"Perfect. Your friends will be here soon, looking for you. I know that. But when they break in and find my suite empty and all your belongings gone, they'll assume you've been taken elsewhere. Then they'll leave. The best part is you'll still be on the property, attending our wedding. When the wild goose chase ends, and they realize they were never anywhere close to you, it'll be far too late for them to backtrack and find you. No body, no crime."

I can't flip him off, tell him what I think, or even give him a dirty look. He wouldn't be able to see or hear anything from under all this garb, anyway. Now I wish I'd taken him out when I had the chance. Never, in a million years, would I have thought he could be this devious.

Then Tabitha walks down the steps, wearing a gorgeous, modern, A-line wedding dress with spaghetti straps and a plunging neckline. Lace appliques cover the skirt. She styled her hair the same as mine. She applied her makeup to look like mine, right down to the eyeliner that changes the shape of her eyes. Even if I could speak through the layers of duct tape covering my mouth, I wouldn't be able to say a single word.

"Ah, *Tawnee*," Raf greets Tabitha. My eyes dart between the two of them, even though they can't see me under this thick black veil. "Are you ready to marry me today?"

"I'm more than ready to marry you, Raf. I've been in love with you for so long, and after my kidnapping, I finally faced my true feelings. I'm so excited to become Mrs. Tawnee Milano-Cruz today." Tabitha's smile beams, exactly like a true bride.

She walks straight to me, searching for my face under the black shawl. "You must wonder why, after all this time, I'd betray you like this. It's really very simple —my loyalty was never to you. Rafael is the one who has paid our salaries all these years. Without him, none of us would have had such a prestigious position. And for marrying him today while pretending to be you, he will set me up for life. Carter and I will be able to sail off into the sunset together, debt-free and without a care in the world. You could have had this for yourself, Tawnee. All you had to do was say yes when he asked you to marry him."

They may have tied my hands behind my back, but my legs are still free. For now. *Time to sweep the leg, Johnny.* My Brazilian Jiu-Jitsu training comes in handy right about now. With a standing leg sweep, I knock her to the ground, pounce on top of her, and squeeze with my thighs until I hear ribs crack. She may sail off into the sunset, but it'll be with a long-term reminder of who she stabbed in the back to get there. The men surrounding me are too shocked at first to react quickly, but when they do, arms grab me from every direction and pull me off her. I squeeze my thighs tighter, lifting her off the floor with me until my legs can't hold her weight and I drop her flat on her back with a thud.

"Enough!" Raf bellows. "Tabitha, go fix yourself up again until you look perfect. We'll be waiting for you downstairs for the ceremony. Carter will walk you down the aisle and give you away."

I glance around, looking for the other members of my team. I'd love to know if they're part of this mutiny or if something has happened to them. They weren't here when we came in late last night after the hostage release. Has Raf killed Jason and John or turned them to the dark side with Tabitha and Carter?

She limps away to fix herself up, but not before throwing a nasty scowl my way. If only she could see the eye daggers I'm tossing her way.

Raf holds up his phone, showing me a live feed of Roman and Silas in the car. "Did you really think I wouldn't have them followed after they dropped you off last night? I know they're on their way here to rescue you. Perfect timing. Let's go get married, shall we?"

Two of the men from behind me walk toward the spare bedroom and return with my suitcases. I know they have packed all my personal possessions, leaving no trace of me behind. There are ways to make everything disappear—security footage, passports, people—with the right amount of money. Raf has that in spades.

"Bring her."

The other two men grab my arms and force me to follow Raf out of the suite, to the elevator, and outside. The wedding planner has been hard at work decorating the grassy courtyard with white linen-covered chairs, a shimmering walkway lined with white flowers and glossy green foliage, and a flowing gossamer-wrapped arbor. Set against the blue sea, sky, and bright sun, it's a ceremony any bride would dream of having.

If she's standing next to her groom of choice, that is.

The chairs are already full of guests, all excited to see Rafael Cruz get hitched. My goons force me into a chair in the middle of the row, next to other women in varying degrees of similar dress, where I'm less likely to be noticed. The music starts, quickly followed by *oohs* and *ahs* from the crowd. The only reason I even glance over at Tabitha is to see if she's grimacing from her cracked ribs and shallow breaths.

She's in a lot of pain.

That makes me smile on the inside. I can't physically smile under all this duct tape.

They must have told the minister to zip through the formalities because he takes no time in getting to the vows, the I Do's, and pronouncing Mr. and Mrs. Cruz as man and wife, sealed with a kiss and exchange of rings. When the guests stand to clap and cheer, my bodyguards force me up and quietly slip away from the adoring fans waiting to throw birdseed at the happy couple.

When we reach the fleet of Rolls-Royce limos, one man stops me, harshly jerks me to face him, and lifts my veil. "Your name is Tawnee Lia Milano? Is that correct?"

Anger burns in his eyes and his face is scrunched

up in disgust. This instantly feels very different from just a few minutes ago.

I nod my head slowly, afraid to confirm his question. How would he know my full name?

"This is her. This is the one. We're taking her back with us."

"But Rafael said—"

"I don't care what he said. He lied to us about her name. She is the one we've been looking for after all. We're taking her now." He puts the veil back in place, shoves me into the back seat of the car despite my kicks and fighting, and instructs the driver to go.

As we drive away from the hotel, I continue to struggle against them, trying to reach the door to fling myself out of the moving car, then one of the men punches me in the face, knocking me out.

When I come to, everything is upside down. Then I see feet below me, moving swiftly. Shifting to get a better look, I realize I've been flung over one of the brute's shoulders, and he's carrying me toward a small jet. I begin to fight again, knowing certain death awaits me if I allow them to take off with me aboard that plane.

"Be still or I will break your neck and leave your body right here for the animals to eat while you're still alive." His angry growl sends shivers down my spine because he means what he says.

I look around to figure out where we are, but all I

see in every direction is flat sand and heat monkeys jumping in the distance. Nothing distinguishable for miles. Without knowing exactly how long I've been out, I make an educated guess that I'm outside of Dubai, in the UAE, on my way to Saudi Arabia.

As a woman, they will strip my rights away from me the moment I cross into their country—no voice of my own, no way to get across the border, and no value as a fellow human being. And that's the best-case scenario I can hope for now. The odds of Roman—or anyone—finding me are statistically impossible. Not improbable. Impossible.

He deposits me in a seat at the rear of the plane where two other women wait. When he rejoins the other men at the front of the aircraft, the two women act quickly to untie my numb hands and remove the tape from my mouth and hair—as much as they can. When the blood rushes back into my hands, the pain is excruciating. With the first noise I make, the women shush me and nervously glance toward the men. One massages my hands while the other woman applies oil to my hair to loosen the adhesive residue. Seems they have more than a little practice at remedying these medieval torture tactics.

After she removes the last of the tape, the lady working on my hair removes a new scarf from her bag and wraps it around my head and neck, covering my hair and every inch of exposed skin. With my arms untied, I'm able to wear the abaya correctly, making it much more comfortable than before. But from the way the man spoke my name, I'm not convinced an abundance of comfort will be found when we land.

"Do you speak English?" I whisper to the ladies.

"Yes," the younger of the two whispers back. "I am Anisa, and this is my sister, Farrah."

"I'm Tawnee. Where are they taking me?"

"To a village on the outskirts of Riyadh." Anisa watches the front of the plane closely. Her discomfort with talking to me is clear.

"Why? What do they want from me?"

The sisters lock eyes, silently deciding whether to answer my question.

"Please tell me. I do not understand why they want me or what they expect from me." That's not a complete lie. I have ideas, but they're unconfirmed suspicions. To know what my next move should be, I need confirmation.

"Because they know you're the woman who's trying to take over our oil business and overthrow our Crown Prince." Farrah sounds as though she completely believes the rumors that are no doubt running rampant about me throughout the kingdom.

Exaggerations and fabrications only add to the hysteria, making me public enemy number one across the country. Next, they'll say I'm after their husbands. Not a chance, sister.

"Farrah, I promise you neither is true. Look at me —do I look like I have the money to buy the controlling shares in SAOR? I don't own shares in any company. Also, I have no interest in being your new Crown Princess, or whatever that title would be. All I want is to go back to my home in my country. How can I do that? How can I get home?"

"This is not possible, Tawnee. The mutawa—the virtue police—have you in custody now. They can hold you indefinitely for such severe offenses." Anisa is clearly the more empathetic of the two.

I know what the religious police are about—they're the plainclothes officers who roam the streets to enforce their public morality laws however they deem fit.

The sisters take their seats when the plane starts to move and stay silent for the two-hour flight. I know exactly how long we were in the air... because I count every second of it. If I have any hope of escaping back to Dubai, I need a way to calculate the distance and direction. Getting out of this country is my one and only goal.

When we land, the morality police—which is a complete oxymoron to me, because I believe it's immoral to mistreat women—snatch me up out of my seat and haul me off the plane and straight into the back seat of yet another car. When we stop, it's at a dull, tan building, mostly made of clay. The windows are all covered by a thick rattan wood. An eight-foot fence lines the edge around the entire rooftop of the building to prevent the prisoners from escaping or jumping to their death.

I'm thrown into a dimly lit cell, with only a hard cot, a thin blanket, and a toilet. Male guards patrol back and forth along the path in front of the bars, simultaneously sneering at me with disgust and leering at me with lust in their eyes. Pitiful sounds echo throughout the sparsely furnished common room. Women cry from every corner of the prison—some scream, some make strange animal noises, and others sound as though they're talking to themselves.

None of this bodes well for me.

A loud bell rings and all the guards congregate in one corner of the room, unroll their rugs, and bow to begin their mandatory prayer time. While they're all busy, I crouch on the floor at the edge of my cell, closest to the woman beside me, and loudly whisper to get her attention.

"Hey, what's your name? Mine is Tawnee. Do you understand English?"

"Yes. Most of my country does. My name is Lara."

"Why are you in here, Lara?"

"Because I ran away from my brother."

"I'm sorry, I don't understand what you mean."

"He was my guardian, but he was very cruel. He used to beat me and make me into his slave. When I ran away, the police caught me and put me in here. My brother refuses to get me out, so the police can keep me as long as they want, or they can sell me as a bride to anyone they choose."

My heart breaks in two for her. She's resigned to her fate and doesn't have the strength to fight it any longer. "Lara, I'm so sorry, but maybe we can help each other. Is there a way out of here? Any way out?"

"No, there's no escape from this place. I've been here more than five years now, and my brother still refuses to take me back. Even if I could escape, I have nowhere to go."

"You can go with me. If we get out, I will take you with me."

"We won't be allowed out of the country without my male guardian's approval. Since I no longer have a male guardian, I can't get approval to leave. You can't either. Even as a foreigner, you're required to have a male escort at all times when in public." I'm sure her argument makes sense to her—this is her culture and what they have ingrained in her since birth. I'm not as willing to accept the rule of another over me.

"Lara, if we break out of jail, it'll be without the help of a male guardian. We'll also sneak across the border without the permission of a male guardian, because we'll be badass prison escapees by then. Who needs a guardian when you're a badass?"

"There's a moment when they leave us alone in the

infirmary after the electric shock torture. The woman who runs the infirmary is the commander's wife, so none of the male guards can stay in there with her. If we could somehow pull ourselves together inside that room, we could make a run for it."

"Do they take everyone for torture at the same time?"

"No, it's scheduled by which cell we're in. You and I will go together in two days, according to our cell numbers."

So much can happen in this hellhole over the next two days.

Is it wrong that I wish for our torture session to come sooner?

CHAPTER 21

Roman

"**D**ude, run over them, knock them out of the way, push them off the road. Do something!" I yell at Silas, knowing there's nothing he can do about gridlock traffic on the main road in Dubai that runs parallel to the beach.

"Don't look now, but we're being watched. There's a guy in the car two lanes over, one car back, who's been following us. Assume the worst when we rush in." Silas checks the rearview mirror again, watching our tail while they watch us.

"Are you above being a pirate?"

"Not at all. It's my dream job. What's your plan?"

"Pull in to that marina and let's commandeer one of those boats from the rental place. Since we're making a water entrance to the hotel anyway, we might as well do it in style. We can ditch our stalkers while we're at it."

"Great idea. There's no way they'll get over in this bumper-to-bumper traffic to follow us out there. Now to get past the guys on the docks."

"Leave them to me. You and Nick pick out a fast boat and let's haul ass."

Silas barely wedges between the line of cars and the pedestrians on the sidewalk to get us out of traffic and onto the side road. The instant we moved out of line, the cars behind us surged forward, cutting off anyone who may have thought about getting over. Before our vehicle comes to a stop in the marina parking lot, I'm already out and running toward the docks.

A party of at least seventy people is lined up to board a large yacht. The deckhands are busy checking in each person and assisting them on board. The captain is in the cockpit, running through his last-minute inspection, and the guests are lively and animated in their formal dresses and black-tie tuxedoes.

I stick out like a sore thumb.

There's no way anyone will buy the line I'm late for this party.

All the more reason for me to distract the couple of guys who don't have their hands full already. I trot toward them, frantically looking around, and stop when I get just past them. They turn, and their gazes track my movement.

That's it, fellas. Eyes on me. I'm over here.

"Have you seen a little girl wander by here? She's five, wearing a pink princess dress. She has a little tiara on her head and a purse on her arm. She was beside me one minute and gone when I looked down the next. I'm afraid she got on one of these boats, pretending it was hers. Or, God forbid, she fell in the water. You haven't heard a splash, have you? You don't think she's under one of these boats, do you?" I'm laying it on thick, letting the alarm overtake my voice and my face.

Panic-stricken, they leave the guests to the other workers and rush to help me. If I keep them busy checking the multitude of yachts lining the five rows of docks, Silas and Nick can manage to get one of the smaller, faster fishing boats untied and ready to take off without being seen. The engines on the party yacht are loud enough to mask a vessel the size we need… for a few minutes, anyway. They'll realize it soon enough.

The two men split up and board each boat, checking every nook and cranny inside after they've finished with the outside. I would feel bad for my blatant lie and their dedication to finding the lost child if a life wasn't truly in danger right now. But Tawnee is my first and only priority—so I can't focus on anything except reaching her.

While the men are busy, Silas and Nick slip past me and hurry to the end of the dock where the smaller center console boats are tied. Nick unties one of the lines while Silas starts the engines, then he unties the second line before pushing off. The longer he lets it idle in neutral, the better off we are. When they drift far enough away from everything that Silas can put it in gear to go forward, Nick motions for me to join them. I rush to the end of the dock, Silas swings by close enough for me to jump on, and we haul ass out of the marina and around the bend to the hotel.

I haven't worked out how we'll get up to Rafael's suite yet. The elevator requires a room key to move off the lower floors, making it almost impossible. We arrive at the hotel in no time, thanks to the powerful engines on the back of the fishing boat. They're designed to take the fishermen out far and fast, so they can be the first to the prize. Now if I can just make it to my prize in time. Silas sidles up alongside the concrete retaining wall around the hotel so Nick and I can jump off to secure the boat's fore and aft lines to the palm trees.

We race across the green grass and through the middle of an ongoing wedding reception. I don't think much about it until I catch a glimpse of Tony lurking in the back. After he checks our surroundings, he motions for me to join him around the corner. I'm well aware it could be a setup, but I'm willing to take the chance. His expression before he saw me was genuinely distressed. I'm going on a hunch that he truly wants to share information with me.

When I turn the corner, Tony's leaning against the side of the hotel with his head hung low and his shoulders drooping.

"What's happened, Tony? Where is she?" I can barely catch my breath, but it's not from exertion. My heart is racing a hundred miles an hour.

Then it stops beating when I realize what I just ran through.

"Did he force her to marry him somehow?" I'm about to lift Tony off the ground by the lapels of his dress jacket if he doesn't start talking.

"No, he let something far worse happen to her." He begins talking and doesn't stop until the entire sordid story is out in the open. "He was in league with a handful of Saudi oil investors in a bid to take over the oil company. Most of the Saudi men are very traditional—and very resistant to change. They didn't want their state-owned company on the New York Stock Exchange. They didn't want foreigners to have any piece of it, but they were willing to do business with Raf under the pretense they'd get it all back. Only Raf never told his business partners that he bought the oil shares under Tawnee's name. He did that to protect himself because he knew the Saudis would be enraged if they found out he planned to keep his shares. He's still an outsider, you know. His business partners could have snuffed him out at any moment.

"Raf thought he had more time to convince her to marry him before things got out of control. He could put the company in both their names without her ever knowing. By then, it wouldn't matter if they got to her —he'd be in control of it all without having lost anything. Later, he could dump the shares at more than twice the price, knowing the Saudi people would buy them up to regain control. Or he could decide to keep them long-term."

"Okay. What went wrong? Whose wedding was today? Where is she now?"

"What went wrong? Everything. He overestimated his charm and underestimated Tawnee's love for you." That "you" was a little forced and a little bitter. "Tabitha pretended to be Tawnee today—fake identification included—and married Raf. When his Saudi business associates heard Tabitha say Tawnee's full name, they immediately realized who she was... and that they didn't need Raf anymore. Raf never dreamed they'd double cross him, but then he never seemed to consider all the angles of his cockamamie plans. That's why he's had so many advisers over the years—he didn't build this empire alone like he tells everyone."

"You advised him, didn't you? That's why he kept you so close to him."

"Yes, I did. But he wouldn't listen to me on this one. I told him those men couldn't be trusted. I told him that Tawnee wasn't here for his money or his status, that she wasn't that type of person. He believed everyone wanted him for his wealth and nothing else, though, so he quit caring about others at all. He hid it well, but I knew better. Tawnee and I butted heads more than a few times over the years when Raf was being an ass and putting her in more risk than necessary. I couldn't tell her that, though."

"Why are you telling me this now? And where is she, Tony?"

"His four Saudi business partners took her before the wedding was over. They didn't even wait until Raf and Tabitha made it down the aisle as man and wife. One of them punched Tawnee, knocked her out, and threw her in the back of a car. I tried to stop them, but I was too late. Raf was furious when he found out because he sank a lot of money into those shares and they just cut him out of it altogether. He doesn't care about her, though.

"I'm telling you all this for three reasons. First, I just quit my job because Raf refused to go after them and save her. Second, you've got to save her because she's about to die. They would have taken her outside of Dubai to a private airstrip to board a jet bound for Riyadh. That's where they were every time Raf had a video conference call with them. And third, because I love her. I've been in love with her for a long time, but I know she never felt that way about me. I was willing to step aside and let her marry Raf if that's what she wanted—at least he could provide for her in a way I never could. But now, I'm done with him, I can't help her, and I'm hoping you can."

"What were their names, Tony? Who are his associates? I need names to find out where they'd be and where she'd be held."

"Here are their names." Tony hands me a folded piece of paper from his pocket. "And I can tell you where they'll hold her —where they hold all the women they to torture and get away with whatever they want. Dar Al Reaya, the female torture chambers in Saudi Arabia where they send all the victims to pay for the crimes they didn't commit."

Ice-cold blood runs through my veins at the mention of that name. I've heard of those places. I know what they do to women in them. My Tawnee is a prisoner in one of those godforsaken locations, where the guards get their rocks off by torturing, raping, and mentally abusing women who have no one to care about them. Sometimes they sell the women in an arranged marriage, where they face the same horrors, only in some man's house instead of a typical prison cell.

"So, they'll torture her, break her down, and make

her transfer her shares to them... then they'll kill her anyway."

"Exactly. Raf is a coward. He wouldn't even try to save her from their clutches. In his twisted mind, he blames her for making him lose all that money. I mean, her name is the one on the company, after all. Right?" His laugh is humorless and full of disgust.

"Where is Raf now?"

A helicopter takes off from the landing pad that hangs off the top edge of the building. Tony looks up at it and points. "On his way to his 'honeymoon with Tawnee.' He's getting out of town before any Saudis come back for him. They're going to Paris."

Without looking, I know Silas and Nick are behind me. They have been there the whole time, ready to give support when I need it. "One of you tell me you have pull in Saudi Arabia to get us across the border without visas."

"Sorry, man, but I don't. Had it been Russia, maybe I could have helped. The border crossings into Saudi Arabia are heavily guarded, and the airport customs and immigration area is just as strict. They don't want foreigners in their country."

"You know I don't have Saudi contacts. Sorry, Roman," Nick adds.

"I can help." A man steps out from behind the landscaping, seemingly out of nowhere, and I didn't even know he was there. I jerk my head to the side, and my eyes fly wide open.

I openly gape at him for a minute. Something about him is very familiar. "Oh my God. Shadow? Is that you? Where have you been?" I can't believe my eyes.

"We've been working, Roman." He motions to the man who steps up next to him.

"Reaper? What the hell is going on? What have you two been doing?"

"Holy shit. I didn't even recognize my own brother." Silas laughs and steps back to get a good look at both men.

"That's because he's wearing a dress, Silas. I bet you've never seen either of them in a dress before."

"Roman, they're not dresses. They're called thobes, and nearly every Saudi man wears one exactly like it. We had to blend in and appear to be one of them while doing recon."

"You two can speak and read Arabic?" My tone is notably skeptical.

"Yes, we can. We had to learn it for this mission. Imagine being caught while dressed up as a Saudi man and not being able to speak the language. Our paperwork is all set, and we're your sponsors to enter the country. They will hold Reaper and me responsible for your behavior while there, so don't make us look bad."

"I would never. I'm just going to kill anyone and everyone who gets in my way. But I'd never make you look bad while doing it."

"Do you have a way home, Tony?" Nick asks.

"Yes, don't worry about me. Just hurry and get Tawnee out of there before it's too late." He walks off with his shoulders hunched and a shuffle in his steps.

"What's the plan, Shadow?" I'm back to business. Tony is a big boy. He can find his way home.

"Tell me, how do you feel about wearing a dress?" The huge grin on his face not only confirms I'm fucked but also that Shadow will enjoy this particular screwing more than he should.

CHAPTER 22

Roman

"Y ou've got to be fucking with me right now." I look at my reflection in the mirror and still can't believe my eyes. "This will never work."

"It'll work because you'll be sitting in the back seat, keeping your mouth shut like the good little girl that you are." Shadow points his finger in my face as he issues his implied threat.

"Just so we're clear... your ass is the first one I'm kicking when we get back home."

"Is that any way to speak to your male guardian? No wonder I'm throwing my daughter in the detention center. She's disrespectful, disobedient, and just plain ugly." Shadow walks off laughing, leaving me to stare at my reflection again.

I'm in a head-to-toe black triangular tent. There's no other way to describe it. I have an opening for my eyes—one slit in the fabric—that's it. "They will never believe I'm a woman, Shadow. Look at me. I'm too tall and too broad to be a Saudi woman."

"It'll be fine. They won't pay much attention to you, anyway. Plus, we'll be in a Land Cruiser, not some tiny compact car. We'll put you all the way in the back, in the third-row seat."

"Whatever works, man. I don't care. Just get me to her."

We pile into the SUV, but we're so much farther behind the men who took Tawnee than we already were because every move we make takes planning, discussions, and contingencies. My impetuous nature still has a hard time dealing with all the waiting this job requires. It's not that I don't understand the reasons—it's knowing Tawnee needs me and I'm not there to protect her.

We're driving across the UAE to the border of Saudi Arabia, roughly 600 miles, because they will definitely question my status as a woman in an airport. But with the Saudi license plate and registration, we're simply returning home from a family visit to Dubai. Once we're inside the country, Shadow has a private plane waiting to take us the rest of the way to the capital. All we have to do is make it past the border guards first.

Piece of cake.

When I look like an enormous woman in a country where the average female height is barely over five feet tall.

I can't help where my thoughts stray on the six-hour journey to the border. Only six, thanks to the liberal speed limits throughout the UAE and Shadow's lead foot. We roll up to the covered booths, where groups of soldiers wait for the nod to descend on someone trying to gain illegal entry. My instincts tell me to account for every threat—the location, the type of threat, and estimate the likelihood of an attack. But I'm scrunched down in the back seat to make myself appear smaller. I purposely keep my gaze low to avoid eye contact with anyone outside the vehicle. And my demure little girl act is keeping us all alive.

The guard takes the documents from Shadow, and they have a brief conversation in Arabic. The reason I don't look at them now is that I'm afraid he'll speak to me and I have no way to reply. I'm at a complete disadvantage in this country on every front. But there's no part of me that wants to back out of this. My girl is in an even worse position, and I know she isn't giving up. She doesn't have it in her to surrender.

I release a huge sigh of relief when we're waved through the checkpoint without an extensive search. When we pick up speed again, I finally feel safe enough to speak.

"Can I take this ridiculous outfit off now?"

"Silence, woman. You're not allowed to speak until spoken to first. Learn your place."

"Shadow, you should know that I'm telling Elle every mean word you say to me. She will make you pay for it when we get home."

"That's cold, man."

The entire vehicle breaks out in laughter, releasing some of the stifling tension that's made it hard to breathe all day.

"Seriously, you can't take it off yet. They're known to have random roadblocks just to harass people, make sure they have all their paperwork in order, and that they're following all the religious laws. We can't let them see your face."

"Good point. I'll keep it on. But you should know this thing is really uncomfortable and I'm developing claustrophobia under here."

"I get it. You hate wearing a niqab and an abaya. But a lot of women in this region like them. It's usually by personal preference, but in this case, your father has deemed you unworthy of staying with the family. So you have to wear it to cover your disloyal face."

"The entire world needs therapy, man. You. Me. Them. Everyone."

After another two hours on the road, we finally reach the private jet that will carry us the rest of the way.

When we land outside of Riyadh, I calculate they had a ten-hour head start on us, and we're still not caught up. The men we meet on the hard-packed sand landing strip are obviously also CIA, putting their lives and their covers on the line to help a fellow brother-in-arms.

"Are you sure you want to go through with this?" One man approaches me, wearing the traditional thobe and headdress.

"Without a doubt. Holy shit. You're Jason, aren't you? You worked with Tawnee."

"Yeah, that's me. John and I were on assignment to follow Rafael Cruz." He nods toward the other man helping us. "We had to pull back when everything got crazy with the whole fake wedding bullshit. We have tabs on where he'll be, though, so we're helping get Tawnee back first."

"We appreciate the help. Why didn't you tell us we were on the same team when we first met? You must have known Silas and I were CIA."

"Sure, we did. Silas's reputation precedes him. But then so does Shadow's, and we were under orders not to give anything away. We knew we couldn't trust the others, so we just kept playing along until we couldn't anymore."

"We're glad to have you on our team. What do you have for us?" Nick asks.

"I don't know where you'll stick this to keep them

from finding it, but I'll leave it up to you to find a spot." He hands me a small military-grade stun gun.

"Well, if they grab my crotch on the way in, they'll get two handfuls of a big cocky surprise anyway, so I think I'll add this to the package." I lift my dress and stuff the stun gun into my briefs.

The guys chuckle, but they know the seriousness of what we're about to do… and the slim-to-none odds of pulling it off successfully.

"We'll be right here with our finger on the engines, ready to roll when we see you coming. Try not to bring too much company back with you. I really don't want to test my pilot skills against the Royal Saudi Air Force fighter jets." John shakes my hand—equally in a symbol of wishing me good luck and in saying goodbye to me for good.

"Roman and I are going to the detention center now. The rest of you should stay here—nearby. I don't know how long it'll take us to get in and out, but it doesn't make sense to put everyone's lives on the line. If you don't hear from us by morning, get out of the country and get yourselves to safety." Shadow makes it a point to look at each man individually when speaks, driving his point home.

"You're my brother. I'm going in beside you." Noah steps up next to him. "My nickname is Reaper for a reason."

"Noah is my brother—literally—and I'm going in

beside him. Roman is my junior officer. I'm going in beside him." Silas steps beside me.

"None of you are going anywhere without me. We're in this together." Nick puts his hands on his hips and stares us down.

Shadow drops his head and stares at the ground. "Noah, your wife will murder me if I go home without you. And Silas, your wife is a trained agent. She'll kill me in my sleep if I go home without you. Nick, your wife and her nanny will have my head and my balls on a pike."

"You don't think Elle would do the same to us if we let you go in there alone?" Silas counters.

"Look, I'm the one going in as a woman. I think you all should stay outside. You can get ready to give us a hand when we get out, and they're hot on our asses. That way, we have the element of surprise on our side inside and outside of the facility."

"I don't like it." Silas shakes his head.

"How many fathers tour the facility when they send their wayward daughters off to a torture center? None. They kick them to the curb and drive off on their merry way. If I have four male guardians escort me inside, they'll know right away something is up. We can't raise all those red flags."

"He's right, Silas. Let the kid have this one. We'll cover the outside and push them back long enough for Roman and Tawnee to make a break for it." Noah claps his brother on the shoulder. "You know this is the right plan."

"Shit. Okay, fine. Let's get this over with. Everyone ready to go?"

"I've been ready all fucking day. Let's go." I slide into the back seat, putting on the shamed demeanor of an unruly adult child.

Shadow drives us through the capital city until we reach the outskirts on the other side and the night grows darker. He drops the guys off about a block from the destination so they can get in place. The lack of consistent streetlights only amplifies the misery and gloom of the women's prison. I've heard horror stories about these places—the women who were arrested for having premarital sex because they were raped, the morality police threw them in prison for not meeting their religious standards, and some women were imprisoned for having a job without their husband's permission. Daily lashes. Torture by electric shocks. Prolonged solitary confinement.

He parks in front of the center to drop me off and talk to the guard. We had already decided he'd tell the guard my vocal cords were damaged, so I don't speak, rendering me worthless to him since he can't marry me off. He'll ask to see where I'll be kept, ensuring I don't have to answer any questions between the door and my cell, but then the rest will be on me.

Escape from my cell.

Find Tawnee.

Get us both out.

Alive. That one is important.

By morning.

No pressure.

Shadow bangs on the door, and a guard opens it almost immediately. They talk while I keep my head bowed, not daring to look at them while they discuss how terrible I am. Shadow grabs my arm, pushes me forward, and I follow in line behind the guard. While they speak in a language that makes no sense to me, I scan the area for exits, the total number of guards, and the proximity of the cells.

As we pass the inhabited cells, I search each one for Tawnee. My anger grows with every woman I see on the stroll toward my cell. Abused, neglected, and forgotten—every one of them. Rocking in the corner, talking to herself, crying or screaming, and every variation in between. Then I stop dead in my tracks when I see a woman passed out on the floor, swollen bruises and scratches across her face and neck, and wearing torn clothes.

After several steps, the guard notices I'm not right on their heels anymore and turns to yell at me. I don't care what he's saying. I don't care how mad he is. Nothing else matters.

Because that woman on the floor who has been beaten unconscious is Tawnee.

And culpable or not, this motherfucker is guilty as sin in my eyes.

He comes closer, getting in my face to scream at me, his spittle spraying on me while his horrible breath could knock me out on its own. Under normal circumstances. But nothing about this is normal. My rage has burned past the point of madness. Now, I'm emotionally numb. The cold and calculating side of me has emerged, and he only wants to witness the carnage.

Shadow searches my eyes and realizes something is horribly wrong. His gaze jumps to the cell beside me, and the ruthless assassin he's rumored to be comes to life.

The guard continues to spew his vitriol, and I've heard enough of it. With a quick jab to his nose, I knock him backward. He stumbles over Shadow's foot and falls to the ground. I move to stand over him, jerk the ridiculous garb I'm wearing off me, and punch him directly in the throat. His hands wrap around his own neck, then he sputters and coughs as he tries to breathe, and he flails on the ground when his oxygen reserves expire. I could easily end his suffering rather than letting him slowly suffocate to death, but I don't want to.

I grab the keys off his belt and unlock Tawnee's cell door. Men's voices carry down the hall, growing closer to where we are. The other guards on duty tonight, no doubt. The man who's barely moving on the floor probably drew the short straw and had to work through his break time.

"Shadow, you should get out of here before the rest get in here. We don't know what kind of weapons they have access to in here." I whisper to him as I kneel beside Tawnee and remove the stun gun from my briefs.

"You're full of shit, Roman. I'm not leaving you alone now. We still have the element of surprise, and we have more backup outside. Let's get her out of this cell. She needs to be close to the front door when the fighting starts."

After we lift her off the floor, we each wrap an arm around her waist and pull her arms around our necks. With her supported between us, we sprint toward the front door to get her to safety. The chattering voices enter the room and turn to angry shouts. Sirens blare throughout the facility, doors fling open and more men run out, and the automatic door locks slide into place.

A dozen men descend on us, but I don't feel panicked at all. There's no fucking way they're taking her back into that cell. They'll have to go through me to reach her, and there's no fucking way that will happen. Shadow releases her into my arms and prepares to fight off the first wave. I gently set her down in the corner behind me, then take my place beside Shadow.

The guards brandish a variety of weapons. Some carry a flogger, others have a cattle prod, and a few have whips. But we're ready for them. We're trained Special Forces operatives and CIA officers. The more weapons they bring my way, the more I'll have to use against them. The first man moves in too close, and I hit him with the stun gun. He screams loudly from the electric shock, and I wonder if he realizes he's only receiving a small taste of his own medicine. When he goes down, I take the flogger from his hand and give it to Shadow.

Several more rush us at once, and though we don't escape entirely unscathed, they definitely hobble away worse for wear. Shadow now holds out two charged cattle prods, fending off the brave but stupid men who try to advance on us, while I try the different keys on the front door. When I find the correct one, I cradle Tawnee against my chest while I run outside, and Shadow covers my back. Reaper, Nick, and Silas meet us at the curb and jump into the fracas to lend a hand. A crowd gathers in the streets, lights in the surrounding apartments blink on, and angry voices increase in volume and numbers.

"Get in. Get the fuck in, and let's get out of here before the whole neighborhood descends on us." Silas slides behind the wheel and peels away from the building before we've even closed the car doors.

No matter. We disappear into the night, park the

car in a crowded parking lot, and quickly jump into another one. When they eventually find the original vehicle, we'll be long gone—flying far away from here.

"Tawnee, sweets, can you hear me?" She hasn't opened her eyes yet. I don't know if she needs a hospital or a good night's sleep. I don't know if they've drugged her or if she has brain damage and internal injuries.

Nervous glances come from everyone in the vehicle, but no one says anything. We can't get her medical help in this country. Our only choice is to see our original plan through until we're in a country where she's safe. We can't stop in Dubai because the religious police have been known to snatch Saudis off the streets there and take them back home to face their punishment.

"Can we get her to Paris tonight? Or Frankfurt?" My voice sounds hollow, but I'm grasping at straws here.

"They're both about the same flight time away. We're looking at a six-hour flight to reach either city." Shadow scrubs his hand over his face. "Let's get back to Jason and John, put her on the plane, and we can do a field assessment on her. Then we'll talk about next steps."

Next steps?

I don't have any next steps without her. I took a hard-line approach when I vowed to get her back, and nothing can make me back down from my promise. Under the passing illumination of the streetlights, I examine her wounds, her skin color, and make sure she's breathing regularly.

"You have to wake up, sweets. There's something I never took the time to tell you, and I need to say it now more than ever. But I'm not saying it until I know you can hear every word." I place a soft kiss on her forehead and say a prayer, asking God to give her back to me.

Jason and John wait inside the plane with the engines fired up, knowing we're coming in hot. When we board with her, John assures us he can take off alone so Jason can tend to her wounds.

"Scoot back just a little, Roman. I was a medic in the Army and a paramedic on the truck when I got out of the service. I promise I'll take good care of her."

I move to the floor and let them stretch her out on the long bench seat. I feel the thrust of the jet engines when we start down the runway. The plane lifts off the ground, but John keeps us low, avoiding radar for as long as possible. Jason continues his assessment of her, checking her pupils, her breathing, and her heart sounds. Her pulse is a bit slow, but that's not unusual for her condition.

"She doesn't have any obvious signs of internal bleeding—either in her torso or her brain. My guess is they gave her a dose of pain medication, or something similar, to knock her out after they tortured her. Her wounds are still very fresh. My advice is to let her sleep for a couple more hours then we'll decide if we should land somewhere for medical attention." Jason sits back on his heels and looks at me, waiting for a final decision.

"Okay, that's our plan, then. Keep monitoring her and reassess after a couple of hours. I'll stay right here beside her and watch for any change in her condition."

After the longest ninety minutes of my life, John announces we have cleared Saudi airspace and are on route to Paris unless we tell him differently.

"Tawnee, sweets, can you hear me? Hey, Tawnee, can you wake up for me now?" I kiss the back of her hand and stroke her hair, being careful not to touch any of the bruised or scratched places.

Feeling helpless, I look at Silas and wait for advice.

CHAPTER 23

Tawnee

I hear Roman's voice, calling my name, but I can't open my eyes to see him. He sounds so far away, and my eyelids feel so heavy, as if they're nailed shut.

Every inch of my body hurts. Snippets of memories flash in my mind, like a movie reel that tries to play but keeps getting stuck. I try to focus on what I remember, but a dense fog has settled on my brain and I can't think straight.

Then it all comes rushing back at me at once.

The men who took me.

The prison guards who tortured me.

The woman in the infirmary who gave me an

injection of something, though she wouldn't tell me what it was. She wasn't pleased that they'd been so rough with me on my first day. Apparently, they prefer to dish out the torture in metered doses so they can remind the wayward girls on a daily basis. She mumbled to me, in English, about how I wouldn't be able to take my punishment tomorrow because they'd had too much fun with me today.

Lovely lady, that nurse.

"Tawnee, sweets, you have got to open your eyes now so I know you're okay, or we'll be forced to land wherever we are right now and take you to the hospital. It's now or never—this is your last warning." Roman sounds so distraught.

I fight against my welded-shut eyelids and finally manage to pry one open. The ecstatic expression on his face from my opening one eye makes me wonder if I look as banged up as I feel. He gently wraps his hand around mine, not squeezing but sharing his strength with me just the same.

"Thank you, God." He kisses the back of my hand over and over. "Tawnee, can you speak? Do you want to go to the hospital right now?"

"No." My voice is hoarse and barely audible, but I force it enough for him to hear me. "I'll be okay."

"Do you know if they gave you any medications?" That's Jason's voice. I manage to open the other eyelid and focus on his face.

"Yes. An injection to make me sleep."

"Okay, I'm putting the portable oxygen on you just to be on the safe side. We'll take turns staying up to watch you until we reach Paris. John's flying the plane, and he's an excellent pilot. Between all of us, we've got you covered." Jason smiles, and I realize I'm happy to see him. Those two didn't turn to the dark side after all.

"No need to take turns. I won't be able to sleep until I know she's all right. You guys should rest while you can, though. I'm not leaving her side." Roman leans in and softly kisses me on the lips. Even though it's only been about twenty-four hours since I last saw him, it feels like an eternity that we've been apart.

"Never again," I whisper.

"Never." He shakes his head. "You're stuck with me forever, sweets. There's no getting rid of me now."

My eyes are too heavy to keep open, so I let them close on their own. Sleep overtakes me again, but this time, it feels different. A warm hand holds mine close to his heart, and I feel him at my side throughout the entire flight. He checks on me, he makes sure my oxygen mask is on correctly, and he whispers sweet nothings to me. Wrapped in the warmth of his love, I'm able to relax and let the dreams flow. Dreams of him and me. Dreams of our future. Dreams of our love. The best dreams I've ever had.

But not better than the real thing.

When the medicine starts wearing off and the grogginess fades, I open my eyes and find Roman still sitting guard over me. He's sitting on the floor and must be uncomfortable after all this time. After I slip the oxygen mask off my face, I move against the back of the bench as much as I can then pat the empty space.

"I don't want to hurt you." He looks up and down my body. I don't bother to look at the scratches and gashes and bruises. I can feel them without needing to see them.

"You won't hurt me."

He turns off the oxygen canister then gingerly moves to join me, facing me as he lies down. "I thought I'd lost you for a while there. You wouldn't wake up, even when I carried you in my arms."

"That was only because of the medicine she gave me. I'll be all right after a little R&R."

"I'm sorry I didn't reach you in time to stop them. I'll never forgive myself for that." He closes his eyes then squeezes them, fighting back the emotions inside.

"None of this was your fault. Not one single thing that happened. Don't you dare try to take the blame for it. This is all on Rafael, and he's the one who will pay for it. Not you." I run my fingers through his hair then along the scruff of his beard.

"Tawnee, there's something I have to tell you, and I

should have told you a long time ago. I shouldn't have kept this from you."

"What is it?"

"I love you. I've always loved you, and only you. I will only ever love you. You are my soul mate…the other half of my soul."

"I love you, too, Roman. You're the only man I've ever loved, and I still love you after all this time."

His kiss holds more urgency this time. It's not as soft. He's not as afraid of hurting me. It's perfect.

"You're right about one thing. Rafael will absolutely pay for this. He won't get away with it."

"Neither will Tabitha or Carter. They were both in on it too. I will hunt them to the ends of the earth if I have to."

He lifts his hand to my face and skims his fingers from my forehead, along my cheek, and down to my chin. His eyes search mine before lingering on every wound, no matter how large or small. There's a question in his expression, but he's afraid to ask it.

"What do you want to know, Roman? You can ask me. I won't break, I promise I'm not that fragile." I smile as widely as I can without wincing to convince him.

"Your clothes were torn when I found you…"

"No, they didn't rape me. Not that they were above it, but they didn't. One of the guards grabbed at me. I stepped backward, trying to get out of range, but he snagged my clothes instead. The fabric ripped from the force."

"What did they do to you?"

"Electric shocks, slaps, punches, kicks—they stopped short of lashes. The woman who gave me the injection suggested that would come soon, though. They wanted the SAOR shares. Seems Raf did set me up, huh?"

"He certainly did. But they wouldn't believe that you couldn't give them what you don't have, right?"

"They didn't believe me at first, but I think they began to after the abuse went on so long and my story didn't change."

"Interesting. Were the men who took you also guards at that place?"

"No, I don't think so. The guards treated those four men with much more respect than anyone else in there. I wish I had their names to give you."

"I have their names." That shocks me speechless. I raise my eyebrows, waiting for him to continue. "We arrived at the hotel right after the fake marriage ceremony. Tony stopped me and filled me in on everything. He gave me the names of all four Arab men and said he quit his job because of what Rafael did to you."

"Tony quit his job because of me?" I must not be hearing him correctly.

"Yeah. Seems Tony has been in love with you for quite a while, but he knew you didn't feel the same. He still tried to look out for you, though, and sway Raf's decisions when he could."

"Knock me over with a feather... I never would have thought any of that."

Roman shrugs one shoulder. "This may come as a total shock to you, but sometimes men have no clue how to express their true feelings. So, they resort to doing stupid shit instead."

I start to giggle at him. Then he chuckles along with me, and before I know it, we're both trapped in a fit of laughter. "Stop making me laugh—it hurts." I hold my side, but to be honest, I don't want to stop. This carefree moment feels too good, despite my sore body, to let it go just yet.

"You can't blame this on me. All I did was tell the truth. Is it my fault that sometimes we men can be functional idiots? If I had any kind of power, I wouldn't get into half the trouble I do. So, if anything, this is mostly your fault."

"Your deductive reasoning prowess blows my mind. Care to explain how this is my fault?"

"If you weren't so smart, you wouldn't recognize my stupidity. Then it wouldn't be such an inconvenience to you. Have you tried being less intelligent? I think it could really help you just be happy all the time."

"Yes, you're exactly right, Roman. I mean, everyone says ignorance is bliss for a reason, right? I could live in complete bliss if only I were just a smidge stupider, right? That's your story, and you're sticking to it?"

He looks down and pulls his lips between his teeth to keep from smiling. When he regains his composure and lifts his eyes to mine, the love shining in them makes my heart skip a beat. "You know I wouldn't change one single thing about you, sweets. I fell in love with a strong, independent, intelligent woman, and I'm more in love with her today than I've ever been."

Tears of pure happiness spill over onto my cheeks. "You can't say things like that to me in my current state, Roman. All that strength, independence, and intelligence melts away, and all that's left is a blubbering, emotional woman."

His smile is warm and understanding. "I love that woman just as much. We'll balance each other, Tawnee. You don't have to be 'on' all the time. If you'll trust me to be your rock, I promise I'll never let you down again."

"I trust you with my life, Roman."

Shadow walks over and kneels on the floor beside us. "Hey, Tawnee. How are you feeling now? Should we divert to Rome, or do you want to wait until we get to Paris? It's no trouble—we can protect you either way."

"I'm okay, Shadow. I'll just rest until we get to Paris. I can't thank you enough for coming to get me out of there."

"My pleasure, darlin'. I'm just sorry it took us so long to reach you."

"There was a woman in the cell next to mine. Her name was Lara. Did either of you see her when you passed by?"

"No, sweets, there was no one in there when we walked by. I was counting cells and bodies until I found you," Roman replies.

"I think they killed her for talking to me, and it's my fault. I initiated the conversation, and I encouraged her to go along with me. We were planning to escape together as soon as possible."

"That isn't your fault, Tawnee. She obviously wanted out if she was so willing to put her life in the hands of an American stranger. The risks were worth it to her, because either way, she's free now. If all those women weren't being held prisoner in there, I'd call in a drone strike and raze that place to rubble." Shadow's hand curls into a tight fist, anger roiling through him over the inability to stop their cruel practices. "I'm glad you're already feeling better, though. We were worried about you. I'll leave you two alone to rest now."

Snuggled against Roman's warm body, I close my eyes and fall back asleep. When we start our approach for landing at our destination a few hours later, my entire body still feels like one big sore muscle. But the medication has largely worn off, so I'm much more alert and ready to face the next part of this journey. Though no one has shared any information with me, I know we're stopping over in Paris for much more than refueling the private jet for the next leg of our trip.

"Does anyone have my passport?" I ask tentatively.

"Now that you mention it, this one in my bag may be yours." Noah winks and hands over my passport.

"How did you get this?"

"We had a gut feeling Rafael would betray you. If that happened, I wanted to make sure we protected your identification, so I took it for safekeeping before you left the beachfront house."

"I'm surprised I didn't even notice. I was so focused on what I had to do that I didn't even check for it."

"That happens to all of us at some point in our careers. Don't sweat it. That's why we have each other's backs."

"Who wants to tell me what we're really doing in Paris, then? This is where Raf and Tabitha are on their fake honeymoon, isn't it?"

"I'll tell you exactly what I'm going to do here, sweets. I will find out where Raf is staying and get word to his Saudi partners. When they show up, I will kill every single one of them in a very unpleasant way. Then we can finish our trip home."

Roman isn't joking in the least. Though his expression is passive and his tone is neutral, he's deadly serious.

"And the other two?"

"If they're with him, they will die with him."

"No qualms? No second thoughts?"

"None. They conspired to kill you, Tawnee. They were active participants in sending you to the executioners—or worse, life imprisonment in a place where women wish for death long before it finds them. They had no qualms, no second thoughts, and no remorse. When I get ahold of them, I won't have any either. Maybe God will have mercy on them because I sure as hell won't."

"You're exactly right, Roman. I'll help you... in Lara's memory."

When the plane touches down, the guys exit first to give me some privacy to change clothes. Roman stays to help me, though I tried to convince him otherwise. I know what his reaction to seeing the still-fresh wounds will be, and I want his head clear when we go after Rafael. But I should have known he wouldn't leave me to struggle alone.

When every stitch of clothing is removed, he circles me and takes note of every abrasion I have. Every location. Every imprint of a hand, fist, or boot. He commits all my wounds to his memory. Then he turns, picks up the pile of clothes one by one, and takes his time to help me into them.

"I promise, he will feel everything you felt and more." He finishes with an extended kiss to my forehead.

CHAPTER 24

Roman

"I can tell you where Raf is staying. He always stays at the same hotel in Paris. He wouldn't give up his favorite place just to avoid me." Tawnee and I descend the steps of the jet and walk across the tarmac at the private airstrip.

"Good. Will it be hard to get to him at this hotel?"

"No, not like at the last hotel. It's still a high-end resort, but much more accessible to the public. We can even get a room there, and he'll never know. He'll be in the penthouse suite on the seventh floor, where he'll have meals on his private terrace overlooking the Eiffel Tower. He'll think he's safe and secure in his upper-class suite."

"That's okay, sweets. Let him be smug right up until the end. I have special plans for him."

Inside the terminal, we move through immigration without a hitch. The private airport is small but busy. Most of the visitors passing through here are CEOs of major corporations, royalty, or other officials in high places, so the immigration personnel are proficient at their jobs. Tawnee receives more than a few raised eyebrows because of her injuries, but she assures everyone that she's just grateful she walked away from the car wreck with the terrible drivers in Dubai. Their empathetic nods end any further questioning.

"Two rental cars are waiting for us. Where are we headed?" Jason asks.

"The most luxurious hotel in Paris," Tawnee replies.

"I'm making our reservations there now. There will be several unhappy guests when they arrive and learn their rooms have been given away, but our cause is more important than theirs." Shadow clicks away on his special CIA phone, hacking through firewalls and employee log-ins to gain access to their reservation system. "Done. Roman and Tawnee, I put you two in the royal suite just below his. Let me know if you need any help getting into his make-believe fortress."

"Thanks, Shadow, but we've got it. He's not going anywhere except to the morgue. I promise you that."

"You already have a plan in mind?" Shadow asks.

"Yes, I do. An especially cruel one that I'm looking forward to carrying out."

"How can we help?" One side of Shadow's mouth lifts in amusement. He wants in on the action.

"Have you ever been a waiter?"

"Are you kidding? There's not much I haven't been while undercover."

"Perfect. I'll be waiting inside his suite when you bring up his special delivery. You're welcome to stay for the show."

"Let's finish this. I love cosplay."

Shadow leads the way to the rental cars. We divide up in the two vehicles and drive toward the hotel. On the way, I turn to Silas for the other part of my plan.

"We need some partially fake news to go viral and draw out our Saudi friends. They need to pay Raf a visit here in Paris so we can end the threat to Tawnee and my dad at the same time."

"Partially?"

"Yes. The pictures we release need to show Raf and the real Tawnee in their wedding photos. Then reveal she's the woman who bought the shares, but Raf is taking over as CEO, effective immediately. His first act in his new position will be to dump the stocks and try to bankrupt the oil company. They won't allow that to happen—it's a matter of national pride. They'd buy the shares back no matter who was selling them, but putting Raf's name and location out there will bring our friends out to play. They won't let him take all the money and run."

"Devious. I love it. It'll spread like wildfire within an hour after I post it, I'll make sure of it." Silas retrieves his computer and begins doctoring the photos and writing a thorough press release, including the exact address where the newlywed couple is honeymooning.

"I figure we have about eight or nine hours before the goon squad lands. Sweets, where can I take you after we check in?"

"Straight to our royal suite." She smiles up at me. The bruises on her face and neck do nothing to detract from her beauty.

"I see your sassiness is making a full recovery already." I quirk up one eyebrow at her, but she knows I love that answer more than anything else she could say.

"I'm guessing it has a huge bathtub that would be perfect for at least two people to soak their aching muscles in until their skin shrivels up like prunes. Then there's room service, with chocolate-covered strawberries and champagne as an appetizer. Maybe a nice juicy steak and lobster tail for the main course. Thick, plush robes and fuzzy slippers to laze around in. Then we can get dressed, scale the wall outside the hotel, and kill a few people before bedtime."

"You are the perfect woman and traveling companion. Has anyone ever told you that?"

Chuckles fill the car, and I'm struck by how fortunate I am to be surrounded by the best friends a man could ask for. I only wish Blake were here to lend a hand, but I'm thankful he's standing guard over my dad right now. He's not exactly in the clear yet. Even eliminating the four we know of doesn't guarantee others won't come for him later, but he'll never be without the protection of the best people in the world.

"There are probably a few places I need to go first. The Saudi men took all my clothes with them, so I have nothing else to change into. I don't even know whose clothes I'm wearing right now." Tawnee's gaze drifts to the window, not exactly focusing on anything as the memory plays in her mind.

"The last people to use the plane left them behind. Sorry if the fit is a little big on you," Jason says from the front.

"They're fine—I'm glad they're not tight. That would be uncomfortable with all these bruises. Thank you for finding them for me, Jason."

"My pleasure, Tawnee. You know, John and I both wanted to tell you a long time ago that we're CIA, but we had orders. I hope there're no hard feelings about that. If it makes you feel any better, we've always had your back, though."

Tawnee's jaw drops open, and she looks up at me. "Did you know that?"

"Only recently—as in the last few hours. Everything is running together. I may have forgotten to tell you that part with the whole thinking you were about to die in my arms thing."

"All right. I forgive you."

"Thank you."

"You're welcome. Just don't let it happen again."

"Yes, ma'am."

"I have to tell you both—I really like this version of Roman. Pliable. Easy-going. Takes orders well. Blake will never believe our boy has changed so much." Silas turns in the front seat to look at me as he speaks. I reply by pretending to scratch my eye with my middle finger. "I can see you, Roman. Don't make me tell Tawnee on you."

I wrap my arm around her shoulders and pull her close to me, planting a kiss on her temple. "Tell her whatever you want about me. Just be sure to include telling her how much I love her."

"We're in the most romantic city in the world, and the only one who has his woman with him is Roman, of all people. How the fuck did this happen?" Silas asks and shakes his head.

"Silas, do you have all the details of my secret company?" Tawnee's question intrigues me.

"Yes, ma'am. Our analysts found every last detail

about it after Roman suggested we search by your name."

"It's in my name alone? No one else's?"

"Just yours." Silas turns around again. His eyes narrow, and a wily grin begins to form.

"And the shares? They're all mine?"

"That's right. Let me guess... you want to dump them for real?"

"Yes, that's exactly what I want to do. Can I?"

Silas checks his watch and mentally calculates the time difference. "Wow. We're working through a lot of time zones. We left Riyadh around midnight their time. Flew six hours to Paris. Now we're an hour behind Riyadh and six hours behind New York. So, when the stock exchange opens in nine hours, you will absolutely be able to sell them."

"Do you have the log-in and password for the account they're in?"

"I can't believe you'd even ask me a question like that, Tawnee. That hurts me. What kind of officer do you take me for?"

"That means yes, he has it and has been closely monitoring it. In fact, he's probably already transferred them to a new account that Raf doesn't know about." If I know anything about Silas, it's that he's always two steps ahead of the enemy.

"Finally. Some respect for the senior officer." Silas smiles and turns to face the front. "When you're ready for them, Tawnee, they're all yours. Since you got them legally, there's nothing we, the government, can do about your investments. Enjoy the fruits of your labor." He jots down the account information and hands it to her.

"I never dreamed I'd have a sugar momma. This is so exciting." The moment the words leave my mouth, Tawnee playfully jabs me in the ribs.

"I'd be a dead sugar momma without you. Our prenup will say I get to kill you if you ever leave me."

"Show me the dotted line. I'll agree to those terms and sign it right now. I've already experienced how dark my life is without you, and that's not a place I want to return to ever again."

She nestles closer to me, lying her head in the crook of my shoulder and wrapping her arm around my waist. "I wish you could feel how happy you make me, Roman. Silas, when my shares are sold and they settle the accounts, what do you think about bringing the whole family here for an extended vacation?"

"I think that's the best idea ever. You won't hear any objections from anyone."

"Good. We could use some fun, family time after all this is over."

It'll all be behind you in a few hours, sweets. One by one, I'll cross the names of those who betrayed you off my list. Then we'll focus only on everything good in our lives and celebrate our reunion in the best way possible.

"THAT'S IT? ALL I HAVE TO DO IS SET THE PRICE I'M selling them at and wait for someone to accept it?" Tawnee checks the information on the screen for the fifth time before executing her trade.

"That's it. Just make sure the price per share is the minimum you want because that's all you'll get." Silas has been so patient with her. She still thinks of this as stealing no matter how many times he's explained she's the legal owner of all the shares. She can't steal from herself.

When she submits the order, she sits back and stares at the screen. "Now, we wait?"

"Yeah, but I promise we won't have to wait very long." Silas chuckles to himself, knowing the news he submitted online earlier has already created such a buzz in Saudi Arabia, we can hear the hum all the way from Paris.

We checked in to our procured, not stolen, room and went on a shopping excursion the minute the stores opened. She was so excited to buy new clothes and shoes in Paris. She rolled her eyes at me so many times in the hours she dragged me from one store to the next that I warned her they'd get stuck in that position. She thinks I'm hopeless because I don't get what the big deal is about the clothes here. We can buy clothes anywhere.

It's obviously a chick thing.

She retorted it's a chic thing.

Then she laughed when I asked what the difference was.

Whatever. She's happy. I'm happy. She has new clothes that I can take off her later. We all win.

"When will I know if they sold?" She refreshes the screen. Again.

"As soon as people start snatching them up. At the end of the day, all the day's trades will be called, and most of the money will be transferred to your account right away, but they have three days to pay up. You'll have access to the full amount after the end of those three business days." Silas has explained that a few times already.

"Okay, it's done. I'll check back later and see how much has moved. Why don't we order some room service? I'm hungry, and we need to finish making our plans for Rafael."

Silas glances up at me, and I nod.

"Tawnee, we have orders to neutralize this threat for national security reasons. But I can't approve for you to go with us. Please trust me. Jason and John will stay here to protect you while Roman, Nick, Noah, Shadow, and I handle the rest. If you get involved, I won't be able to protect you from French or US laws." Silas carefully explains the precarious situation we're in, and I can only hope she understands.

She glances up at me, the anguish and distress immediately clear in her expression. "He did this to *me*, Silas. Not to you or anyone else. But you're telling me I don't have the right to defend myself?"

"What we're doing isn't self-defense, sweets. You know that. It's the preservation of our way of life, which happens to coincide with fulfilling a deep need for vengeance in me. Please let me take care of this for you. Trust me to do that."

She taps her nails on the tabletop for a solid minute, considering her options against our request. "All right. I'll stay here. But if anyone comes into my room, they're fair game to me, and you two will stay out of it."

"Deal," Silas and I reply at the same time.

"Will you at least include me in the planning session so I'll know what's happening?"

"Yes, we will. You need to be prepared in case anything goes off plan. I don't want you getting caught unaware."

We order enough food and drinks for an army then call the rest of the guys up to our suite. While we eat, talk, and laugh, the time ticks away. Silas's phone pings with incoming information at the same time as Shadow's. The two team leaders have just been alerted to an incoming threat.

"The four camel-men of the Saudi apocalypse just landed in Paris, didn't they?" My question is rhetorical. I already know that's what their alert is about.

"Yeah, they're here, and they're searching hotel databases for Rafael's name to verify this is where he is. This hotel is full, so they'll be looking for their own room next. My guess is they'll only stay one night— long enough to do the job and get back home the staff finds his body." Silas pushes back from the dining table and stands. "It's time to put our plan into action. Roman, I'm going to change clothes and will meet you in the stairwell. Shadow, you have your uniform, right?"

"I do. I hope he's a big tipper. I hate serving ungrateful people." He walks out with a spring in his step, headed back to his room to change with the other guys on his heels.

I turn to Jason and John. "Don't let her out of your sight or out of this room until we come back. I don't care if every fire alarm in the building is going off—if I'm not at that door, do not open it."

"Got it. We'll keep her safe." John assures me as he steps up beside her. "Don't worry about us. Just focus on getting the job done upstairs."

After I change into my nondescript black clothes, I meet Silas, Shadow, Nick, and Reaper in the stairwell. Shadow carries a silver platter covered with a white linen napkin. The covered plate is compliments of the chef. Having heard Raf was in the building, the chef wants to welcome him personally.

"I'm going in. The terrace doors are wide open, just as Tawnee said they would be. After a quick climb up one floor, I'll be inside his room in no time. Give me ten minutes, Shadow, then deliver his gift."

"Ten minutes—mark. Get to climbing, Roman."

I rush back into my suite and straight to the balcony directly below his expansive terrace. I scale up the ornate concrete decoration and over the wrought-iron fence. From my vantage point, I see Rafael lounging on his couch while watching TV. I expected him to have it on the news or a business channel, but I realize he's so confident in his underhanded dealings, he's not the least bit worried anything will go wrong.

Kneeling behind the small round table with two chairs, I watch for any other movement inside the suite. If Tabitha and Carter are in there with him, I'll deal with them first. My guess is they're in a separate room. His insistence on having the three-bedroom royal suite to himself in Dubai tells me he doesn't share well with others. After eight minutes, I feel confident he's alone, and I move into place inside the suite. Right on time, Shadow knocks on the door and announces he's with room service with a perfect French accent.

When Raf opens the door, he barely acknowledges Shadow. "I didn't order anything, so you can take that off my bill immediately."

"This is compliments of the chef, sir. He heard you were staying with us this week and wanted to send your favorite rare delicacy to you, free of charge."

"Really? What is it?"

"Pufferfish, sir."

"Chef Olivier does know how to tempt me. Bring it in—I can never resist pufferfish."

Shadow walks in with the tray and waits for Rafael to give him instructions. "Where shall I put it, sir? Would you care to dine at the formal table?"

"No, just put it there by the couch. I'm watching this show, so I'll just enjoy my fish with the wine I've already opened."

"Very good, sir. With compliments from the chef, we hope you enjoy this small treat."

"I'm sure I will. Thank you." Raf pulls out a €100 bill, hands it to Shadow for his tip, then closes the door in his face before he can respond.

Raf sits on the couch and removes the silver dome cover, humming to himself when he sees the thinly sliced pieces of fish. He leans back on the couch, taking the plate with him, and mindlessly pops slice after slice into his mouth while watching TV. When he has scarfed down almost the entire fish, he sets the nearly empty plate on the coffee table and starts punching his lips and tongue with his fingertip.

I grab him around the neck from behind and force him down onto his back. When he opens his mouth to protest, I release several drops of the pufferfish's deadly toxin down the back of his throat.

"You've already eaten enough tetrodotoxin to kill thirty people, but those extra drops I gave you will ensure the job is done faster. The tingling you felt on your lips and tongue was the neurotoxin already going to work on your nervous system. With as much as you've consumed, you'll be paralyzed in the next few seconds. You'll lie here, fully aware of what's happening to your body, but unable to do a fucking thing about it.

"Before you die, I want you to know what else is happening right now. Tawnee is here—she's alive and well. We rescued her from that women's detention center you let your piece of shit friends throw her in. All those shares you were waiting to cash in are still in her name, and she just opened the order to sell them all. By the close of business today, she'll have more money than you ever dreamed of having. But there's more—she doesn't know this part yet. I'm waiting to give her the rest of the documents as a wedding gift.

"Look at this picture, Raf. It's one of the real Tawnee and you getting married. We also have a copy of your marriage license and a copy of your will. The will you changed eight months ago to leave everything you own to her. So, you can lie here, you fucking coward, and die in your own piss and shit as you lose control of your bodily functions. You think about how you had it all when you had her, and how you lost it all when you betrayed her and left her for dead in a Saudi prison."

When I release him, he remains rigid and still on the couch. But his eyes confirm his brain still functions at full capacity. He'll be dead within twenty minutes, but I'm not going anywhere until I see it with my own eyes. No fucking ghosts will come back to haunt my love.

His breaths become ragged and shallow as his diaphragm short-circuits from the poison coursing through his body, shutting down his organs. The light in his eyes is extinguished, and there's no way anyone can bring him back now.

One down.

When I step out into the hallway, Silas, Shadow, Nick, and Reaper have all four of Tawnee's kidnappers on the floor. "Bring them in here with Raf."

We lift their limp bodies and haul them into the suite and arrange them in the other chairs. After a few drops of toxin into each man's mouth, and the leftover contaminated fish on the plate, the cause of death for all five will be easily explained. Since pufferfish isn't on the hotel menu, it will clear the chef of any wrongdoing, and they'll assume he brought the delicacy in from somewhere else. It won't be traced back to anyone in this city; we've already made sure of that.

The five of us walk back down to my suite with a weight lifted off our shoulders and smiles on our faces. We can go home soon—or we can bring the family to us for a while first—because the menaces to society have been dealt with expediently. When I reach the door to our suite, my heart jumps up in my throat when I see it's not latched shut.

I gently push it open the rest of the way and peek inside. Tawnee has Tabitha subdued on the floor, while John holds Carter with his hands cuffed behind his back.

"What the hell happened here?" I know I specifically told them not to open the door unless it was me.

"These two idiots got the room numbers mixed up and tried to get into this suite. When Tawnee heard their voices, she bolted for the door before we could catch her. But we got them, anyway. INTERPOL is on the way to get them and help process the paperwork for the other mess—our director called theirs and explained the situation. Carter and Tabitha are going to spend a long time in prison," Jason explains.

"Is that what you want, Tawnee? For them to live their lives behind bars?" I want to make sure because we still have time to make them disappear.

"Yes, I decided death was too quick and easy for them after what I've been through. They'll spend the rest of their lives thinking about what they did to me, though. In separate prisons. In separate cells. Alone."

She made the right choice. But then, so did I. Rafael never would've gotten what he deserved, and those four kidnappers would've been national heroes when they returned home. Now, they'll all go home in pine boxes.

For all intents and purposes, this is over. For Tawnee and me, we're finished with their deception, betrayal, and greed. My focus is solely on her from now on—whatever it takes to make her happy.

That's my new hard line perspective... my only rigid stance going forward.

CHAPTER 25

Roman

"You want to tell me what really happened in here?" I turn to Tawnee when the last of our squad leaves the room.

The slightly guilty expression on her face gives her away. *You're totally busted, sweets.*

"Whatever do you mean?"

"I gave those men strict instructions before I left. That door should have been barred from the inside. They should have tied you to a comfortable chair with silk ropes and sat in your lap to keep you from opening it. So, do you feel the need to confess anything?" I put my hands on my hips and straighten my back, and using my intimidating glare, I wait for the truth.

"I confess... I regret nothing." She lifts on her

tiptoes to kiss me. Her lips are so soft, and I'm so grateful to feel them again.

"You're trying to distract me. I know your tactics." I manage to state my accusation between luscious kisses. "Not that I'm complaining... much. I'd just like to know the truth."

She pulls back and looks up at me from under her lashes. I know the very second when she accepts the inevitable.

"All right. Here's the full truth. You took off on your own to exact your revenge against Rafael when I'm the one who was wronged. I appreciate your doing it on my behalf, but it's not the same, Roman. There are some things I need to do and standing up for myself is one of them. But I agreed to your plan, even though you still haven't told me what you did to him, for the record—so I had to improvise.

"Jason and John follow the rules pretty well, so they had set up surveillance in the lobby to keep tabs on who was coming in and out. When John saw Tabitha and Carter coming back in, laughing and enjoying themselves, I may have snapped. Just a little. Not like a Roman-level snap, but enough. As Raf's head of security, I still have access to his messaging network, so I used Jason's phone to access it. Raf was never tech-savvy enough to handle it on his own. So, I messaged them as Raf and told them the hotel had to change their room, but their keycards would still work."

"They didn't know that's impossible? The front desk would have to re-key them to work with this lock."

She shrugs. "Tabitha and Carter never questioned Raf like the rest of us did. I guess they just thought he magically made it happen. Anyway, when they showed up at the door, Jason, John, and I were ready and waiting for them. Tabitha was easy to overpower since I cracked her ribs when she confessed to stabbing me in the back. John and Jason had no problem restraining Carter. And you know the rest."

"But you decided to let them live." I'm questioning if I'm worthy of her love. She shows mercy and forgiveness while I charge full steam ahead and let a man die a cruel death.

"I gave it a lot of thought, and I even wavered when I had her in my grasp. But something she said to me stayed with me. She planned to ride off into the sunset with Carter and the money Rafael promised them. Spending her life with him was her ultimate goal, regardless of who she hurt along the way. Then I realized how devastated I would be if you and I were separated for the rest of our lives. I realized how devastated I've been since the day we split up. Doing that to Tabitha and Carter would be worse than ending their lives, putting them out of their misery. Their hell is only starting... and they'll be in it for a long time to come. They don't deserve death."

"And Rafael? What do you think he deserved for his offenses?"

"He deserved to die. He planned this scheme for a long time. All the paperwork he had drawn up and forged. The trip to Dubai under false pretenses. The wreck that put us all in danger. He had someone attack your dad. He arranged my kidnapping, and he knew where they'd take me. Then that led to Lara's death. Even though I don't have proof that she's dead, I heard her screams after they caught us talking. If she's still alive, she's wishing for death. This is all on him.

"He hurt so many people simply to make more money that he didn't even need. He already had more than he could ever ask for—money, possessions, respect, admiration, and loyalty—but none of that mattered to him in the end. It's as if everything he did was a game to him to see how much he could get away with before someone stopped him."

"I'm glad you feel that way because his death wasn't an easy one. He suffered. He felt every second of it right up until the end. And I wouldn't change a single thing about it. I'm sorry you feel I took away your right to exact your own revenge. Maybe I did. But when I carried you out of that shithole, I thought you'd die before we could get out of the country. Maybe it was selfish of me to leave you out, but I couldn't take the chance of something going wrong and losing you for good. I can handle anything any man throws at me, but I'm not strong enough to lose you. So, when Silas pointed out we couldn't cover for you if things went sideways, I jumped at the loophole to keep you safe."

"Tell me how he died."

We sit on the couch, and I proceed to tell her every step I took, every word I said, and every reaction Rafael had to the toxin up until the moment he took his last breath. She listens intently but silently, taking everything in. I can't help but wonder what she thinks about me now. Will this change her feelings for me? Will she feel unsafe around me and walk away?

"What are you thinking, Tawnee?"

She purses her lips and slowly nods her head, considering how to frame her response. "I'm impressed. That was a great idea—very imaginative. I especially like how it can't be traced back to anyone so there's no fall guy in this scenario. Thank you for taking care of everything and seeing it through until the end. And thank you for taking care of me. I understand your reasons. All I ask is you include me in the discussions in the future instead of deciding for me. And I promise not to be so independent that I don't listen to your concerns. Deal?"

"Deal. Let's shake on it." I extend my hand, and she tentatively accepts it after a moment's hesitation.

Then I drop one knee on the floor in front of her.

"Tawnee, will you marry me? Will you promise to stand beside me regardless of how stupid I act? Will you be the woman who snaps me back in line and keeps me from self-destructing? Will you sleep beside me every night, donating your body to the Roman Scientific Study Foundation from this day until death parts us? Will you be my everything for the rest of time?"

She uses her free hand to whisk away the tears that escape from her eyes. Then she nods enthusiastically. "Yes. Yes, I will, Roman."

I reach under the sofa cushion and retrieve the small velvet box I bought during our Paris shopping excursion. While I hold it, she opens the hinged lid and gasps.

"I can't believe you bought my ring and proposed in Paris. When did you become such a romantic?" She smiles through the tears that fall freely from her eyes now.

"Like I said, we can buy clothes anywhere. But an engagement ring from Paris is something to brag about." I take it out of the box and slide it onto her ring finger. "Perfect fit. Just like you and me, sweets."

She slides off the couch onto my leg, and I gently pull her into my arms. "I'm yours, Roman. Always."

"And I'm yours, sweets. Always have been. Always will be."

She brushes her lips across mine, and fire immediately engulfs us. Within seconds, I'm stripping off our clothes and burying myself deep inside her right there on the floor. Her body shudders and shakes beneath mine. Every soft moan urges me on. Every fingernail scratch down my back only makes me go harder. When beads of sweat cover our bodies and drip from my brow, we find the edge of ecstasy and leap off the cliff together.

As I stand, I gather her in my arms and carry her to the bathroom. After a long, hot shower, I wrap her in the thick, warmed towel and use a second to dry her off. "I didn't make your wounds worse, did I?"

"No, baby. You made me feel better all over." The peaceful smile on her face makes me proud, because I know I put it there.

"You called me 'baby.' You've never used a pet name with me before."

"Then I'd say it's way overdue, wouldn't you?"

"Absolutely."

After she finishes drying her hair, we retreat to the bedroom to sleep after a long and trying day. The minute our heads hit the pillows, the laptop chimes with an alert. She groans in frustration but checks it all the same. Not knowing what it was about would drive her crazy all night.

"Is this a joke? Holy shit, Roman! I keep forgetting about the time difference between here and New York. Look at this!"

She shows me the final settled amount from selling her shares. All I can say is, I'm glad I'm already lying down, because I'd be face-first on the floor otherwise. "That is unbelievable. But I'm thrilled for you, sweets. I mean, what else do you say to *that*?"

"You're thrilled for *us*, Roman. Not just me. We're really getting married, aren't we?" Her tone is uncertain, but I'll squash that doubt immediately.

"As soon as possible—just try to stop me. I only assumed you'd want a prenuptial agreement after the recent developments. Oh, there's one more thing I legitimately forgot to tell you about with all the excitement. Rafael had a fake will made six months ago, showing you left everything to him in the event of your death. But, about eight months ago, he changed his actual will to leave his entire estate to you. So, on top of the shares you just sold, you're also set to inherit everything else he owns."

"Are you kidding me, Roman?"

"No, sweets, you really get it all. Houses, properties, bank accounts, his holding company—"

"Not about that! About wanting a prenuptial agreement. After all this time and everything we've been through—including today—you nonchalantly throw that comment out there. Have you lost your mind?"

"I honestly just thought—"

"Well, stop thinking. You're not allowed to think for either of us anymore. I'll handle all of that going forward."

"Yes, ma'am. You'll get no more thinking from me." I can't help but smirk. "I'm not trying to be an ass. I'm willing to do whatever it takes to protect you, Tawnee."

"I know you will. That's why I don't feel the need for anything else. Some say that's naïve, but I can live with that. You put yourself in danger to rescue me. You've taken care of me, whisked me out of the country, and gotten rid of all my problems. As far as I'm concerned, half of this is already yours as payment for your services. You know, as soon as I have access to the funds."

I shake my head. "I'm not interested in an IOU. But I will take an 'I do' as payment."

"Consider my debt paid in full, then. Because I'll 'I do' you so many times, you'll have a permanent smile on your face."

"I don't know about you, but I'm wide awake now. What do you want to do?"

"Let's go wake up all the guys. They need to call everyone back home and start making plans to join us in Gay Paree. Do you have any idea how many more clothing shops there are here? It could take weeks before we work our way through them."

Not exactly what I had in mind, but also not a bad idea.

"There's only one clothing shop I want you to go to. The rest of the time, you won't need any clothes."

"Oh yeah, and where's that?"

"A bridal shop for your dream wedding dress."

"What kind of ceremony do you think we should have?"

"I don't think. That's your job, remember?" She swats me with the pillow, and I laugh. "Sweets, listen. Most guys don't care about that. I'll show up where and when you tell me to, and I'll be happy to wear whatever you pick out. Except one of those Arab dresses. I have to draw the line there after the past few days."

"I promise—no thobes, headdresses, or anything related. I can't wait to see you in a custom-tailored Armani tuxedo. I bet you'll look so hot."

"I can't wait to see you in absolutely nothing all day, every day, on our honeymoon, because I already know for a fact you look hot in your birthday suit." I waggle my eyebrows at her, and she rolls her eyes at me. "Time for a confession, Tawnee. I know you're not a materialistic person—you never have been. But I questioned how you would ever choose me over Raf. I knew I'd never be able to give you the finer things like he could or take you on trips around the world on a whim."

"You give me what he never could, Roman. I can feel you when you're near. Electricity runs through me when I simply touch your hand. You've offered all of you, holding nothing back from me. My soul recognizes you as its mate. You're the other half of me."

"You're the best part of me, Tawnee."

Now that we're unable to sleep, we get dressed and share all the wonderful news with our friends who have had our backs every step of this journey. After we pop the cork on some champagne and toast our announcements, the guys contact our friends and family at home to fill them in. They're all excited to start making travel arrangements to join us on a European tour. When we finally head back to our room, we stand in the window, staring at the Eiffel Tower lights as they twinkle against the night sky.

"Roman?" she whispers to me, though her back is flush against my chest.

"Yeah, sweets?"

"If I ask you to give up something for me, would you resent me for it later?"

"I highly doubt that, Tawnee. How could I ever resent you? Tell me what you want." My curiosity is piqued.

"I want you to quit your job. We'll have more than enough money—neither of us will ever have to work again." She turns to face me, searching my eyes for an answer.

"What do you want to do with all our time if neither of us works?"

"I want to be the voice and an advocate for those

women in the Saudi prisons. How can I escape and never think about the ones who are still stuck in there? They're probably facing worse punishment because I got away. I'll have the resources to build a platform for awareness of their plight and to help stop the inhumane treatment. That's what I really want to do, and I'd love to have your help with it."

"You've got me, sweets. I'll be right beside you every step of the way. I have one condition, though."

"And that is?"

"You're never going anywhere in the Middle East again. Ever. Travel to that area of the world is strictly off-limits unless we have the entire US military as an escort."

"Agreed. You don't have to ask me twice."

We both know she'd never be safe there, and I'm not willing to risk her life for anything, no matter how noble the cause. I'm just glad to hear we're on the same page. Otherwise, I'd have to look into investing in building a house with secret rooms, hidden passages, and interesting dungeon furnishings to keep her in until she came to her senses.

EPILOGUE

Tawnee

About an hour outside of Paris, we found the most gorgeous castle, complete with a moat, and beautifully manicured adjacent grounds.

"This is perfect for a wedding, Roman." I can't help but gush over the towers, balconies, and turrets lining the 52-bedroom, genuine 1500s French chateau-turned-hotel.

"Sweets, you know we can't officially get married here unless we've been a resident for thirty days. Refusing to leave France after an extended vacation does not meet the residency requirements."

"I know, spoilsport, but it's still fun to pretend."

"Gerald and I are into the pretending, too. He pretends to be the big, bad wolf, and I pretend I don't want to be eaten." Liz walks by and blurts out way more personal information than I ever need to hear.

"Liz, come on. Keep that shit to yourself." Silas shakes his head and sticks his fingers in his ears. "I think my ears are bleeding."

"Let me tell you something, Silas Steele. You and Shadow are both just jealous because you lost the chance to experience your reverse harem fantasy with me. Gerald is my main man now, and we're not into sharing. We're devoted to each other, and there's nothing you two can do about it."

Shadow mumbles under his breath beside me. "I don't know whether to congratulate Gerald or have him committed for a psychiatric evaluation."

Silas steps up to my other side and mutters, "Never use the words pretend, role-play, prophylactic, or flogging around Liz. It never ends well."

"So, Liz, you never told me how you ended up dating Gerald." I'm not letting these guys off the hook that easily. I love how she makes them squirm, even if I think she's crazy, too.

"Well, sweet pea, it was like this. Blake, Rebel, and Bull brought him home to the Casa de la Steele. That's fancy language for the Steeles' house. Anyway, you know someone stabbed him in that third world country over there."

"Liz, Dubai is far from a third world country." Noah stops her. "They're very wealthy."

"Anyway, before I was so rudely interrupted, I was saying someone stabbed Gerald, so they brought him to Miami so I could patch him up. You know, these boys can't exactly do their job without me. While he was on the mend, Gerald and I had a lot of time to talk. He couldn't give me a good explanation for why he'd been single for so long.

"He finally said it was because his wife had died, and he was afraid of getting hurt again. So, I took my flogger and whacked him across the back of the legs with it. He screamed out, 'That hurt!' and I told him it was supposed to hurt."

"Naturally." *Where the hell is this going?*

"That's when I explained to him that regardless of whether he loves again, he'll still get hurt. He'll still feel pain. There will never be a time in his life, while he's alive, that he can escape all pain. Then he finally understood me."

A time in his life... while he's alive? Is there a time in his life when he's dead? I can't ask these questions because I'm genuinely afraid of the answer.

"After that, I put the flogger away until he was ready for it. But when he asked for it on his own, that was a beautiful thing. I knew then he was ready to love freely and not worry about getting hurt. That just freed us up for so many other possibilities. Ball gags, whips, chains—I don't even know what some of those toys are called. Doesn't make them any less fun, though."

When I glance around, all the men have their hands over their ears and are running—*running*—away from us. The women are all wiping away tears of laughter. And Gerald, sweet Gerald, is standing next to Liz with the biggest smile I've ever seen anyone wear.

There's a man in love if I've ever seen one.

We continue our stroll around the castle before piling back into the stretch limousine. I've felt a little guilty for enjoying all the spoils of our victory so extravagantly. But if I've learned anything, it's that we only have one life, and the best we can do is live it to the fullest.

"Please, sweets, for the love of all that is holy in this world, can we go back to Miami now? I've loved every minute of the last three weeks I've spent with you in France, but I'd love some time alone with you. Completely alone. Locked in our own home. Tell you what—I'll even have a moat built around it the second we get back, complete with a drawbridge that only I have the access code to open." Roman pleads with me, keeping his voice low enough so the rest of the crowd can't hear.

"Okay, I suppose we have been away for a long time now. If the others are ready to go back, we can alert the pilot and head home tomorrow."

"Thank you, thank you, thank you. Have I told you

how wonderful and sweet and beautiful and precious you are today?"

"Yeah, I think that's what I heard you say right about the time you ran away and left me alone with Liz."

"There's a standing rule with this group. I'm not proud of it, but I have to live by it."

"And that is?"

"It's every man for himself when it comes to Liz. If you fall, it's up to you to get yourself out of there on your own. That's the only time we'd purposely leave a man down behind." He smiles and winks, but I know every one of these men would take a bullet for her.

Though they won't take a flogging from her.

"Hmm, I'll have to remember that. It may come in handy one day very soon."

The smug smile disappears from his face, and it's quickly replaced by a concerned, haunted stare. Now it's my turn to smile.

"As fun as this vacation has been, is everyone ready to go back home?" Roman asks the group.

"Ready when you are. This has been an amazing vacation, and we appreciate your generosity so much. I think we all needed this time to relax and unwind." Brianna, Noah's wife, grabs his hand and squeezes. "Noah works way too much. I've tried to get him to slow down and not take so many cases."

"I was actually hoping this group would take on a

different type of case—one everyone can take part in. But I don't want anyone to feel pressured. This isn't a tit-for-tat. Only join if you're sincerely interested."

"Tell us. The suspense is killing me!" Chaise, Bull's wife, bounces in her seat.

"Roman and I have plans to start our own nonprofit organization to work to help end human rights violations in Saudi Arabia. It won't be easy, but I feel very strongly that we have to try. Even if all we can do to start out is put public pressure on our government to stop doing business with them, or levy economic sanctions against them until they stop their travesties against women and the other minority groups they target. After seeing it firsthand, I can't turn a blind eye now."

"I'm in, Tawnee. You know I was an investigative reporter. I can dust off my writing skills and start publishing scathing articles about their mistreatments." Brianna reaches over and grabs my hand, showing her support.

"That's a great idea. Bri. I've worked in human resources for years. I can help you with setting up your nonprofit and writing the bylaws. When we're ready, I'll be right beside you on Capitol Hill to make our case." Chaise adds her hand on top of Bri's.

"While we're at it, I'll chime in. I'm a nurse, and I'll use my medical expertise to help in all sorts of ways. I can detail what happens when they deny women healthcare. I can help examine those who have escaped and document their injuries." Heather, Rebel's wife, puts her hand on top of ours.

"I'm still a Hollywood movie director and an actress. I will use my public voice to affect change. Count me in." Elle, Shadow's wife, plants her hand with ours.

"My sister and I have a variety of special skills. We can get all the information you need, and no one will ever be the wiser." Kira, Silas's wife, adds her hand.

"I'm an author—I'll be glad to write a book about it, get on the interview circuit, and get more people involved." Savannah, Nick's wife, joins her hand with ours.

"I'm Liz. I'm a superspy and a force to be reckoned with. I'll put those men in their places—under my feet." Liz places her hand on top.

"I'm feeling all the girl power in this vehicle. Tell you what, I'll just kick whoever's ass tries to get close to you ladies. Consider me your full-time bodyguard." Roman kisses me on the temple and squeezes me to him.

"The rest of us are with Roman. We'll carry your purses and kick asses, too. Just point us in the right direction, and we'll do what you need us to do." Noah grins, content to pitch in wherever he's needed.

"Thank you, all of you. I don't know how far we'll get, but every little bit has to help. Right?"

When we get home, I immediately start planning our wedding. It's been a long time coming, and we're both finally ready to make that leap. Since Roman and I first met in Miami, and so many of our pivotal moments occurred at the beach, that's where I've chosen to have our wedding. It seems fitting to make our new beginning match our original one.

I'm wearing a sexy backless mermaid dress with thin spaghetti straps. The scalloped top meshes perfectly with the beach theme, and the white lace chiffon sets the tone for an elegant evening wedding. The length is perfect to wear my jewel-embellished barefoot sandals, with the strap extending down the middle of my foot and looping over my toe. Roman is wearing a white linen suit that fits him perfectly.

As I walk down the aisle to meet the man I love, the one who drives me crazy, makes me laugh, rocks my world, and would move heaven and earth for me, I realize I'm the luckiest woman alive. When we say I do, exchange rings, and kiss for the first time as husband and wife, I genuinely feel as if my life is finally starting.

And what a beautiful life it'll be.

Two Years Later

THE OFFICE BUILDING BUZZES WITH EXCITEMENT AS they release the news from the Middle East. The newly named Crown Prince has allowed women to drive in Saudi Arabia. The fight is nowhere near over since the detention centers are still dotted throughout the land, and male guardianship rules are also still firmly in place.

But we'll take this win for the team and press on until we reach the next milestone.

Brianna is working on another exposé story, having met with two sisters who managed to flee their home for the country of Georgia, pleaded for asylum from any country that would help them, and they were finally given safe passage to Canada. Their stories of male domination, abuse at the hands of family members, and no rights to choose whom they wanted to marry make my skin crawl. If this venture helps just one of those women, all the hours we put into the cause are worth it.

Chaise walks by, stops, and backs up. She can't pass by me without rubbing my belly, as if the protrusion is there for good luck.

"I can't wait to be an aunt again. Hello, baby, it's Auntie Chaise. Again." She bends and speaks loudly to my stomach. "He can hear me, you know. He'll know my voice as soon as he's born."

I shake my head when she hurries on her way, late for another conference call with a senator's office. Her brother, Silas, used some of his DC clout to arrange the direct meetings to give us a chance to push for more concessions.

Roman steals up behind me and wraps his arms around my now extended waist. His hands slide down across our baby bump as he kisses my cheek. "Hello, sweets. How are you and my baby holding up today?"

"We're tired. He's heavy, Roman. I can't comfortably sit down, lie down, or stand. I think he'll make his grand entrance into the world any day now."

"I have to admit, I'm ready for that day. Then you'll be forced to take time off and spend it with the baby and me. We'll allow close family and friends to come over, but we will lock the rest of the world out. No senators. No CEOs. No foreign dignitaries."

"Oh shit."

"What? What's wrong?"

"You just wished it into being. Quick, wish for a fast delivery. Say it!"

"What are you talking about, Tawnee?"

"My water just broke, Roman. It's running down my leg right now, like I just peed all over myself. This baby is coming today."

"Oh shit. Let's go—your suitcase is already in the car." He takes my hand in his, then stands up on the chair in the middle of the expansive room.

"Can I have your attention, please?" he yells at the top of his lungs. Everyone stops and stares at him, waiting for him to continue. "Tawnee and I are leaving the building... because we're having a baby today! We love you all—but we're out of here as of right now since she's in labor."

Cheers and clapping fill the room, and with my pregnancy hormones, my emotions get the best of me. With tears in my eyes, I thank all our employees for their tireless work, their well-wishes, and their support.

On the way to the hospital, Roman keeps my hand in his to share his strength. It's scary, knowing a tiny human is about to be ejected out of my body through an opening that frankly doesn't seem big enough. But he reassures me the entire way, letting me know he's right beside me with all his love. Those sentiments continue all the way to the birthing room, where the nurses prepare me for the inevitable conclusion to this condition.

Once I'm settled and comfortable, our family begins streaming in. Silas and Kira, with their children, Amber, Laci, and Ryan. Those two have been busy the last couple of years. Then Nick and Savannah, with their twins, Gavin and Kinsley. Blake and his girlfriend, Julia. I still have hope for them.

Our extended family also comes to show their love and support. Noah, Brianna, Bull, Chaise, Rebel,

Heather, Shadow, and Elle—all our brothers and sisters in love if not in blood.

I can't leave out Liz and Gerald. They married soon after Roman and I tied the knot, and they've lived in wedded bliss since that day. Gerald has said many times the reason he waited so long to fall in love again was that his soul knew he had to wait for Liz. They're precious together, even if Liz is still crazy and makes me laugh every day. At least I can honestly say I love my mother-in-law and my father-in-law as if they're my own parents. After losing both my parents in a tragic car wreck when I was in my early twenties, I'll take this family over being alone any day.

When the nurse comes in to recheck me, she announces it is time and shoos them all out of the room. With Roman by my side cheering me on and giving me encouragement, we welcome our son into the world. After the staff finishes their work and leaves us alone, we enjoy some much-needed quiet time—just the three of us.

"Hello, Ethan Matthew Scott, my little love." I nuzzle his cheek and gently kiss his little button nose. "He already looks like you, Roman."

I look up at my big, strong man and see tears glistening in his eyes for the first time in all the years I've known him. "I can't even remember all those years I lived without giving all my love away now. I wouldn't know how to go back to that life, and I'll never want to.

I'm the luckiest man alive, with the most beautiful wife anyone has ever seen and the most perfect baby boy ever born. I promised you this on our wedding day, and I'll say it again now. Our little family is my entire world. You have all my love, all the time, no matter what."

"I love you too, Roman."

With Ethan asleep on my chest and Roman asleep at my side, all three of us wedged into this twin hospital bed, I drift off to sleep happier than I've ever been, loved deeper than I could hope for, and giving more love than I even knew was inside me.

This is the perfect life.

Haven't read Nick Tucker's story yet? Get it now in *Fine Line*.
Silas's story is now available in *Blurred Line*.

Want more of Nick Tucker?
Read *Her Dom* and *Her Dom's Lesson*!

❧

Want more of Nick, Silas, Roman, Reaper, Bull, Rebel, and Shadow, and Liz?
Find them and more the *Steele Security series*:
Wicked Games,
Wicked Ties,
Wicked Nights,
Wicked Intentions,
and *Wicked Shadows!*

Have you met Damon Marchetti, the sexy anti-hero

mafia capo? Danger, intrigue, murder, betrayal, and oh-so-steamy times are waiting in Warning, Part One, Warning, Part Two, and Warning, Part Three!

Find all my books on Amazon at
amazon.com/author/adjustice

Are you on Facebook? Join my reader group! No requirements or expectations — just readers having fun! :)

ABOUT THE AUTHOR

A.D. Justice is the award-winning USA Today bestselling author of the Steele Security Series (Wicked Games, Wicked Ties, Wicked Nights, Wicked Intentions, Wicked Shadows), the Crazy Series (Crazy Maybe, Crazy Baby), the Dominic Powers series (Her Dom, Her Dom's Lesson), the Immortal Obsessions series (Immortal Envy), and a few stand-alone romance novels, such as Saving Grace, Completely Captivated, Just One Summer, Intent, and Mistletoe Not Required.

When she's not writing, she's spending time with her own alpha male character in their North Georgia mountain home. She is also an avid reader of romance novels, a master at procrastination, a chocolate sommelier, a twister of words, and speaks fluent sarcasm. An avid animal lover, A.D. Justice has two horses, three cats, and two very spoiled dogs.

While the primary focus of her books has been romantic suspense, she has expanded into different sub-genres of romance. Stay tuned to read what she has in store for you!

Connect with her online!
Newsletter
Facebook Reader Group
Website

f facebook.com/adjusticeauthor

○ instagram.com/authoradjustice

BB bookbub.com/authors/a-d-justice

a amazon.com/author/adjustice

BOOKS BY A.D. JUSTICE

Steele Security Series

Wicked Games (Book 1)

Wicked Ties (Book 2)

Wicked Nights (Book 3)

Wicked Intentions (Book 4)

Wicked Shadows (Book 5)

The Crazy Series

Crazy Maybe (Book 1)

Crazy Baby (Book 2)

Crazy Love (FREE Short Story)

Dominic Powers Series

Her Dom (Book 1)

Her Dom's Lesson (Book 2)

The Vault

Warning, Part One

Warning, Part Two

Warning, Part Three

Crossing Lines

Fine Line

Blurred Line

Hard Line

Immortal Obsession

Immortal Envy (Book 1)

Stand-alone Romance Novels

Saving Grace

Completely Captivated

Intent

Just One Summer (Novella)

Mistletoe Not Required (Novella)

ACKNOWLEDGMENTS

Writing a book is much harder than one would think. The finished product only takes a few hours to read, but months to agonize over every single word, plot point, and character action. Only speaking for myself, I can honestly say I put my heart and soul into the story, taking time away from family and friends (and cleaning house. Oh, so messy!) to write just one more chapter.

When I finally reach those two little magical words, a weight lifts from my shoulders, and I'm able to breathe again. That is until I start the next book, which is usually while my editor works on the recently completed one.

My writing journey includes chatting with other authors I trust and admire to give feedback and suggestions. Others encourage and support me along the way, taking a chance on a new plot twist or storyline that's not mainstream, and who aren't afraid to step outside the box and give "different" a chance. These are my people—my tribe—whether they realize it or not.

Acknowledgments are hard to write because I never want to leave anyone out or make anyone feel their place in my life isn't important. **If you've ever read my books, you hold a special place in my heart.**

There are a few select people I want to recognize for helping make this book special to me.

First and foremost, I thank my Lord and Savior, Jesus Christ, for His eternal love, mercy, and forgiveness of a sinner like me. Without Him, I am nothing. Yes, when I say I fall short, I realize I fall way short, but thankfully, there's no such thing as being too far from Him. He knows my heart.

Someone recently called me a hypocrite for adding this to my acknowledgments. Since I openly admit I'm a sinner, I don't see it the same way she does. To me, a hypocrite implies someone denies any wrongdoing WHILE actually doing wrong. Adding this is my way of sharing my belief and thanking Him for the many blessings in my life, even though I'm well aware I don't deserve them.

Michelle Dare, you've been the bestest BFF ever. You listen to me whine and cry and puff up, only to tell me to suck it up and get over it already. I LOVE YOU! You're still stuck with me.

Victoria Renteria, you are an AWESOME alpha reader—even though you ditched me at the end of this book and went on a family vacation (the audacity!!!)—then you laughed about it. THAT is real friendship. Thank you for your time, feedback, and for making me add *just a little more*. MUAH!!!

T.K. Leigh, I don't know what I'd do without your bad influence and spot-on advice virtually every day. I'm so fortunate to have you in my tiny circle and count you as one of my very best friends in the world. I love you to death!!!

Lisa A. Hollett with Silently Correcting Your Grammar, my editor and my friend, thank you once again for working through another book with a penciled in due date then helping make it as perfect as possible at moment's notice. I hope your other clients aren't like me! :)

Wander Aguiar, the photographer for the covers in this series, is always wonderful to work with—although he does make choosing one photo very difficult. Fortunately, I was able to find three that perfectly fit this series.

Sommer Stein with Perfect Pear Creative Covers, thank you for creating the awesome covers for this series. I'm constantly in awe of your amazing talent.

Candi Kane with Candi Kane PR, you are a godsend! Thank you for all your help and support. I think I'll just keep you.

To all the bloggers, thank you for the cover reveal posts and the release day shares. You don't get nearly enough credit for all you do. We need you more than you know!

To the readers, whether you love, like, or hate this book, thank you for taking the time to read it. Thank you for your reviews, even if all you say is you liked it or not. Thank you for your support—you have no idea how much every little bit means to me. You are the best

_____

All my love to you,
Angel